"What do you feel?" Caine demanded.

Placing his hands on the bed on either side of her, he shifted his weight very close, as if he were going to kiss her neck.

His magnetism pulled at her, but more than that she felt his heat; glorious, primal heat. "I feel how hot your skin is, even though you're not touching me."

"That's lust and desire. I want you."

His declaration made her feel light-headed.

What does all this tell you about me? About us? he demanded, suddenly serious.

Emma blinked. She *had* just heard him speak in her mind. She searched his gaze, sensing that whatever words she spoke next would be very important. "That you're different."

His expression hardened. "*We're* different. You and I. Tell me, damn it!"

The ferocity in his expression scared her because she thought he was going to push her away. "You're unique, and we have a connection that's undeniably mind-blowing, but...I don't know what you want from me!"

PATRICE MICHELLE

Born and raised in the Southeast, Patrice Michelle worked as a financial analyst before giving up her financial calculator for a keyboard and never looking back. Thanks to an open-minded family who taught her that life isn't as black and white as we're conditioned to believe, she pens her novels with the belief that various shades of gray are a lot more interesting. She's a natural with a point-and-shoot camera, likes to fiddle with graphic design and, to the relief of her family, strums her guitar before an audience of one.

Visit Patrice's Web site at www.patricemichelle.net to learn about her upcoming books, read excerpts and join her newsletter.

SCIONS: REVELATION

PATRICE MICHELLE

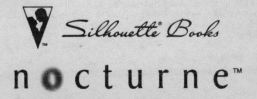

Silhouette Books

nocturne™

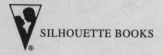 SILHOUETTE BOOKS

ISBN-13: 978-0-373-61800-2
ISBN-10: 0-373-61800-X

SCIONS: REVELATION

Recycling programs for this product may not exist in your area.

www.silhouettenocturne.com

Printed in U.S.A.

Dear Reader,

Welcome back to the dark and seductive SCIONS world! I hope you're looking forward to learning the answers to the prophecy and how they relate, not just to the hero and heroine in this third book, but to the first two books in this trilogy as well.

Ever since I introduced Caine Grennard as Landon's loyal packmate in *Scions: Insurrection,* I couldn't wait to share his story with you. Darkly sexy, dedicated and on-the-edge in a rebellious sort of way, Caine is the kind of alpha hero you can't help but fall in love with, yet whom you also ache for, because those rebellious tendencies are what ultimately land him where he is at the beginning of *Scions: Revelation.*

Young, enigmatic Emma Gray never felt as though she fit in with girls her age. The social scene just wasn't her thing, not to mention that her life was pretty full, between family obligations and her job at a café in town. So she's taken by surprise when something finally entices her away from her calm and predictable world.

Emma has no idea that meeting Caine will completely change her life. And neither does Caine.

I hope you enjoy Caine and Emma's tempestuous journey as they follow their hearts and wind their way through the layered machinations of others, while duty, honor and loyalty fiercely test their future together. Only after every intricate twist and turn of the prophecy is revealed can Emma and Caine finally find their own path to happiness.

All the best,

Patrice Michelle
www.patricemichelle.net

To my family, thank you for always believing in me!

Acknowledgments

To my amazing agent Deidre Knight for believing in my writing and finding a home for my books, to my editor Ann Leslie Tuttle for her astute editorial input and endless drive to make the story better, and to Charles Griemsman—the go-to guy for pretty much everything. I can't thank you enough for all that you do!

Thank you to my brainstorming partner-in-crime Rhyannon Byrd for always being there!

Prologue

No one will ever look at me the same again. Caine Grennard's hand shook as he lifted it toward the mansion's main door. Clenching his fist, he focused to calm his rage before he turned the knob. As he entered, the Lupreda sitting in the living room and standing in the hall turned and stared. Every single member in the wolf pack was there now. Only a few had witnessed his fight with Brian.

It had been a great battle—painful and bloody, but satisfying to kick the jerkoff's ass and finally put him in his place. Brian, the surly, ready-to-mutiny Lupreda, wouldn't dare disparage Landon as Alpha Wolf again, at least not in Caine's presence. Yet all the satisfaction Caine had when the fight was over disappeared the moment he realized he couldn't shift back from his dominant werewolf form, known as Musk form among the Lupreda, to human.

Was the pack waiting to see if Caine had gone full zerker—
to see if he was permanently stuck between man and wolf, like
the other three Lupreda in the past?

He saw it in their eyes: the worry, the condemnation. Brian
had the nerve to smirk. Caine wanted to kick his ass all over
again. When Caine's gaze locked with Landon Rourke's, the
Alpha's stoic expression told him nothing. Resentment burned
in Caine's stomach.

Landon uncrossed his arms and pushed his tall, broad form
away from the thick column separating the living room and
the foyer. "Everybody, out!"

The Lupreda scattered, moving so fast that Caine saw only
blurs zooming past. A pair of folded jeans landed with a
thump on the floor in front of him.

He looked up and caught a glimpse of Kaitlyn's red hair
through the rails in the catwalk overhead before she disappeared. Landon's half human–half Lupreda mate was one of
a kind. Only she would anticipate the turmoil and self-doubt
that had festered within him while he'd paced in the woods
for two agonizing hours, waiting for his body to finally shift
back to human form. Kaitlyn intuitively sensed something as
simple as a pair of jeans would help him feel more human as
he faced the pack's leader.

Caine quickly pulled on the jeans and buttoned the fly. As
soon as he met Landon's steady gaze, the Alpha tossed something in the air toward him. Catching the metal, Caine curled
his fingers into a fist around it. The chain felt both hot and
cool against his palm.

"Put it on," Landon said in a hard tone.

Caine tensed and glanced at the silver chain in his hand.
He'd been there, done that. All the Lupreda had experienced

having a thick silver collar locked around their necks to keep them from shifting to wolf form until the Sanguinas vampires were ready to hunt them as prey. Ever since the vampires got sick from humans' poisoned blood over twenty-five years ago, and they'd retreated from their land into exile, Caine had relished his freedom. He swore he'd never let anyone put silver around his neck again. He sure as hell wasn't doing it willingly, even if he was at risk of going zerker.

Clenching his hand around the chain once more, Caine met Landon's steady stare. "No."

Landon's green gaze narrowed. "I won't have you going zerker. You'll wear it if you want to stay here."

If Caine couldn't shift to Musk form on the fly, he couldn't protect his pack. He'd be nothing to his brethren. Useless to his Alpha, the man who'd mentored him all his life. Why didn't Landon see that?

Caine shook his head and flexed his jaw. For as long as he could remember, his faith in Landon as the pack's true Alpha had never wavered—even while Landon had lived away from the pack for eighteen years—yet now that Landon had recently become Alpha, he was the one who would force Caine to leave.

"I guess the decision's made for me." Turning, Caine slipped the chain around the neck of the carved wolf statue sitting on its haunches by the door and walked out of the Lupreda's mansion—the only home and family he'd ever known.

Chapter 1

Why would an alluring smell make me feel so free? Emma Gray wondered as she waved good-night to her boss before pushing the café's door open. Her pulse raced and every nerve in her system worked overtime. She hurried across the street, heading toward the nightclub Squeeze. Despite her social hang-ups, she was finally going into that nightclub. Come hell or high water.

She stepped up on the curb and inhaled, trying to recapture the glorious smell's deep earthy notes, the essence that brought her out here in the first place. She knew if she could conjure it, the scent would help solidify her resolve and calm her stomach that felt like a snake had taken up residence inside, coiling tighter and tighter.

Nothing but car exhaust, lingering hints of rain and alley trash filled her nostrils. Damn.

She'd always had a keen sense of smell, something Jared, her boss at Jared's Java and Pastries café, often relied on. "You think these eggs are still good?" he'd ask as he held the carton under her nose, to which she could accurately predict, "You've got two days before you have to chuck 'em." Jared thought her talent was "wicked uncanny." Emma thought her "gift" was just plain weird.

Until yesterday.

She was cleaning up coffee cups left by some of the patrons, whose lingering musky smell on them made her body tingle all over. She smiled and she didn't know why. But she just felt…exhilarated, like she was flying down from the highest hill on a roller coaster—buckled in and safe, but completely free.

Then, tonight at work, she'd caught the scent again and her heart nearly jumped out of her chest, she'd been so excited. This time the smell had been very fresh—as if the person or persons had just been there. She'd lifted her gaze from gathering the cups in the dirty-dish container in time to see a tall, dark-headed guy leave the café and accompany an auburn-haired man to the popular Manhattan nightclub across the street.

Now, here she was, an hour later, her throat closing as she stood at the end of the long line of people waiting to get inside the nightclub. In the two years she'd worked at the café, there'd been many nights that she'd stared out the big display window at Squeeze's black double doors, wondering what it was like with music blaring and patrons packed inside like sardines. But curiosity wasn't enough to overcome her social ineptitude. She wasn't a sexy siren. Just a normal, average-looking woman, who'd rather talk about the latest marketing strategies being used in businesses today than prove how well she could hold her liquor or how fast she could tie a cherry stem with her tongue. Yep, she'd crash and burn the moment she opened her mouth.

If it weren't for that earthy, musky aroma that had imprinted itself on her psyche since yesterday, she wouldn't be standing here. But she had to at least put a face with the appealing, soul-wrenching scent. Maybe then she could let it go.

Techno music thumped and the crowd inched their way through the frigid, damp air, waiting to be let in. As she waited, Emma noted the distinct difference in her own attire: jeans, bulky sweater and black wool pea coat, compared to the other young women her age. Sporting big earrings, spiked heels and heavy makeup, the girls wore clubbing clothes of tight pants, miniskirts and cropped tops underneath their winter coats.

While they giggled and flirted with the guy manning the door, Emma's insides churned. *These girls have mastered the art. I could never compete.* With each step closer to the entrance, Emma's body tensed to the point she thought she might pass out. *Breathe. They're people, just like you. Well, except for the I-suck-at-flirting-and-idle-chitchat part.*

"You don't look twenty-one," the burly guy at the door said after he'd checked Emma's driver's license to make sure she was legal.

"I *am* twenty-one, but it doesn't really matter. I'll only be in there for a few minutes." She'd always been told she looked young, but was it because she didn't have on any makeup or was it because she wasn't wearing three-inch heels? She was sure her five-foot-six height made her appear much shorter and younger than the girls he normally let in. Even if half those girls were probably three years younger and sporting fake IDs.

"You still have to be twenty-one to be allowed in." Frosty plumes expelled from his nose, reminding her of a dragon.

Emma followed his frown to her feet. Her boots had mud spatters all over them from her jaunt through the woods this morning, looking for Casper. She instantly regretted not changing her shoes before she went to work. Meeting his gaze, her smile turned sheepish. "I'm going for the grunge look."

The streetlight shone on the man's bald head as he scanned her clothes. Crossing his arms, disdain laced his tone. "We have a dress code for a reason."

Emma stiffened and outraged, embarrassed heat shot up her cheeks. She didn't need to be reminded her pea coat had threadbare elbows and a frayed collar or that her jeans were so old and worn they were *naturally* faded. "Are you saying I'm not good enough to enter this club?"

She *had* to get into the club so she could at least see the guy with the innerving scent, even if she didn't speak to him. Maybe his face would ring a bell or something. There were no guarantees he'd come to the café again just because he'd been there two days in a row. Plus, working up the nerve to enter the club was a big deal for her. Seeking out this guy was a perfect excuse for her to finally get a peek inside Squeeze without feeling like she was there on a social basis.

A snotty look crossed the bouncer's thick jowls. "That's exactly what I'm—" At that moment, a thin guy burst through the club's double doors, took a couple of steps and hurled on the sidewalk. Baldy turned to him and growled, "Hey, go puke somewhere else, moron."

When he walked over to send the guy on his way, Emma's heart rate ramped. She didn't have the flirtatious skills the girls in front of her had used to make him wave them in with a lopsided, dopey smile. Instead, she'd challenged the guy. *Way to go, Emma.* Better take the opportunity to quickly slip inside the club while he was occupied.

Inside, the nightclub was so dark, the neon manga murals painted on the walls on either side of the entryway glowed vividly. When the closed door opened with a swift jerk behind her, Emma's pulse jumped. She pulled her pageboy hat low on her head and ducked past a tall guy, moving farther into the room.

It didn't take much effort to be sucked into the crowd; the nightclub was that packed. It was like she'd entered another world, full of drinking, dancing and erotic decadence. Emma was enraptured and invigorated by the laughter, talking, partying and *life* going on around her. And the smells. There were so many: thick, sickly smelling perfume, heavy musk-based cologne, strong deodorant soap aromas laced with sweat…all were mixed in with alcohol's distinct sharp scent.

Hanging above the DJ on the other side of the club, glittery gold cages held half-naked girls sliding up and down poles. The sunken dance floor three feet below the main floor was so crowded that she couldn't tell where one person began and the other ended. The partiers were one big mass of arms, legs, bobbing heads and gyrating bodies, moving to the beat of the music.

Fog floated through the room in a heavy haze, carrying with it images of excitement, aggression and…lust. She saw it in the way the people moved, the way they touched. Especially one group of three, who were dancing on the fringes of the dance floor.

A tall, broad-shouldered man with pitch-black hair danced in front of a woman with short dark hair, while her blond girlfriend plastered herself to his backside. When the blonde raked her nails down his cotton T-shirt and then along his denim-covered thighs as she leaned close and bit his shoulder blade, Emma's stomach tightened. The man laughed and turned to say something in the blond woman's ear. Emma could tell by the way the woman's eyes narrowed into pleased slits that his comment was very suggestive.

She felt like a voyeur watching the three of them, their bodies moving in tandem to the suggestive beat of the music, but Emma couldn't look away. She was totally mesmerized by the sight. The man held the brunette's waist with a gentle touch that surprised her. When he ran his lips along the woman's throat, Emma found herself tilting her head as if he were kissing her.

Her pulse thrummed and her palms turned sweaty. Sudden heat spread through her body, making her dizzy. Seeking a distraction, she unbuttoned her thick jacket and gazed around the room, looking for the auburn-haired man. He'd be easier to spot in a crowd than the dark-headed guy. When she returned her gaze to the threesome on the floor once more, the man lifted his head and stared right at her.

Embarrassed to be caught staring, Emma quickly turned and made her way through the crowd toward the bar. Maybe the two men were having a drink. Frat boy and sorority girl were making out on the stool to her left. She ignored them and leaned across the bar to scan the patrons sitting on either end.

The bartender's military-style buzz cut shifted forward with his raised eyebrows. "What'll you have?"

Emma nodded. "I'll have a dark beer." More than once she'd shared a beer or two with her aunt. Mary might be in her mid-sixties, but she could hold her own against any sailor out there.

"Come on, baby. You don't need a drink," a woman said beside Emma, drawing her out of her musings.

Glancing to her right, Emma froze. The man from the dance floor had walked up to the bar. But it wasn't his face that shocked her. It was his smell…that intriguing musky scent she'd come looking for. The blonde stroked his waist and hips, dancing in place behind him, while the brunette hung on his right arm.

Emma stared at his profile as he raised his hand to get the bartender's attention. Nothing about him looked familiar. She knew she'd never met him in her life, yet his scent evoked something strong within her. Appearing to be in his early thirties, he wasn't pretty-boy handsome. From his nose, to his square jaw, to black eyebrows over dark eyes, his looks were a bit harsh but intriguing.

He turned and whispered something to the brunette beside him. The blonde slid her hand along his backside, then wrapped her arm around his waist and tugged him against her. "You have to dance with me next," she said, rubbing her body on his.

Emma smirked. *You mean he wasn't already?*

"Here's your beer." The bartender interrupted her observation, setting Emma's drink on the wood bar top, then he turned to the man on her right. "What'll it be?"

The dark-haired man glanced at Emma's imported beer. "I'll have what she's having."

The bartender walked away before she could hand him her money. Emma thrummed her fingers on the bar top and waited for him to return. She refused to look at the guy beside her. Had she imagined *him* walking inside the club with a red-headed guy? Or maybe the other guy had girls climbing all over him somewhere else in the club.

Apparently, the brunette didn't like that the man she hung on had glanced Emma's way. Emma felt the female's avid stare as the woman moved to stand in front of him, while the blonde literally crawled all over his back. The bartender returned with another beer and the man handed him a large bill. "That's for hers, too," he said, nodding to Emma.

He had an engaging smile and smelled like sin incarnate, but Emma wasn't flattered. Handing the bartender her money, she swept her gaze over the two ladies hanging on the man and said, "No thanks. I think they've got all your sides covered," before she walked away.

Caine stared after the petite woman who'd just slammed him. He was taken aback but amused by her comment. The brunette kissed his jaw and said in a husky voice, "We'll be right back."

The blonde backed away with her friend and waved. "Bathroom break."

As he watched the women walk off, he realized he hadn't learned their names yet, but his mind was on the woman who'd turned down his offer to pay for her beer. She had the most arresting eyes. They were so light brown that the color appeared almost yellow. What was her name? He scanned the crowd, looking for her pageboy hat among the crush of people. She'd disappeared.

Laird walked up and ran a hand through his short auburn hair. "Better learn to tie a knot. That bathroom line is long." Frowning, he glanced around the bar area. "How the hell did you manage to lose *two* women while I was gone?"

"Talent," Caine grunted, then took a drink of his beer.

"Now I know why you weren't answering your cell."

Caine immediately tensed at Landon's terse tone behind him. He swiveled and met the Alpha's steady stare. Out of the corner of his eye, he saw Kaitlyn, Landon's mate, ordering drinks at the other end of the bar. "Why are you looking for me? Wasn't kicking me out of the pack enough for you?"

Landon's face turned to stone and he crossed his arms over his wide chest. "Leaving was your choice."

Resentment churned in Caine's stomach. Ninety days of loneliness and feeling completely alienated from his own kind fueled his bitter tone. "You didn't give me an option."

Kaitlyn walked up carrying two mugs of Guinness. At the same time, the song ended and the multicolored spotlights around the dance floor were doused, sending the bar into momentary darkness. She gasped and stared at Caine. "Do you see it?" she addressed Landon.

A new song started up and the colorful lights sprang back to life, reflecting off Landon's tense jaw. "I do." Grabbing the drinks from her hands, he set them on the bar. "Let's go."

Laird's attention pinged between Landon, Caine and Kaitlyn. "Am I missing something?"

Caine shrugged and took another swig of his beer. "I'm as clueless as you."

"More than you realize." Landon's cold tone spoke volumes. "Leave immediately and meet me at my office."

Caine stiffened, ready to refuse.

The Alpha got right in his face. "As far as I'm concerned, you're still a member of my pack and my responsibility. Get your ass moving, *wolf*."

After Landon and Kaitlyn walked off toward the entrance, Laird said, "Where'd the ladies go? Did you find out their names?"

Caine shook his head. "They went to the bathroom. If the lines are like you say, they'll be a while." He set down his beer, wishing he'd gotten the hat girl's name. "Come on. Let's get out of here."

When they left the club and the heavy doors shut behind them, Caine caught a glimpse of the girl in the hat walking up the road and his pulse raced. "Get the car and meet me around the block," he called to Laird, then took off in her direction.

As he headed her way, she pulled her gloves out of her pockets and shrugged into them. Caine briefly stopped to grab the paper she'd dropped. In a matter of seconds, he was just a few feet behind her. "Hey, Hat Girl! Wait up."

She gasped and jumped, coming to a halt. "You scared the crap out of me. Don't sneak up on people like that."

"You dropped this." Caine walked up and handed her the napkin before sliding his hands into his jeans pockets. "You shouldn't be walking the streets by yourself at night. Let me walk you to wherever you're going."

"Thanks." She shoved the napkin in her pocket. "Don't you have other women to attend to?" she said before she continued walking toward a parking deck up ahead.

Caine chuckled and fell into step beside her. "Things aren't always what they seem."

She raised an eyebrow. "So I imagined those two women trying to become your second skin?"

Touché. "And yet I'm here, talking to you," he said in a husky tone.

She shrugged, unimpressed. "Everyone likes a challenge."

She was a good six inches shorter than him, but with her thick jacket and her hair tucked up under a black pageboy hat, he couldn't tell much else about her physically. No earrings swung from her ears or lipstick coated her lips. High cheekbones made her oval face more interesting than beautiful, but she had something about her…something elusive, and damn he liked her snap. "Is that what you would be? A good challenge?"

Her yellow gaze slanted briefly. "I would be the *ultimate* challenge."

No smug smile, no pretense at all. Just the determined set of her jaw and the way she walked—graceful and self-assured. She exuded the kind of self-confidence some people work all their lives to acquire but never really accomplish, yet she was so young. He'd guess a little over twenty.

They'd reached the entrance to the parking deck and she stopped. "I can take it from here. Thanks."

Caine was stunned to be summarily dismissed. Women, especially those younger than him, were usually drawn in by his smile alone. He searched her face, looking for some kind of clue to her underlying strategy. No artifice reflected in her intriguing eyes. "Will you at least tell me your name?"

She smiled and his groin hardened and his chest cinched tight in a deep primal response to her natural beauty.

"Hat Girl will do. Good night."

She turned to walk away, but Caine caught her gloved hand. Drawing her fingers to his lips, he said, "I'm glad I met you, Hat Girl."

A car horn blew and Caine jerked his gaze to the road behind him. Laird leaned out the car window. "Come on, Caine. Landon's waiting."

Small fingers folded around his, drawing his attention. Her lips were tilted in amusement, a delicate dark eyebrow elevated. "Things aren't always what they seem?"

Caine grinned. "Exactly."

Pulling her hand from his, she backed away. "It was nice to meet you, Caine. Your friend is waiting."

"I'd like to see you again."

Her low laugh made his heart beat faster.

"I'll be around."

Caine didn't like her evasive answer. He realized he'd been so caught up in trying to learn more about her that he hadn't taken the time to catch her scent. He'd be able to track her that way. Something close to panic gripped him at the thought she'd disappear and he'd never see her again. "At least tell me your name or give me your number."

"I've got to go. I have a long drive ahead of me."

"You don't live in the city then?"

She shook her head.

The horn blew again and Caine barked toward the car, "I'm coming, Laird."

When he turned back, she was gone.

"I have to deal with Landon for taking our time getting there. You don't," Laird grumbled as Caine climbed into the passenger side.

Caine shut the door harder than necessary. "He'll get over it."

Laird drove down the road. "Stubborn lone wolf."

Caine shrugged off the conflicting emotions that squeezed his chest at Laird's flippant comment. He never really understood what Landon went through while he'd lived away from the pack on the fringes of Lupreda land for as long as he did…until now. "It doesn't matter. I'm out of the pack anyway."

"It took you two hours to shift back, Caine!" Laird growled and steered the car onto a side street.

The past few months of solitude in the city, while working double shifts to pay for rent and food, had given Caine plenty of time to think about those two long hours in the woods. Going zerker was not going to happen to him.

"It's not the same without you. Landon's Second should be with the pack. You *can't* enjoy delivering packages."

Laird's comment jerked Caine out of his musings. "Second?"

"Damn straight." Laird pulled his car into a space on the street in front of Landon's New York City office. Cutting the engine, he drilled Caine with a steadfast stare. "Everyone knows it. It was only a matter of time before Landon made an official announcement."

It was true he'd assumed the role of Second the moment Landon took over as Alpha, but Caine thought Laird would take over once he left. Roman was too laid-back to assume Second responsibilities. All Caine had ever wanted, all he'd ever trained for, was to be Alpha one day. With the threat of turning zerker a very real possibility for him now, he wouldn't be allowed to enter the annual Alpha run.

Laird grabbed his arm when he started to get out of the car. "Just put the damned necklace on."

Caine's ingrained loyalty burned within him. Even though Landon had forced him to leave, he still respected Landon more than any wolf, even more than Garius, the head Omega and oldest retired Alpha. "It might've been over twenty-five years ago, but I can still feel the weight of the vampires' damned silver collar around my neck. I refuse to be shackled again."

"You can take the chain off with each full moon and run with us as a wolf. Your family wants you to return."

Family. The concept both fascinated and frustrated Caine. Unlike Caine and Landon and the wolves before them who were created in a lab by the vampires, Laird's generation were the first werewolves born into the pack. Caine's friend knew what it felt like to have siblings and parents. Laird had both pack and *family* ties. Now that the pack thought he was close to going zerker, Caine felt they'd turned their back on him. What was that human saying, "Blood is thicker than water"? Laird's parents would never walk away from him, zerker or not.

Caine shook off the sense of isolation that had consumed his thoughts while he'd been living away from the pack and climbed out of the car. As he walked up the sidewalk beside Laird, he knew the Lupreda were worried about him. Living among humans was his only option. Humans didn't rile his need to call forth his Musk form for dominance like his fellow pack mates did, like Brian had. They were a safe, if not somewhat boring, race…all except for one, apparently. Hat Girl.

With the zerker issue breathing down his neck, he felt as if he was losing touch with what little humanity ran through his veins. Maybe that's why the human appealed to him. She represented something that was slipping away from him as fast as sand through his fingers.

"Caine. You with me, bud?"

Caine blinked when he realized he was staring unseeingly in front of him. Landon Rourke Private Investigations came into focus in bold black letters on the door a couple feet away. He smirked. Landon was going to have to change that now that Kaitlyn had left her job as NYPD police detective to join his agency. Tapping on the door, he walked in when Landon called for them to enter.

"'Bout damn time." Landon scowled and leaned against his desk which was currently turned on its side.

"Shit!" Laird stared at the shambles before them.

Caine's gaze jerked to Landon. "What happened?"

"I think it's obvious," Landon said in a dry tone.

Caine walked around the ransacked room. Sniffing the air, he stepped over filing cabinets with drawers wide open. Paperwork was everywhere. Nothing. Not a glimmer of a scent. Knowing Landon's sense of smell wasn't as strong as the rest of the wolves in the pack, Caine frowned. "I'm assuming you asked us here to help you scent, but I don't detect any lingering smells."

Laird lifted a turned-over chair. Inhaling near the wood, he shook his head before he set it upright on the floor. "Me neither."

Landon stood. "That's not why I asked you here."

Kaitlyn walked into the office from the back entrance, carrying a small hard case. Opening it, she removed a strange-looking flashlight with a green shield in front of it. Handing Caine and Laird each a pair of orange-colored safety-style glasses, she said, "I borrowed this equipment from a friend's office at the lab."

"You borrowed?" Caine grinned and slipped on the glasses.

"It'll be back where he left it before work resumes tomorrow morning." She tucked strands of her shoulder-length red hair behind her ear and walked over to the light switch.

"You *know* we can see in the dark, Kaitlyn." Laird chuckled, then put on his glasses.

She flipped off the light switch. "Just humor me. I'm hoping this will work."

Laird lifted his hands in the air. "See. No difference. Everything looks the same."

Kaitlyn turned on her flashlight and swept it past them to the room in general. "What about now?"

Caine froze as the special flashlight scanned the room. He saw defined sparkling handprints all over the place—on the desk, the filing cabinets, on the paperwork and file folders, even on the chair Laird had just checked.

Kaitlyn was showing Laird and him what she and Landon had the ability to see without this special equipment. "Damn it to hell!" Caine ground out, then glanced at Laird when Kaitlyn turned the flashlight on him.

Sparkling handprints covered his friend's face, his chest, his arms, his hips, even his crotch. "Son of a bitch!" Laird hissed. "Those two girls crawling all over us like a couple of cats were—"

"Panthers," Caine finished with a snarl, his gaze snapping to Landon's. Now he knew why Landon was so furious when the lights went down in the club.

"I don't think the panthers have a clue that Kaitlyn and I can see the trail they're leaving behind," Landon said.

"Either that or the Velius don't give a damn." Caine walked over and flipped the light switch back on.

"Velius or panthers. No matter what name we call them, it's like they're taunting us." Laird snorted.

"Well, one thing's for sure…" Katilyn retrieved the glasses from Caine and Laird. "You two need to stay away from the club until we can figure out a way for you to detect them."

Frustration and anger boiled deep in Caine's chest. The club was his only connection to the woman he'd met. He didn't know her name. He didn't know her scent. "The women don't know that we know they're panthers. If Laird and I go back tomorrow night, we could follow the two of them and find out where their pride is located."

Landon shook his head. "They know I killed one of their own while trying to protect Kaitlyn's mom. But they must think we have something more on them or they wouldn't have tossed my office looking for it. If Kaitlyn and I go back to the club, we'll tip our hand. If you and Laird go back…" Landon paused and ran a hand through his short, light brown hair. "You can't see or smell them, Caine. What if the two women weren't the only panthers there? You could try to follow them and get ambushed."

Laird snorted. "We can take out a bunch of cats."

Kaitlyn put the flashlight and the glasses back in their case, then faced Laird and Caine. "I'll go with you two to the club tomorrow night."

"Hell no, you won't!" Landon growled.

Kaitlyn sighed. "My hybrid status makes it impossible for them to smell me. I'll wear a wig and glasses or something to make me look different. My heavy coat should mute your mark's scent, but you'll have to stay away from me once I take a shower."

Landon moved to stand in front of her. "I said no, Kaitie. I can't be there to protect you. End of discussion."

Kaitlyn glanced at Laird and Caine. "I'd like to talk to my mate alone. Caine, I'll call you tomorrow."

As he and Laird headed out the door, one thing Caine knew for certain…no matter the outcome of Kaitlyn and Landon's discussion, he was going back to Squeeze tomorrow night. The club was his only connection to the young human with the intriguing light brown eyes. He didn't plan to give her up.

Chapter 2

An electric current slid up her arm from the point their fingers touched, making Emma's stomach tumble. Caine was holding her bare hand. No glove separated them this time. He stood in front of her, and the dark smile on his face made him look both sinful and sexy as hell.

"I'll be around." She tried to walk away, but he didn't let go.

Instead, he spread his fingers wide and threaded them with hers, locking their hands together. "I don't want you to go." He glanced at their hands. "And I don't think you want to either."

The warmth from his palm seeped into her skin, warming her chilled fingers. She followed his line of sight. Her fingers dug into the back of his hand, clasping tight.

Emma jerked her gaze to his. "I—"

"Dance with me, Emma." Using his hold, he pulled her

close. When her chest aligned with his, he wrapped his arm around her waist and locked her against him.

The rough rasp in his voice ignited her body. She loved the way her name sounded coming from him. Much better than Hat Girl. Her nerves played havoc with her mind. He wanted to dance? She glanced at the rows of cars flanking either side of them. "We're in a parking deck—"

"Listen and you'll hear the music." He leaned close, his lips a breath away from hers.

As his hand slid up her back under her coat and sweater, the searing heat from his palm branded her bare skin, and she began to hear the steady thump of a seductive beat in her head—deep music with erotic undertones, meant to seduce the senses, to lull her mind and insecurities.

Emma realized she was dreaming. Even though she was a little sad that this arousing scenario was in her subconscious, the knowledge freed her from worry that she'd make a fool of herself by saying something stupid. This "dream Caine" was a figment of her imagination. She could be uninhibited and he would respond as if she'd said and done all the right things.

Wrapping her arms around his neck, she pressed her body close to his muscular chest and whispered in his ear, "You take the lead and I'll follow."

Caine's dark eyes blazed. "Things aren't always what they seem, Emma."

The low register of his voice made something fundamental twist deep inside her. His hard body pressed against her, combined with his invigorating smell, caused her pulse to whoosh in her ears. Her heart beat faster and the sound grew louder until all she heard was a blaring *whaaah, whaaah,*

whaaah. She stiffened in his arms. The pace felt off. The steady noise was harsh and jarring.

Emma jerked awake to the annoying sound of her alarm clock. Five in the morning. Ugh. She'd set the alarm so she could go in search of Casper before her aunt woke. The older woman would be frantic if she knew he'd gotten out again. The dang cat had slipped through Emma's legs when she'd opened the door last night after she'd returned from the club. Hitting the off button, her heart thrummed as she lay back on her bed and squeezed her eyes shut, hoping to recover the dream. But the wisps of the surreal fantasy slipped away.

Her dream about Caine made her realize how attracted she'd been to him. She hadn't admitted it to herself last night. Rolling over, she punched her pillow when she considered the fact she hadn't given him her name. Most likely, he thought she was being coy and evasive, giving him the "challenge" he thought her to be. Ha! The truth was, she didn't know what to say to someone like Caine—a man obviously assured in his seductive skills with women. Pushing him away was the best defense mechanism she could come up with at the time. Socially adept, she was not.

Growing up home-schooled and living in the boonies over an hour from the city pretty much guaranteed she grew up smart but not very skilled when it came to making friends. She didn't give Caine her name on purpose. That way, she could imagine all kinds of sexy scenarios between herself and this mysterious guy with his evocative smell, so long as she didn't have any embarrassing "real-life" moments with him to get in the way.

Emma sighed as she stood up and dragged on a pair of jeans and a sweater. Staring out the frosted window into the dark early-morning sky, she grabbed her coat. A few minutes later, Emma tugged the coat tight around her to ward off the frigid air and entered the dense woods surrounding their home, calling out in a low voice, "Casper!"

Once she'd reached the stream a half mile from their home, she peered up and down the babbling flow of partially frozen water. Casper considered this area his personal hunting ground. She had no qualms leaving him out here on his own, but her aunt had other ideas, to the point the older woman had even put a lock on his cat door to keep him inside at night.

Emma was freezing her butt off and ready to get back home to a cup of hot cider. "Casp—" she started to call again when a small bundle of pitch-black fur darted across the embankment twenty feet upstream. She stepped forward to take off after him, at the same time a few drops of ice-cold rain hit her nose. Smiling in satisfaction, she turned to head back home. Casper might like his freedom, but he hated being wet even more. He'd be meowing at their back door soon enough.

With each step Emma took back toward her house, something didn't feel right. The air felt heavy and thick as if an ominous hush had fallen over the woods surrounding their small stone house—waiting for her to return. The tiny hairs on the back of her neck stood up as she neared her home. Heart thumping, she picked up her pace and broke into the clearing to see steady rain sliding in quiet rivulets down the high-pitched roof over the front porch. Still, she couldn't shake the feeling…

She came to a halt when she saw fresh, deep tire marks in the gravel driveway, as if a big truck had come and gone. Her pulse thundered in her ears at the sight of the front door standing wide open. Icy fingers of fear for her aunt traced down her back. Her boots made heavy thumps across the wooden front porch as she ran inside screaming, "Aunt Mary!"

The house appeared empty, eerily quiet. She raced toward her aunt's bedroom and her voice echoed in the hall as she gave another shrill cry for her aunt to respond. Emma's stomach knotted with each step she took. The lamp lay broken on the floor beside her aunt's bed—the only indication of trouble, other than the open front door. Emma rubbed her neck and glanced around the bedroom.

Her aunt's purse was still on the dresser untouched. So was her jewelry box. They hadn't been robbed. Feeling as if her safety and privacy had been completely ripped from her, Emma crept back down the hall toward the front of the house, trying not to panic for her aunt. Their car was still in the driveway, so unless her aunt had walked out, she didn't leave on her own. Where had her aunt gone? Completely perplexed, she pulled the front door closed.

As soon as she shut the door, a piece of paper fluttered to the floor. Emma's heart seized and she stared at the bold, black letters scrawled across the white surface. *Want to talk to you. Go to the club again tonight. Be there at ten. No police.*

To the club again? The note had to be for her. *No police?* Did that mean the person had taken her aunt to make sure she would comply? Emma bit her lip and swallowed a sob. Even though she was alone in her house, she felt as if every move she made was being scrutinized, like she were a fish floundering around in a fishbowl.

Running down the hall to her bedroom, she grabbed her purse, her cell and keys, then headed back to the front of the house. She couldn't stay here another moment. Her home had been invaded and being an hour away from the city felt—for the first time in her life—too secluded.

Casper's angry meow drew her attention and Emma grabbed a towel and unlocked his cat door at the bottom of the back door. He tried to dart past her, but she was too fast, grabbing the cat up and drying him off with brisk strokes. The cat yowled his displeasure and scratched her to be free. The moment his feet hit the floor, he made a beeline down the hall for her aunt's dirty-clothes basket—his bed every night.

Emma considered taking the cat with her, but Casper was as undomesticated as they came. He was used to the wide-open wooded spaces, not a crowded city full of concrete. Her aunt wouldn't forgive her if he got run over. Sighing, she filled Casper's bowls with enough food and water to last a few days and made sure the cat door was in the unlocked position so he could come and go as he pleased.

When she started back through the kitchen, her gaze landed on her aunt's plastic pillbox. Emma had filled the seven days of the week full of meds for her aunt yesterday. Renewed panic ramped inside her as she slipped her aunt's medicine box into her purse. Mary needed her pills or she ran the risk of a heart attack.

Closing the front door, Emma locked it, then quickly bolted for her car. Suddenly, the dense woods appeared sinister, surrounding the area around her house in a shroud of damp darkness. Emma's heart hammered out of control. Every sound seemed to echo in her head: the gravel under her boots, her erratic breathing, even the crows in the trees above squawking incessantly.

Once she'd pulled her car onto the interstate that led to the city, the rain began to come down harder. Emma gripped the steering wheel tight and sobbed in worry for her aunt. Her first natural instinct was to call the police, but she couldn't jeopardize her aunt's life. *No police.* What if the kidnappers got angry and hurt her aunt?

Why did they want to meet me at the club? Who was doing this? She'd only talked to one person last night. Then again, Caine had really wanted to know her name or her number. At the time, she'd assumed she'd just intrigued him with her evasive responses. Dear God, had he followed her home? Could Caine be the one doing this? Had she somehow unwittingly brought some psycho-stalker to her home? She began to shake all over.

Where could she go for a place to think? Whom could she trust? Right now her boss, Jared, was the closest Emma had to a friend. He'd always been understanding about her situation with her aunt's medical needs and endless doctor appointments. She tried to call Jared's cell, but her cell's coverage was spotty this far from town.

An hour later, as Emma parked her car behind Jared's Java Café—space was surprisingly available in the wee hours of the morning—it started sleeting. Rain and sleet coated her hair and coat by the time she climbed the metal stairs that led to Jared's apartment above the store and banged hard on the door.

Bleary-eyed and bare-chested, his short blond hair in bed-head disarray, Jared yanked open the door with a baseball bat in hand. "What the fu—" He lowered the bat to his side. "Emma?"

She stood there, shivering and incoherent. "Ja—Jared. I need a place to stay for a bit." Her legs barely held her upright.

The bat clattered to the floor and he caught her before she collapsed. "Emma!"

When he lifted her in his arms and kicked the door closed behind him, Emma began to shake all over. She was soaked through. Her breathing came in erratic pants and her teeth chattered. "So c-c-cold."

A half hour later, Emma emerged from Jared's bathroom, steam rolling out behind her. Tucked in a thick terry towel, her wet hair hanging around her shoulders, she turned down the hall and entered the kitchen.

Jared raised a blond eyebrow right before he poured her a mug of coffee. He'd shaven and pulled on jeans and a sweater while she'd taken a shower. When she sat down at the small two-seater table, he set the coffee in front of her. "Want cream?"

She nodded mutely.

Grabbing the milk from the fridge, he pushed the carton toward her and sat down in the chair across from her. "Start from the beginning."

Seeing him like this, outside of a boss-employee situation, he appeared so much closer to her age, even though he'd just turned thirty last month. Emma glanced down at the coffee mug tucked between her hands. "I—um, it's complicated." If she told him everything, he'd insist she call the police. She couldn't put her aunt in harm's way. What she needed was a safe place to stay and think.

"What happened? Did you argue with your aunt or something?"

She met his concerned, deep blue gaze and wished she didn't have to lie. "Yes, I brought up moving to the city. She refused to budge. We had a huge blowout."

He glanced at the streaks of dawn just showing through window and his eyebrows shot up. "This early in the morning?"

Unable to meet his steady stare, she quickly made up the

rest of the story as she poured milk into her coffee. "I was supposed to start my classwork early and get it e-mailed off to my professor before I had to take my aunt to her doctor's appointment later this morning, but I couldn't sleep. I tried to talk to my aunt about possibly moving closer and that's when the fighting started." Glancing up at him, her voice trembled. "I just needed to get away for a bit. Can I stay here?"

"Don't you have to take your aunt to the doctor in a few hours?"

His question twisted a knife of worry deep in her gut. Her aunt was a tough cookie. Not much scared the woman. *Please let her heart be able handle all that's happened to her,* Emma silently prayed. *And whoever took her better not have harmed a single gray hair on her head!* "My aunt called a friend to take her so I could come into work on time."

When he didn't answer right away, she grimaced. "At least I won't be late for work today."

Jared smiled. "There is that." Standing, he walked over and picked up his phone from the counter. "I can't have you serving customers in a towel. My clothes dryer's on the fritz. I'll call my little sister to bring you some girl stuff. She's about your size. Until then, I've got something you can borrow."

Relief lifted some of the weight off her chest. "Thanks, Jared."

He looked up from dialing. "Your shift starts in a few hours. You can use my bed to catch up on some sleep."

She cast a gaze over her shoulder to the living room. "I'll crash on your couch if that's okay."

Once Jared hung up with his sister, he walked into his bedroom and then came out and placed a stack of clothes in her arms. "Here's something to wear until my sister gets here."

Emma waited until Jared was in the shower before she

quickly changed into his clothes and then lay down on the couch. She didn't think she could sleep, her head was so jumbled up with worry for her aunt, but she forced herself to close her eyes and lay very still even as her mind raced.

A half hour later, Jared passed by the couch and lifted his coat off the rack by the door. "I'm leaving." His hair was back to its normal finger-combed blond waves and he smelled like soap. "My sister should be by later with some stuff for you." He shook his head at his jeans bunched loosely around her hips. "If she doesn't make it in time, we'll just have to declare it sloppy casual Friday." Chuckling, Jared turned and opened the door. "See you downstairs later."

"Thanks, Jared." Emma's eyelids felt so heavy, she lay back on the couch and closed her eyes. As thoughts about her aunt filled her mind, her entire body sank deeper into the cushions, and she suddenly realized why she felt so tired. She hadn't taken her vitamin last night or the night before because she'd run out. Sometimes it really sucked living with a vitamin deficiency.

Her aunt would kill her if she knew Emma forgot to tell her she needed a refill on her pills. She'd lost count of the number of times Mary had pointed a finger at her, pale blue eyes squinting in her wrinkled round face. "I don't want to lose you like I did your mom. It's not something you grow out of. It's in your genes, Emma Marie Gray. Don't skip a single day."

Closing her eyes against the tears that threatened, Emma prayed she got to hear those stern words from her aunt again. As the hours crept by, she grew more and more tense. A light knock on the door jarred Emma from her worried thoughts.

"Hey, it's Jared's sister, Tanya. I brought you some stuff," a muffled female voice called through the front door.

When Emma jumped up to answer the door, she almost fell over. Dizziness ensued and her ears rang. Shaking her head to clear it, she quickly pulled open the door. A woman with spiky, short blond hair blew her slant-cut bangs out of her eyes and handed Emma a black duffel bag. "Here ya go. I hope I picked some things that'll work for you."

As soon as Emma took the bag, Tanya turned and headed back down the stairs, waving to her. "I have to take off or I won't make it to work on time."

Knife-sharp frigid air gusted against the door, slicing through Emma's lungs as she called after Tanya, "Thank you so much." Shivering, she cast her gaze upward. The rain had stopped, but the sky was heavy with bumpy white clouds. Snow was coming. Emma closed the door and glanced at the kitchen wall clock. She had a half hour to get dressed and make it downstairs before her shift started.

Once she'd changed into Tanya's pink retro Go-Gos T-shirt and a pair of dark jeans that fit a little too snug compared to how she normally preferred her clothes, Emma glanced at her long, black, bed-head hair and immediately searched through the duffel bag for a rubber band. After looking through makeup, shampoo and other girly stuff, she remembered Tanya had short hair and gave up her search in an effort to "finger-comb" her hair into some kind of order.

Damn, she had all the pep of a slug. She needed to get her vitamin prescription refilled. Pronto. Grabbing her cell phone from her coat pocket, she found the phone book in a kitchen drawer, looked up the pharmacy then quickly dialed the number.

"MedCare pharmacy," a woman said in a cheery tone.

"Hi, this is Emma Gray. I'm calling to refill my vitamin prescription."

Keys tapped in the background. "I'm sorry, but I don't have a prescription listed for an Emma Gray."

"It's probably under my aunt's name. Try Mary Gray."

"I'm sorry, but I can't give out that information, since you aren't Mary Gray. I can tell you that we have never filled a prescription here for vitamins under the name Emma Gray."

Completely bewildered, Emma hung up the phone. Had her aunt filled her prescription at another pharmacy? She doubted it. Mary was a creature of habit in the highest order. When she found a pharmacy she liked—any store, for that matter—she stuck with it, even though she'd moved away from the city. Plus, Emma had always driven her there and waited in the car while Mary got the prescription filled.

Pulling her vitamin bottle out of her purse, she held it under the kitchen light to see if maybe she'd dialed the wrong number. No, the number on the label was the number she'd called and the label was in her name, not her aunt's. Emma squinted when she noticed what looked like writing underneath the label.

Once she peeled the white printed label back, she was surprised to see a phone number handwritten on the back of the label. Her hands shook as she dialed the phone number. The phone rang and rang. She was about to hang up when a recording came on.

"Leave a message." A man's raspy voice came across the line. At the beep, Emma spoke quickly. "Hi. My name is Emma Gray. I found your number written on my bottle of prescription vitamins. I believe my aunt, Mary Gray, might have purchased them from your pharmacy. Can you please return my call?" Emma gave her cell phone number and then hung up. She was about to put her cell phone back in her pocket when she realized she'd left her charger at home. Turning the phone off to save the battery, Emma slipped it back into her coat pocket and mentally reminded herself to check her voice mail as soon as she got off work.

Sliding the empty pill bottle into her coat's inside pocket, Emma slid her arms into the jacket and grimaced that it was still slightly damp. As she started to head out the door, she saw Jared's red baseball cap on the rack. Grabbing the hat, she tucked her rumpled hair underneath it before she ran down the stairs. Jared would never let her live it down if she were late this time.

While Emma went through the day's paces of ringing up customer's bills, making lattes, heating up bagels, muffins and other pastries, her mind turned over question after question.

Why did someone go to such lengths just to talk to her? Was her aunt okay? And what was up with her vitamin prescription? Why had her aunt led her to believe she'd gotten them at MedCare Pharmacy? A thought suddenly occurred that shocked Emma; she knew they were strapped for money with her taking classes, but good grief…was her aunt buying prescriptions off the black market? Is that what all this was about? Emma didn't know what was and what wasn't the truth at this point. All she knew was, that damned empty pill bottle sat in her jacket pocket, weighing as heavily on her mind as her aunt's safety.

She might be upset at her situation, her mind completely on edge, but as the day wore on, she began to feel better and more alert than she had in a long time. The coffee smelled stronger, the pastry aromas sweeter. Her energy level had shot up, too. Then again, the heightened sensations were probably due to the three espresso shots she'd had earlier. She

was so wound up that she felt as if she was perched on a pre-
cipice, waiting for something to happen.

The indescribable sense of awareness stayed with her all
day, prickling her skin, sharpening her senses with each
passing hour. Emma was so tuned in to her surroundings that
she found it hard to filter out the normal conversational "white
noise" going on around her.

A couple more people entered the shop and their voices
carried to her finely tuned ear while she wiped crumbs off a
table with a wet cloth.

"You don't need coffee."

"But I *like* coffee."

"Wuss."

The first voice sounded familiar. Emma's head snapped
up and her gaze zeroed in on the two guys who were heading
to the counter. The auburn-haired man was wearing only a
T-shirt and jeans. No gloves, no scarf or hat, just a T-shirt…
in twenty-degree weather? The nut. He probably *did* need
coffee.

As she stared at them in surprise, Caine's eyes locked with
hers. Pulling his hands out of his black leather coat's pockets,
he paused and smiled. Heat shot everywhere throughout her
body at once. Her primal response, mixed with fear and anger,
welled up inside her, bubbling hot and building steam. She
blinked several times to focus her jumbled, conflicting
emotions to one—anger. Emma turned away, her stomach
twisting in knots. She scrubbed the table with the cloth, trying
to decide what to do.

"Hey, Hat Girl," Caine said in a low voice, tapping the bill
of her cap. Emma slowly lifted her head and stared at him.
His friend was at the counter ordering.

She narrowed her gaze. "Why are you here? I thought I was supposed to meet you at the club tonight."

"Huh? Laird wanted a coffee and I remembered the café logo on the napkin I handed back to you last night. I came by hoping this was a place you frequented—"

Setting the cloth down, she stepped into his personal space and hissed, "Where is my *aunt?*"

A look of confusion crossed his face. "Your aunt? What are you talking about?"

"Emma, I need your key. The drawer's jammed again," Scott called from behind the register. He was trying to ring up Caine's friend's order.

"Coming," she responded. She was so tense that she thought she might lose it any second. Her attention snapped back to Caine. "Why did you take her? Answer me!"

His big hands surrounded her fists in a firm hold and his brow creased in a deep furrow. "I don't know what you're talking about. What's going on?"

Emma sucked in her breath at the tingling, near burning sensation where his hands covered hers. She jerked away and backed up a step.

Caine frowned. Glancing at his palms, he rubbed his fingers across them and mumbled, "That was…intense."

Emma's physical reaction to his touch frightened her. She honestly felt like she was going to jump right out of her skin. Electric didn't begin to describe the sensation. More like shocking. Caine had seemed taken aback by her question, like he didn't have a clue what she was talking about. "You didn't follow me home, did you?"

He fisted his hands and his black eyebrows slashed downward. Jaw flexing, he said in a suddenly serious tone, "No."

Cool wind rushed in, heralding a group of talkative business-men into the café. Emma glanced at the side counter. The milks and stirrers needed to be replenished. Coffee drinkers got cranky when their condiments weren't readily available. She would normally ask Scott to do it, but he was busy with a crowd at the register and John was in the back unloading supplies.

"I have to go," she said, even as a sense of relief released some of the tension from her chest—at least as far as Caine was concerned. She was glad he wasn't the bad person her mind had begun to think he might be, but…who else saw her at the club last night? She didn't *know* anyone in town. Shaking her head, she blew out an unsteady breath and said, "My apologies for what I said. I was mistaken," then grabbed the cloth and headed to the supply closet.

Emma stood in the back of the supply closet, trying to reach the stirrers on the top shelf when Caine leaned over her shoulder and lifted the white box down for her.

The instant his hard chest pressed against her back, his body heat made her skin prickle all over. Emma quickly stepped away and turned to face him. "Um…thanks."

Before she could walk off, Caine clasped her shoulders, his expression intense. "Emma. Talk to me. Tell me what's wrong. Maybe I can help you."

His hazel eyes were interesting, an intriguing mix of forest green and brown. The colors seemed to meld and pulse in intensity as he talked. Hearing her name in his deep baritone sounded more intimate and personal than Hat Girl, way more personal than her dream. It sent a delicious thrill zipping along her spine. The warmth and comfort of his hands soaked through her T-shirt, even as the cotton barrier buffered the electric effect that had happened earlier. Something about the

look on his face and his firm grip felt dangerous and excit-
ing…and strangely trustworthy, while his inviting smell made
her want to tell him everything, to trust him completely.

It would be so easy to ask him to be there in the background
at the club tonight, if nothing else but for support, but she
didn't know who, among the faces of strangers at the club,
would be watching. What if they did have her aunt, and
Caine's presence by her side angered the people who took
Mary? Emma couldn't take the risk with her aunt's life.

Regretful, she shrugged out of his hold. "I'm fine, Caine.
I have to go."

He didn't say anything as he followed her out of the room.
She felt his heavy gaze track her every movement while she
refilled the stirrers at the condiments counter, felt the heat of his
intense stare trace her every step when she moved behind the
main counter to replenish the skim and whole milk thermoses.

Jared's hand landed on her shoulder, making her jump.
Concern laced his tone. "Hey, you okay? You seem to be in
some kind of a daze."

She glanced over her shoulder to see Caine sitting at a table
near the far window. His friend was drinking a mug of coffee
and talking to him, but Caine hadn't taken his eyes off her.

"Have you talked to your aunt yet?" Jared continued, drawing her attention. "I really think you should stick to your guns
about moving closer to town if that's what you want to do."

Emma tried her best to smile at him, although it probably
came across more like a grimace. "I'll…" She swallowed the
hard knot in her throat. What if she never got to speak to her
aunt again? Unshed tears burned her eyes. "I'll do that."

He tugged on her cap's bill. "You've got a free pass tonight,
roomie, but tomorrow you're going to have to talk to her."

Her smile wobbled. "Thanks, Jared."

"Sure thing." An encouraging smile tilted his lips and he swept his gaze over her Go-Gos T-shirt and jeans. "I'm glad my sister made it by."

"Please thank her again for me."

He nodded. "Why don't you go ahead and take off. We have it covered."

"Really? I still have another forty minutes on my shift."

He laughed. "Take the generosity while it's being offered, Emma."

"Yeah, it happens like…never to me." Scott's curly black hair fell into his eyes. He'd glanced at them over his shoulder after ringing up another customer.

Emma nibbled her bottom lip. "I guess I could try to catch up on my sleep." *And check my voice mail to see if that other pharmacist called back.*

"That couch is hard as a rock. Use my bed. You'll sleep bet—"

Something shattered on the hard floor. Caine's auburn-haired friend lifted his hands and called across the room, "Sorry, the mug slipped."

"Scott…" Emma started to ask him to take care of it.

"I know, I know." Scott grabbed a white towel. He paused as he came around the counter. "Dude, it's in the middle of the room. What'd you do? Throw it?"

Emma had been avoiding Caine's gaze, but at that moment their gazes locked for a split second and her stomach dropped. Sitting sideways in his seat, he'd leaned forward slightly with his fist clenched on the table. He looked intense and on edge—like he was about to launch across the room.

When she turned to leave, Emma decided to exit through the back way. She had a feeling Caine had no intention of giving up on trying to talk to her. Any other time, she'd have been thrilled to have the sexy man's undivided and intense attention, but tonight she couldn't afford to screw up.

Chapter 3

"Give me your damned cell, Laird," Caine snarled under his breath.

Laird shook his head and leaned back in his seat to pull his cell from his pocket. As he handed it across to Caine, he said, "That human's got you some kind of eff'd up, bro."

Caine snatched the phone and quickly punched in Kaitlyn's cell number. Thrumming his fingers on the table, he waited for her to pick up. When voice mail came on, he clenched his jaw and ticked off the seconds before he was able to leave a message.

"It's Caine. We haven't heard back from you. I have something important I have to do at the club tonight. It's a gut call. I'm going."

When he closed the phone and slid it across the table to his pack mate, Laird nodded to the guy who'd just finished cleaning up the broken mug, then frowned at Caine, saying in a low voice, "I really wanted to finish that coffee."

Caine shrugged. "You were being a prick."

Laird smirked. "I smell the blond guy's interest in the girl, too."

When Caine narrowed his gaze, Laird sighed. "I've always trusted your instincts, but going back there without being able to see or smell the Velius will be risky. I know your going to the club tonight has something to do with the woman you were just blatantly eavesdropping on." He glanced toward Emma as she disappeared into the kitchen. "I'll admit, she smells…" He paused, like he was trying to think of the right word to describe her scent.

"Earthy and primal," Caine added, his tone full of gravel.

Laird snapped his fingers and his eyes lit up. "That's it! She smells like the woods."

Caine shook his head and his heart thumped hard. "It's more like she took a long walk in a misty forest. She's all woman, but the scent of rain-soaked leaves and earth clings to her."

When he was close to Emma in the supply closet, Caine made sure to scent her. As soon as he'd inhaled, his predatory hunting senses kicked in. In the small room, her strong scent had made his fingers itch to capture her like prey, leaving her nowhere else to turn. Caine shook off the strange, aggressive emotion that rushed full force to his brain. A human was no competition for him, and yet she'd said she would be his ultimate challenge. One thing was true, she aroused him on many levels.

Instead, he focused on the protective instincts that had sent him in the closet after her in the first place. She'd seemed both angry and fearful when she'd asked why he was at the café when he was supposed to meet her at the club. And what was this about her aunt? He wanted to know who had frightened or threatened her.

"Emma was the woman I was talking to outside the parking garage last night. I met her at the club."

Laird shrugged. "You know where she works now. Talk to her here."

Caine shook his head. "I have to go to the club tonight. I think she might be in some kind of trouble."

"You'd put yourself out there like a lamb for slaughter because of some human woman?" Laird's eyes closed to near slits.

Caine slammed his fist on the table. "Shut up and listen."

Once Caine relayed the strange conversation he'd had with Emma, he finished with, "She was told to go there tonight." He jerked his head toward the counter. "She's staying with that guy, which makes me think she doesn't have any family to turn to. I could tell by her heart rate that she lied to him about why she's staying with him. I don't want Emma going to that club alone."

Laird rubbed the back of his neck. "Damn, I hope Kaitlyn calls us. Do you know when Emma planned on going?"

"No. She just alluded to having to meet the person at the club tonight when she thought I was 'him' and something about her aunt being taken."

Laird jerked his gaze back toward the kitchen door. "Why don't you just ask her?"

Caine ground his teeth. "I tried. She wouldn't tell me."

"No wonder this woman is so appealing to you." Laird's grin was smug. "If you can't charm her, you'd see her as a challenge."

It was a helluva lot more than that, Caine thought, rubbing his fingers across his palm again.

Laird stood and Caine said in a dark tone, "Where are you going?"

"You didn't plan to camp here all day, did you?"

"I was going to try and talk to her when she got off work."

Laird raised an eyebrow. "Let's find out when that'll be."

Before Caine could tell him to mind his own damned business, that she'd be leaving soon, Laird got up and walked over to the counter to speak to the guy who'd cleaned up his coffee mug earlier. "Sorry about the mess, man. When does this café close?"

"We close at eight."

Laird leaned forward, his tone conspiratorial. "My buddy wants to ask Emma out. Any idea when she gets off work?"

"She's already left for the evening," Jared answered as he walked out of the kitchen wiping his hands on a towel. Cutting his distrustful gaze toward Caine, the café owner continued, "Do either of you two plan to order anything else?"

Annoyed with Laird, Caine bit back the fierce growl that rumbled in his chest when the blond man's tone turned challenging. The guy had no idea Caine could smell his testosterone level spiking. Did Emma know how her boss felt about her?

Determined to find her, Caine stood up from the table and said in a cold tone, "Let's go, Laird."

The second they walked outside, Caine concentrated and inhaled. He caught Emma's scent instantly. She was close. Laird followed him around the side of the building. "You scented her?"

Caine nodded and paced around the small beat-up car in the parking lot beside the café. "Her scent is on this vehicle.

It might be hers." Approaching the stairs that led to a second level above the store, his focus zeroed in on the door at the top of the stairs. "She's up there. Must be his apartment."

"You can't go up there, bang on the door and demand that she tell you everything. You'll scare the shit out of her."

Caine clenched his fists in frustration. Laird was right. "Let's go back to my apartment for now. We'll just have to be at the club the moment it opens."

"It would be helpful if Kaitlyn could be here tonight," Laird said as they stood outside Squeeze an hour later. Sleet had been pouring down on them for a good ten minutes.

"I called Roman to help even the odds." Caine jammed his hands into his coat pockets, then swept his gaze over Laird. "The least you could've done was wear a coat and pretend you're affected by the weather like the rest of the humans. You look like a freak wearing nothing but a thin shirt in twenty-degree weather. Your hair is turning to a block of ice."

Laird laughed and plumes of frost floated in front of him. Brushing the sleet out of his hair, he glanced at the long line ahead of them. "You'd think the weather would've deterred some people from coming tonight."

Caine snorted. "When it's the first big snow of the year, humans go a little nuts. Think about how it affects our pack."

"I'm here, boyeeees!" Roman slid across the icy edges of the sidewalk and came to a stop next to them. He flipped his shoulder-length blond hair away from his face, his grin wider than usual and full of mischief. "Let's par-tay!"

Of all the Lupreda, Roman was the most "at home" in the ice and snow. Whereas Laird approached his role of financial planner and investor of the Lupreda's entire portfolio with calculated shrewdness, Roman contributed financially by entering and winning snowboarding competitions. "I get paid to play" was his motto. The first snow of the year always revved him up. "Case in point," Caine said in a dry tone with a pointed look at Roman.

Laird grinned his agreement and rocked back on his heels. "Have you seen Emma yet?"

Caine shook his head and focused on Roman. "I've brought you up to speed with what we know. Got any questions?"

Roman's expression turned serious. "No. I'm good."

Caine cut his gaze to Laird. "Do you have your phone on vibrate in case Kaitlyn calls us back?"

"Yes. You grab yours before we left?" Laird asked.

Caine nodded. "Since I called Kaitlyn on your cell, I want to make sure we don't miss her call."

"Hello, my two favorite dancing partners!" The blonde from last night walked up and wrapped her arms around Laird's waist from behind. "And who's this?" she said with interest, tilting her head and eyeing Roman appreciatively.

"What happened to you last night?" the brunette whispered in Caine's ear while hooking her arm in his.

As Laird started to introduce Roman, Caine waited to see his friend maneuver his way around the fact he didn't know either of the girls' names.

Roman took care of it for them in typical "Roman" style. "Hello, ladies. I'm Roman. It's nice to meet you." He bent over each of their hands and planted kisses on one and then the other.

When the blonde said something about three men being better than two, Caine learned their names were Veronica and Mandy. Although, in this dangerous game of wolf verses panther, he highly doubted those were the girls' real names.

Caine's cell phone began to vibrate in his front pocket and the brunette rubbed her thigh against his. "Hmm, I'll have to use my cell and call you a lot tonight."

His lips tilted in a devilish smile. "Hold that thought." Pulling his cell phone from his pocket, Caine tensed when he saw Landon was calling. If he answered, the women would be able to hear Landon's voice. He couldn't take a chance in case the panthers' hearing was just as keen as werewolves. He hung up on Landon's call and quickly typed a text message—*Catya later! At the club. Now*—then sent it.

Laird's eyebrows lifted. "Who was that?"

Caine slid his cell back into his pocket. "My roommate. I told him I was here and I'd catch up with him later." Wrapping his arm around the brunette's shoulders, he hoped Landon got his coded message.

From the moment Emma walked into the club, men made a beeline to her. To bolster her confidence, she'd taken the time to at least comb through her hair, dab on some lip gloss and change into another outfit Jared's sister had provided.

Emma tensed at every offer to dance or for a drink, wondering which man was the bastard who'd written the note and kidnapped her aunt. After the tenth time she had to turn down someone, she regretted not asking Jared to come. At least with a man by her side, the other guys might've left her alone. But while she and Jared ate dinner together at his apartment earlier, he'd told her that Caine had asked about her after she'd left the café and how much it had really bothered him. He went on to tell her that he wanted to get to know her better outside of work and not as her boss.

With the way Jared's feelings seemed to be changing toward her, Emma didn't want to give him a reason to think she'd return them. She thought of Jared as a wonderful friend, nothing more. Because she couldn't tell him why she was going to the club, asking him to come along would definitely send out a mixed signal. Not to mention, his constant presence by her side could put her aunt in danger.

Emma had helped clean up after dinner, then she'd checked her voice mail once more for a reply from that number she'd called about her vitamins. Nothing. While Jared took a shower, she'd jotted a quick note saying she'd be back and left. And here she was, standing inside Squeeze an hour earlier than her designated time, being hit on left and right. She had absolutely no interest in getting to know any of these men, nor did she care if they found her boring. How ironic, considering her worries while she'd waited in line outside just last night.

Snowflakes melted in her hair as she moved her slim cell phone to her jeans' front pocket and then shoved her gloves into her inside coat pocket. Every sound vibrated within her, knocking her heart, thrumming along her jangled nerves. The people danced frenetically, their movements expressive and reckless, their touches more aggressive than the night before. The scents were stronger, too, almost like the smells themselves had been heightened by the snowstorm swirling outside. The way the wind howled as she walked over from Jared's apartment promised blizzard conditions within the hour. She didn't care. She wanted answers and for her aunt to return home safe.

Emma scanned the crowd and, once again, as if he were emitting some kind of invisible pheromone only she could zero in on, her gaze instantly locked on Caine. He was with the same blonde and brunette from last night, but this time he wasn't alone. His tall, auburn-haired friend danced on one side of the blonde, while another man with longish blond hair danced on the other side of the brunette. They made a train of male, female, male, female, male gyrating to the music.

She set her jaw. Caine might've been asking about her earlier, but it didn't take him long to find a replacement. Turning, she walked away, weaving her way through the intimate, two-seater round café tables around the dance floor. She'd climbed the three stairs and was almost to the bar area when someone grabbed her arm.

"Emma!"

She didn't look at Caine, but pulled from his hold and kept walking.

"Things aren't always—" Caine began, following behind her.

"What they seem?" She faced him with a raised eyebrow, then shrugged. "It doesn't matter. I didn't come here looking for you."

As she started to walk away once more, he gripped her elbow. "The only reason I came tonight was because I thought you might be in some kind of trouble."

"You have an interesting way of keeping yourself busy," she said in a dry tone. Even though her heart tripped at the thought he seemed sincere in his desire to help her, she needed to do this alone. Shaking her head, she continued with a sigh. "I'm fine, Caine. Thanks for your concern."

Caine's hand slid down her elbow until his fingers locked with hers. She shivered at the electric heat that swept through her. The intensity was so…conflicted, almost as if her body wanted to shove him away, yet at the same time felt drawn to his touch. Like magnets with the same ends facing each other—pushing away, while a strong pull remained along the fringes, demanding that the attractive ends finally find each other and slam together.

Lifting their locked hands between them, he used his hold to pull her closer. "I know you feel what happens when we touch, Emma. I can't explain it either, but I want you to trust me. Come dance with me."

The man towered over her. Emma tried to pull free, but he didn't budge. She should be intimidated by his forceful stare, yet she wasn't. She should be angry that he was just dancing with another woman—other *women* but she didn't care. Instead, the moment he stepped close and his primal scent invaded her senses, a strong urge to move as close to him as she possibly could rocked through her. It was irrational. She couldn't explain the attraction or the desire to know why her nerves tingled and sparked under her skin whenever he touched her. But it was there. Intensely strong.

And he wasn't letting go.

She glanced around them to see if anyone was watching. Everyone seemed engrossed in their own activities. Caine's fingers tightened around hers as if he thought she might take flight.

"One dance," she said, *and then I can walk away.* Caine released her hand so she could shrug out of her coat, but the moment she set her jacket on a chair near the bar, he grabbed her hand once more and tugged. He pulled her to the other side of the dance floor and moved to dance along the edges of the crowd, but she shook her head and led him deep into the throng, until they were in the center with everyone dancing around them. It was darkest in the middle and less likely anyone would see her with someone there. The bright colored lights swept the crowd in psychedelic patterns, yet the spot where they stood was the one area the lights didn't shine.

They stood facing each other and the song segued into a slower one. The music thumped and the heavy seductive rhythm poured right into her soul as Caine held her gaze. Wrapping his arm around her waist, he pulled her close. When they began to move to the slow beat, he released her hand and cupped the side of her face. Emma closed her eyes and gasped when the tingling sizzle leapt from her skin to his. Or was it his to hers? She couldn't tell which. Maybe both.

Caine slid his hand into her hair and his jaw brushed her temple when he spoke close to her ear. "Your hair is sparkling all over."

"It's the snow." Emma placed her hands on his dark green button-down shirt, then sucked in her breath at the sensation of his solid chest underneath her fingers. He was hard as a rock and his musky smell was so sinfully decadent she couldn't stop inhaling.

As they continued to slowly move to the music's erotic rhythm, his thumb tilted her chin upward and his dark gaze searched hers. "Your eyes sparkle, too, like they're reflecting golden light. They're mesmerizing."

Embarrassed heat shot up her cheeks. She considered her looks passable and her smile nice, but no one had ever acted as if he was totally enthralled by her. Jared had shown interest, yet the hungry way Caine's gaze searched the planes of her face—like he wanted to taste every part of her—was down-right impossible to resist. Damn, he was good.

"How many times have you said that to a woman?" She

stared at his defined jaw and tried to wrestle control over her scattered emotions. She felt so safe with him, wanted to trust him—that he really *could* help her.

Caine's jaw muscle jumped at the same time he slid his hand underneath her hair. The moment his hot palm cupped the back of her neck, Emma instantly froze in place. Her heart hammered and her breathing turned shallow. Like an animal playing dead in front of a threatening predator, she just stopped moving. She couldn't control the impulse or explain it. It was instinctual and frightening all at once.

"I've never said that to anyone. It was sincere, Emma. I want you to trust me."

When she didn't say anything, his voice lowered. "Look at me."

"Why can't I move?" she whispered. Her gaze snapped to his and her pulse rushed in her ears.

"Maybe because you don't want to," he said as his lips hovered a mere inch from hers. His fingers pressed at the small of her back and his penetrating gaze bored into hers. "Don't you want to know if the fire sparks everywhere we touch?"

The intimate suggestion made her stomach tumble. She fell into his compelling gaze and heard herself say, "Yes."

He moved his hand into her hair and his sexy smile sent her pulse whooshing at a faster rate. "Then kiss m—"

Surprising herself, Emma tilted her head and lifted on her toes to press her lips against his. When their lips met, the conflicting emotions twisting her stomach fled. The heat between them tingled and zapped, frying her mind and her body with visceral lightning-flash intensity.

Every sound around them stripped away; the press of people disappeared. All she heard was their own breathing and the thump of their hearts. She moaned when Caine yanked her against him to press his lips harder against hers.

As he slid his tongue into her mouth, the sensual glide set her skin on fire. He tested her with a steady slow rhythm, his kiss deep and thorough as he explored, tasting her…demanding a matched response. She was so caught up and surprised by how deeply his kiss affected her that her knees actually wobbled. Emma dug her fingers into his shoulders to keep herself upright. His flavor was as irresistible as his earthy primal scent, full of heat and lusty promise.

Her body quaked from the desire she tasted on his tongue and the possessive way he slanted his lips over hers. Emma instinctively locked her hips against his and twined her arms around his neck, her kiss just as aggressive. The vibration of his groan against her mouth felt primitive, passionate…and right. Maybe it was the music, maybe it was his smell or his electric touch. All she knew was, as inexperienced as she was with men, she couldn't get close enough to this one. Her trust in him was inexplicably absolute.

Caine's chest rumbled against hers and his hands slid down her waist. When he gripped her rear in an assertive hold, then pressed his thigh hard against her sex, Emma shivered at the erotic sensations scattering through her. Her body hummed, pulsing with jolts of heat everywhere at once, like she was on some kind of hormonal high. She kissed his jaw and tried to catch her breath. "Closer."

As soon as she spoke, something vibrated against her inner thigh. Emma tensed, then gave a nervous laugh when she realized it was probably his cell phone.

"Sorry, I have to get this." Caine pulled the phone out of his pocket.

After he read the text message, he glanced around the room and tucked the phone back into his pocket. Emma noted his high-alert expression. "What's wrong?"

Caine's mouth set in a firm line and he seemed genuinely torn before he grabbed her hand, his hold tight. "I need to take care of something, but I want you to stay close."

Emma glanced at her watch. She had a half hour before she was supposed to meet with the person who'd left her that note. It was probably best if she did so alone. She pulled out of his hold. "Go do what you need to do." Pointing to the bar area where she'd left her coat, she continued. "I'll be over there." *In an open area where I'll be seen by myself.*

Caine's expression hardened. "I want to help you, Emma. Come with me."

She started to argue when he cursed under his breath and reached into his pocket again, pulling out his cell phone. As he read the text message, she began to back away. "I'll be fine. Just right over there."

He frowned. "Don't move from that spot. I want you to trust me enough to let me help you."

She nodded and turned away. Strangely, now that his smell wasn't seducing her senses, she still believed he wanted to help, even though she didn't think there was anything he could do for her. When she walked up the stairs to a higher spot near the crowded bar, Emma looked around the club for Caine.

He was already on the far side of the room near the entrance, talking to another blond woman. Every few moments, he'd glance Emma's way. Her insides turned to mush. Whatever they were talking about, he couldn't be paying too much attention to the blonde if he kept staring at her.

The song ended and a large group of people from the dance

floor headed for the bar. The mass jostled her, pushing her out of the way as they each vied for the bartender's attention. A sudden painful prick along her hip made Emma gasp in shocked surprise. She tried to turn, but someone spoke next to her ear, preventing her from seeing his face.

"We've been looking for you," a man said in a calm voice. As he spoke, her vision began to blur. When her legs began to collapse underneath her, an arm wrapped around her waist. "Don't fight it. Come along."

"Nooooo," she slurred, barely able to speak, let alone try to fight him off. Whatever he'd injected her with was very powerful and fast-acting. Her ability to resist had completely disappeared.

"That's a good girl," was the last thing Emma heard before she lost consciousness.

Chapter 4

Caine glanced up in time to see Emma stumble and a man with a salt-and-pepper beard and spiky hair hold her upright. When the man turned her around and started escorting her limp form toward the back exit, Caine instantly grabbed Kaitlyn's hand and moved through the crowd as fast as he could. "Emma!" he called, but his voice was drowned out by a sudden loud alarm reverberating through the club.

Someone had pulled the fire alarm.

Pandemonium erupted and people rushed toward the main entrance, creating a wall of people between Caine and the exit where the man had just taken Emma. Across the room, Laird called Caine's name over the screams. Caine saw the two female panthers heading toward the front door. He motioned for Laird and Roman to block their path, but the ladies were quickly swallowed up by the mob.

Landon stood at the entrance of the club, his expression grim and intense as he began to shove his way through the crowd. The moment his Alpha reached them, Caine released his tight hold on Kaitlyn, and a deep snarl unfurled from his throat as he leapt over the crowd toward the exit. He didn't give a damn who saw his inhuman jump. All he cared about was saving Emma. When he landed with a heavy thud near the back exit, he knocked a man in a black shirt back against the wall.

"Watch it!" the man yelled over the alarm.

The main lights came on at that moment, highlighting the man's stark features. He scowled as he pushed himself off the wall. When he started to turn toward the back exit, Caine stepped in front of him and thumbed toward the main entrance. "Go out the other door."

The guy stared at the crowd of people squeezing out the front door, then glared at him before he stalked away. Caine grunted his annoyance at the interruption. He didn't need any witnesses when he shredded the bastard to bits for attempting to kidnap Emma.

The heavy metal door slammed against the building's brick wall as Caine burst through it. His wereclaws were already extended, ready to inflict painful damage. Only an empty alley and a Dumpster greeted him. A howl of fury erupted from his throat as swirls of snow drifted quietly to the ground. He clenched his fists and welcomed the pain his claws inflicted on his palms before they retracted.

A couple seconds later, Landon and Kaitlyn appeared behind him, flanked by Laird and Roman. "Care to tell me what that was all about?" Landon said, peering past the glow of the single floodlight above the door into the dark alley.

"A human woman was just kidnapped," Caine gritted out

before he stepped into the darkness and began looking for tire tracks, clues, anything that would help him find her kidnappers.

"Emma? Who took her?" Laird's brow creased with a frown as he brushed past Landon and Kaitlyn.

"A man with a graying beard and spiky hair." Caine kicked at the offending snow that had begun to cover the tire tracks. In a matter of minutes, he'd lose the scent altogether. Ignoring the cold flakes landing in his hair, he glanced up at Laird, his stomach knotting with guilt. "I saw him drag her toward this exit. I couldn't get to her in time."

"Everyone spread out and scent the entire area," Landon commanded in a hard tone. He walked up to Caine and put a hand on his shoulder. "We'll find her."

Caine's jaw tensed and he gave Landon a curt nod before he turned back to the task of cataloging the scents around him. Emma was scared tonight. He's seen the fear in her eyes and heard the frustration in her voice. Whom had she come to the club to meet?

After several minutes, Laird and Roman approached Caine. "We only detect one fresh, distinct scent," Laird said as he inhaled the frigid air. "There's a human male's scent and Emma's earthy one."

Landon snorted and Kaitlyn put her hand on her mate's arm. "What is it?"

"The scents are all muddled." He rubbed his neck and shook his head. "I can't put my finger on it. Something smells 'off.'" He looked at Caine. "You got them all?"

Why did Emma's scent smell so distinct and different from the human male's to him? Caine wondered, even as he nodded to Landon. "I would recognize the man's scent again if I smelled him." *Whereas I could pick Emma out of a crowd of five hundred people in two seconds flat.* The fire alarm had stopped a few minutes before and he saw red lights flashing around the corner of the building. The fire trucks had finally arrived. Caine turned away to head back inside the club. The moment he walked over the threshold, he saw one of the bartenders lifting Emma's jacket from the chair where she'd left it.

"I'll take that," Caine called out, approaching the man.

The guy eyed the coat, then frowned. "It looks a bit small for you."

Caine's gut tightened. Emma's coat might help him find her. "It's my girlfriend's. She sent me back inside to get it once the alarm stopped."

The dark-headed bartender nodded and handed him the jacket. "That's one less thing to go into lost and found."

Caine gripped the coat tight at the same time Laird and the others walked back inside. "That hers?" Laird asked while Caine felt inside the pocket and pulled out a plastic box with the days of the week marked on the outside and loads of pills in the separate compartments.

He nodded and frowned at the meds, then shoved the box back into her pocket and felt around once more. When his fingers brushed against a set of keys, he pulled them out and held them in front of him. "These might help me find out where she lives."

Ten minutes later, Laird stood watch while Caine shoved Emma's car key in her car's passenger-side door. The crowd had dispersed and the fire trucks had driven off, leaving the street strangely quiet, while the heavy snow continued to coat their hair and clothes.

"How is this going to help you find her house again?" Laird asked over his shoulder.

"Registration," Caine said. Pulling the glove box open, he rifled through the paperwork inside, then held the paper aloft. "Bingo."

A light came on above them, and a guy walked of out the apartment above the café, carrying a trash bag. "Hey!" he yelled down into the parking lot. It was the guy from the café, the owner. "That's not your car."

Caine and Laird took off the moment he went back inside, threatening to call the police.

"Damn, Caine, your woman lives in the boonies, doesn't she?" Roman commented from the backseat after Laird pulled down the long gravel driveway, then cut the engine in front of a small house ensconced deep in the forest near the Greenwood Lake area.

"Apparently she likes her privacy," Caine mused while Landon and Kaitlyn drove up behind them in Landon's truck.

Kaitlyn hopped out and was walking toward the house before Landon had shut off the engine. She'd removed her blond wig, and had pulled her red hair up in a clip. Caine tensed when she quickly withdrew her gun from the holder at her waist and motioned for Landon, her expression suddenly concerned.

Caine and Landon reached her side at the same time. "Do you see it?" Kaitlyn whispered, pointing toward the dark house.

Landon's body stiffened. "Velius," he said in a clipped tone. Stepping in front of Kaitlyn, he approached the house with a guarded stance. When he was within twenty feet, he called over his shoulder, "The house is empty. I don't sense any heartbeats."

Why were the panthers at Emma's house? Caine's chest constricted as he entered the house behind Kaitlyn and Landon, Roman and Laird following in his wake.

The moment they stepped inside, Kaitlyn gave a low whistle. "There are handprints everywhere, like they searched every nook and cranny."

Landon snorted. "They were a lot neater here than at my office." He gestured to Caine, Laird and Roman. "See what scents you can pick up, if any. Right now I only smell one human. A woman."

Roman sniffed the air and walked into the living room, then stepped briefly down the hall before coming back. "I smell one human, as well, and residual earthy scents." He tilted his head to the side. "The human's scent is laced with several man-made chemicals."

Kaitlyn came out of the kitchen holding a few medicine bottles. "You're smelling her meds." She glanced at the name on the labels. "According to these, her name is Mary Gray and she has a heart condition among other things."

That explained the jam-packed pillbox in Emma's pocket. Must be her aunt's, Caine thought. He walked down the hall to peer into the two bedrooms. One room appeared to be someone else's and the second definitely had to be Emma's with an old desktop computer and a stack of schoolbooks. He definitely picked up two scents. Why didn't they smell Emma's like he did? "This doesn't make any sense." His chest tensed as he stood in the doorway to Emma's room.

"Whoa!" Kaitlyn brushed past him and walked into Emma's room. "This room explodes with handprints." She moved to the bathroom and Caine heard her opening cabinets and pulling back the shower curtain. Something wary settled in his stomach when Kaitlyn came back out and she looked at her mate standing behind Caine.

"She's a panther."

"You're wrong!" Caine snarled even as his inner wolf acknowledged the fact Emma had smelled distinctly unique from any human he'd come across.

"*That's* what I smelled in the alley. That faint scent I couldn't place," Landon said in a low tone. "It has been a long time since I've smelled a Velius and her scent was so faint I thought I'd imagined it."

Caine felt as if someone had slammed a hot poker deep inside his chest. He suppressed the sense of betrayal that threatened within him. A panther? "There's some explanation," he said in a curt tone.

"It's all right here," Landon said as he moved to stand beside his mate in the bedroom.

Caine wanted to explore Emma's room, to see what kind of books she liked to read, what she was studying, to check out her taste in music. He didn't want to have to look at her room like this…as if she were a criminal to be analyzed. Kaitlyn approached him and put her hand on his arm. "I'm sorry, Caine, but I just checked out her most private toiletries to be sure before I said anything. They were covered in her sparkling handprints." She gestured toward the room. "Her keyboard, her books, her pillow and sheets, her hairbrush, her toothbrush. Everything carries these sparkles. No other room in the house has this much residue."

"But we smelled her earthy scent," Laird started to say, when Caine cut him off by speaking in his head. *Don't say anything.*

"You scented her?" Landon's stare was shrewd.

Caine knew what that question meant. Landon would want them to hunt her. "Neither of us thought to. She was human."

"Who happened to smell of the earth?" Landon challenged. *Why aren't you telling him?* Laird spoke to Caine in his mind.

Caine's mental reply was terse, not meant to be argued with. *Something's not right. I need to do some digging.* "We were unaware of the Velius' existence until recently when you killed that one to protect Kaitlyn's mom." He paused and glanced at Laird and Roman before he returned his attention to Landon. "Since the Velius were created and set free before our time, we didn't know that's what they smelled like."

"Now you do," Landon said. "Though I'm partially to blame for not cluing all of you in on their scent markers. It hadn't occurred to me to do so, because all the panthers we've run across have masked their scent. Hers was so faint and slightly different than I remembered that I almost missed it."

Emma's not part of this, Caine wanted to yell, even though he couldn't deny her smell or the electric shock that happened between them whenever they touched. It was something he definitely couldn't explain. He'd never experienced that before with anyone, human or Lupreda. "Fill us in on what we need to know about these panthers."

Landon rolled his head from shoulder to shoulder before he spoke. "They can't shift without a specialized injection straight into their system, and they can only stay in their panther form until the injection wears off. Usually after a couple of hours. They're powerful beasts and would be more-than-worthy adversaries, but the Lupreda who created them to hunt for prey wanted to ensure equal footing. The Velius' black coats radiate iridescence and their eyes give off a glow in the absence of light, taking away the panthers' best hunting advantage in the dark—the element of surprise."

While they were in the club earlier, Emma's hair had sparkled and her eyes had flashed in the dim light, attracting him like a jacked-up wolf on his first full-mooned run of the month. Caine's heart sank. There was no denying that she was Velius. *Why wasn't she masking her scent?* He *had* scented Emma, but he wanted to find her first, to give her a chance to explain what she was and why she was pretending to be human.

"Is there anything else we should know?" Caine's tone held a sharp edge. Frustration warred within him. He wanted to believe she was special. He wanted answers, damn it!

"They don't heal as quickly as we do." Landon's features turned to stone and his body tensed. "Maybe this whole thing is some kind of setup. A cat-and-mouse game the Velius are playing with the Lupreda. Panthers are known for their ambush hunting style."

Caine didn't like Landon assuming Emma had played them. She was truly upset at the café and the club. He tensed and started to challenge Landon when Kaitlyn brushed past them both. "Let's check out the rest of the house. Maybe we'll find more answers."

Caine moved to follow Landon and Roman down the hall when Laird spoke to him mentally once more. *You know I trust you, but holding back could put our pack in jeopardy.*

Pausing, Caine narrowed his gaze on Laird. *Spoken like Landon's* true *Second,* he said before he turned away.

Laird's hand landed hard on his shoulder, stopping him. *I'll heed your judgment on this one. You have twenty-four hours to find her on your own.*

Caine didn't speak nor did he look Laird's way. The respect his pack mate paid him was enough. He grunted his appreciation and Laird's hand fell away.

When Caine and Laird walked into the other bedroom, Kaitlyn held up several clear packets full of hundreds of white pills. A couple empty brown medicine bottles and a stack of pretyped labels were in her other hand. It appeared she'd pulled them from a box she'd set on the bed.

She glanced at the writing on the labels. "It says these are prescription vitamins for Emma Gray, but I'll bet you money this is how the panthers are masking their scent." Setting the packets on the bed, she took a pill out of one of the sleeves and handed it to Landon. "Want to pulverize this so I can see if my theory is true?"

Landon crushed the pill between his fingers, then murmured, "Son of a bitch," as he spread it across his open palm.

Kaitlyn nodded. "That's what I thought. The meds might be suppressing their scent, but they're also causing them to leave behind the sparkling handprint residue. At least we have one answer." She met Caine's gaze. "There was only one area of this room that had the iridescent handprints." She paused and pointed to the bottom nightstand drawer. "The person had this box with the medicine hidden under stacks of magazines and newspapers. I think the human woman must've been giving them to Emma." She frowned for a second. "Humans are helping the panthers?"

"Members of the mafia were working with them in the pulser gun-running case a few months ago," Landon reminded her with a shrug.

She shook her head. "This feels different to me. This is a home. There aren't any stolen pulser guns here, nothing malicious or illegal that I can see."

Landon scowled. "The damned pills give them too much stealthy power."

Caine shook his head. He needed answers and Emma was the only one who could give them to him.

Roman walked into the room holding a piece of paper. "This was on the floor behind the front door."

Caine read the note and ground his teeth. Crushing the paper into a tight ball, he tossed it to Landon. "She told me her aunt had been taken. We need to find her. Not only did they kidnap her aunt, but they've taken her, as well."

Landon read the note, then narrowed his gaze on Caine. "This could be an elaborate trap. The Velius' actions so far have been conniving and deadly. We need to proceed with caution."

"She's guilty until proven innocent. Is that it?" Caine's jaw felt like metal that had been heated then cooled too quickly. He was ready to snap.

"Have you forgotten the three zerkers they tortured and killed? I will not lose any more wolves, Caine." Alpha fury vibrated off Landon as he clenched his hand into a fist.

"I'm not volunteering anyone but me," Caine shot back, his neck hairs bristling.

"Nothing is open at this hour," Kaitlyn cut in with a calm tone. "Why don't we start with the pharmacy listed on these labels first thing in the morning." She turned to Caine with a meaningful look. "Maybe we can find out who's supplying the panthers this medicine and backtrack to other connections from there."

Caine gave her a curt nod, then left the room.

When Laird pulled up outside Caine's apartment over an hour later, he spoke in a low tone after Caine slid out of the car. "Twenty-four hours is all I can promise."

"Understood." Caine grabbed Emma's coat and shut the door behind him. Worry for her cramped his stomach as he climbed the stairs to his apartment three at a time. After he'd let himself in the door, he settled on the sofa and inhaled her coat's collar. Fresh soap and shampoo scents coated the material, but her earthy, forestlike smell still lingered faintly. It wasn't enough to scent her, though. He was relieved he'd already set her unique markers to memory earlier.

Unfortunately the snow still falling steadily outside confused his senses, making it impossible to try and find her right now. Not to mention New York was wall-to-wall people and buildings. He could search for a couple weeks before he found her…and that was if her captors kept her in one place. But he would find her. He just hoped like hell he wasn't too late to help her. If he was, no one involved would be breathing when he left the place. He clenched his fists tightly around Emma's coat.

Caine heard a cracking sound and his fingers eased up on the thick material. Sliding his hand into the inside coat pocket, he pulled out a pair of gloves and what used to be a pill bottle before he'd crushed it. As he tossed the gloves to the couch, a couple of the bottle's hard plastic pieces fell away from the label. Caine frowned when he saw black writing on the backside of the paper. Thumbing back the label, he memorized the phone number and stood, pulling his cell phone out of his pocket.

Punching in a number and an extension he'd seen Landon use before for the police precinct, he waited until a woman answered, then said, "Hi, Sandra. This is Caine Grennard. I'm working with Landon Rourke and Kaitlyn McKinney on a case and I'm wondering if you could do me a favor. I need to have a phone number traced. Can you do that for me?"

"I'm not supposed to but…because Landon helped out my little brother, I help him whenever I can. What's the number?"

Caine rattled off the number and waited for her to punch it in. "Hmm, there seems to be a block on it, but I might be able to get past it if you can get them to answer it and stay on, even for a few seconds."

"I *love* today's technology," Caine said with a feral smile. "Wait a few seconds for me to call from my cell and then lock on to the number."

"She's coming around. I sense her consciousness. Go ahead and take her blood quickly," a woman said.

The smell of rubbing alcohol preceded a small, sharp pain at the crook of her arm. Emma winced. Her body felt as if someone had laid a heavy lead cape across it. She was so tired. She tried to open her eyes, but they only rolled in her head. She caught a glimpse of a spotlight above her before her eyelids closed against the stark brightness.

There was something she was supposed to remember. What was it? She struggled to organize her fuzzy thoughts. Something important. Someone could get hurt. Her aunt! Emma moaned and flailed her arms, knocking the spotlight out of her eyes. "The pills," she groaned.

"I know you haven't taken your pills," the same woman replied.

"No," Emma croaked. "My aunt's pills. In my jacket. Take them to her!"

"She must be talking about Margaret," a man said. He moved closer. "Is Margaret sick?"

Emma picked up on the urgent concern in his voice. "Where have you taken my aunt? She needs her medicine."

"It'll be okay," the woman said in a calm tone, then her voice turned harsh, accusatory. "You gave her too much."

Emma wasn't sure if the woman was speaking to her or the man. "Needs her meds," Emma mumbled, her words slurring.

"Go test her blood. Once her head is clear, I'll give her a shot instead of a pill for expediency."

"Not me!" Emma insisted. She didn't need the pills. Her aunt did. The man seemed to know she was talking about Mary, even though he'd called her Margaret. The woman didn't. Why was everything fuzzy and blurred when she tried to see them? Why wouldn't her eyes cooperate? God, her head felt like it was going to explode right off her body. The horrific throbbing seemed as if her head was bouncing on the hard surface she was laying on.

Emma smelled the man's fear spike when he'd asked about Margaret's health. How could she smell his fear? She didn't know how, but the sharpness was undeniable. Yet she sensed nothing, not a trace of a scent, from the woman. It was as if she didn't exist, like a ghost with a voice.

Straps came around her wrists, making Emma's heart rate soar. The woman spoke again. "I wouldn't want you to fall. He gave you too much. 'Wanted to get you out quickly,'" she said, mimicking the man's raspy voice. Leaning closer, she continued. "It's going to take you a while to come out of it. You rest for a bit. I'll be back once we have the test results. We want to make sure you're healthy."

"My aunt!" Emma thrashed and her throat burned with the need to scream. Her voice croaked. Tears of frustration rolled down her temples, wetting her hair. In the back of her mind, she wondered why they wanted her blood, but her aunt was her first priority. "You have me. Let my aunt go."

Cool fingers lightly brushed across her forehead. The touch was so faint that Emma wondered about ghosts once more. "Rest. We'll take care of everything."

A door opened and closed. *They were taking care of Mary.* Relief washed over Emma, but after a few minutes alone in the quiet room, her paranoia rekindled and grew. She lifted her head and blinked to try and see her surroundings. White walls and metallic silvery shadows—reminding her of hospital-style medical cabinets—was all she could make out. The room felt sterile and cool, like an exam or operating room.

They wanted to make sure she was healthy? The thought made her heart hammer against her chest. Were they going to experiment on her? *Did they kidnap me for my organs?* Oh, God. She'd heard stories about such things but thought they were just urban legends. Jerking against the straps around her wrists, she tried to pull free, but her arms where held down too tightly.

Her pulse whooshed in her ears and she blinked several times to try and focus. Nausea rose from her belly, settling in the back of her throat. Her head swam from the burning sensation and she had to lay her head on the table once more to regain her equilibrium and settle her stomach.

She'd taken several deep breaths to calm herself when she heard a light tapping noise to her left. Emma turned toward the sound and saw a shadow outlined by what looked like a window.

Panting in fear, she opened her mouth to scream when a male voice spoke quickly in her mind. *Don't scream. I'm here to get you out.*

The voice sounded so familiar. Someone she trusted. The scream in her mind gave way to quiet mewling in her throat and she blinked again to try and force her eyes to work. It sounded like a window was being jimmied, then lifted, and a few seconds later the man was closer. Had he come inside? But she'd heard his voice clearly a second ago when he was outside. She blinked to clear her confused mind, but his image remained blurred and hazy. When she squinted, desperately trying to see, dizziness ensued once more.

All she could do was close her eyes and nod. What man did she trust? She racked her brain and could only come up with the name Jared. She knew him somehow. She'd gone to him when she was worried about her aunt. *I trust Jared.*

A couple seconds later, he was leaning over her and a gloved hand touched her face. "Emma! Can you hear me?"

She felt a jerk around her wrist and her arm was free, then her other arm was freed from its restraint, as well. She bit back a cry of shock when he lifted her in his arms. He was soaking wet and freezing cold. "Did you take a shower?" she whispered.

The storm and wet clothes make it hard to smell me, he replied. As soon as he set her on the floor, her legs refused to work. She would've collapsed if he hadn't had a good hold on her arm. *I'm going to have to lift you through the window. Think you can help me? Just nod if you think you can.*

Frowning, she bobbed her head in agreement. She realized why he'd sounded like he was inside the room before. He was speaking in her mind, but *why* did she hear his voice in her head? Focusing, she gritted her teeth and forced her wobbly legs to hold her upright. The next thing she knew, he'd lifted her and turned her facedown toward the ground as he slid her legs out the window first. Something crunched along her hip as he slid her across the windowsill. She winced at the pinching sensation.

Hold on to the ledge, then I'll grab your hands and lower you to the ground. Understand? he said in a commanding tone.

Emma nodded, even though the world around her was spinning on its axis. Upside down was suddenly right side up. Her body was dry yet shivering with cold. She was so confused, but strangely she trusted him to keep her safe. His big hands cinched tightly around her wrists and then she hung suspended in the air. "I'm flying," she whispered in awe as she glanced toward the fluffy white cloud below and kicked her feet in glee.

You're flyin', all right, he mumbled. *Focus! I'm going to let you go. The snow should buffer some of your fall, but be ready to roll so you don't break a leg. Got it?*

And then Emma was set free to fly. Her flight of freedom was over way too quickly and she landed on her side with a heavy thump. When her right hip began to throb, Emma remembered vaguely she was supposed to roll. "That hurt," she moaned as he landed on booted feet beside her.

She was scooped up in his arms once more. "I told you to roll," he chided in a low, concerned tone.

Emma realized it was snowing as a burst of frigid air and heavy snowflakes blew against them. The snow was coming down hard, and the whiteout, combined with her blurred vision, made it impossible to see his features. She wrapped her arms tight around his cold coat and settled her face against his cold collar. He smelled wonderful—how could he say wet clothes dulled his smell?—and his body radiated warmth underneath his coat. She inhaled and rubbed her nose along his shirt. "Thank you for rescuing me, Jared."

His grip around her tightened and his brisk steps stopped for a second. Then the wind whistled around them as if they were moving at a rapid speed—like they were gliding. Emma's breath caught against the bitter cold air. By the time he stopped and set her feet on the ground next to a truck, her teeth were chattering and her body shivered uncontrollably.

She blinked and tilted her head when the passenger door's handle came off in his hand. Damn, it was colder out here than she realized for the handle to break like that. She didn't realize

freezing-cold metal crumpled so easily, either, she thought
when he tossed the mangled handle to the ground. Above the
whistle of the wind, someone was yelling off in the distance.
He jerked open the door and she stepped up on the runner, then
flopped into the seat. *When did Jared get a truck? He normally
drove a beat-up Jetta.* Emma's muddled mind pondered as the
driver-side door opened and he climbed inside.

Before she could ask about his new truck, he pushed her
to a seated position and quickly snapped the seat belt around
her. A second later, after he'd messed with some wires under
the dashboard, the engine roared to life. That's odd. Where
was his key?

The moment he jammed on the gas pedal and they began
to move, the window on the driver side burst. Emma screamed
as glass flew everywhere and a man's dark head came through
the window. He snarled and grabbed at her rescuer, throwing
haphazard punches as the truck swerved in the snow.

Emma panted and leaned to grip the steering wheel while
the two men grappled with each other. She had no idea where
the truck was heading. All she could think to do was hold the
wheel straight and pray they didn't slam into a wall.

Jared howled his fury and drove his fist into the man's face,
and then, in a swift move that left her reeling in shock, he twisted
the man's head. The sickening snap gave way to complete silence
right before he pushed the intruder out of the window.

Lights flashed behind them as her rescuer took hold of the
steering wheel and said in a gruff tone, "They're coming.
Hold on tight. They're closing the gates on us."

Pulse racing, Emma had barely gotten the words "What
gates?" out when they slammed into something. Sparks flew
and metal ground against metal right before a piece of chain-

link fence bounced against the windshield, cracking the glass right down the middle.

As they sped down the street, the snow made it near impossible to see more than a few feet in front of them, or even if they were on the right side of the street. Then Emma saw the blinking yellow caution sign that warned of something in the middle of the road—construction maybe? She jerked her gaze his way. "Do you see it?"

"I do." He jammed harder on the gas and kept the truck straight ahead and on a collision course.

When they were within two seconds of hitting it, she panted erratically and screamed, "Turn!" At the last second, he jerked the truck to the right and she breathed a sigh of relief, quickly glancing behind them. The SUV chasing them didn't have time to react. The vehicle hit the cement median and flew through the air. Landing on its side in a metallic crunch and shattered glass, it skidded across the snow-covered road.

Five minutes later, they pulled up beside another truck. Once he'd carried her around and set her inside the cab of the second truck, locking the seat belt around her, he said in a gruff tone, "They're not going to stop that easily. Another vehicle wasn't far behind that one."

Right before he turned the key to start the engine, he lifted something from the seat between them and wrapped it around her shoulders. "Here's your coat. It's going to take a while for my truck to get warm."

As the vehicle lurched forward, Emma realized through all the chaos she missed hearing his deep voice in her head. And now that he'd spoken to her directly a couple times, his voice sounded different than she remembered. Her mind was starting to clear a little, even if her vision was still moving in and out.

All she could make out was shadows in the cab and white everywhere she looked outside the truck windows. She was amazed she even saw the yellow marker in the road. Apparently blinking warning lights and self-preservation were powerful motivators. She turned toward his shadow to see he was holding his hand up to his ear.

"I have Emma. If you want the Velius, here's their address." He rattled off an address, then paused before he spoke again in a harsh tone. "She's all drugged up and can barely say her own name, Landon. I've got someone coming on my tail. I'll shake them and then I'm taking her somewhere safe until she can detox."

The phone snapped closed at the same time she heard the ring tone shut down sequence that indicated he'd turned off the cell phone. Her rescuer had spoken long enough for her to realize… "You're not Jared," she whispered in a shaky voice.

He didn't say a word. Instead he set the phone on the seat, pulled off his glove and reached over toward her. Emma swallowed a small scream and tried to cringe away as he slid his fingers under her hair and curled his fingers around the back of her neck. She gasped when his touch locked her still in her seat. Warm heat and an inviting smell enveloped her as an electric sensation spread all the way to her belly and beyond.

Emma gripped his wrist and her heart jerked as her body recognized what her impaired sight and muddled mind couldn't. Tears streaked hot trails down her cold cheeks. "I know you, but…but my mind is all confused." She shook her head in frustration.

"It's nice to be *kind of* remembered," he said before he pulled his hand away.

They turned onto a highway and the vehicle fishtailed on the slick surface, making her stomach roil. Emma closed her eyes and put her hand over her mouth. Her stomach heaved again. "You have to stop," she moaned.

"Emma, we need to get you out of here. They're not far behind."

The urgency in his voice went right over her head when her mouth began to water. She was going to puke. "Stop the truck now!"

Quickly jerking the vehicle to the side of the road, he slammed on the brakes. Emma managed to unbuckle and get the door open just in time. She leaned out and tossed everything in her stomach onto the stark white snow until only dry heaves racked her body. Vaguely, she realized that he was holding her hair back from her face when he said near her ear, "Are you okay?"

Emma moaned and nodded. Taking the bottle of water he offered, she swished the water around in her mouth, then spit once more into the snow. Straightening, she set the container inside the door holder before she closed the door. Snow coated her hair once more, making her shiver all over. The truck began to move again and she closed her eyes, trying not to think about her stomach. When her head lolled from one shoulder to the other in exhaustion, she felt a tug on her shoulder and a strong hand pushed her head down toward his lap. "Lay down, Emma. We've got a hell of a drive ahead of us in this snow."

"Going home," she mumbled with a heavy sigh as she put her coat on his wet thigh and laid her head down on top of it. The sensation of the vents blowing warm heat over her and the swishing of the windshield wipers lulled her tired body.

He gave a strange, almost sad-sounding laugh as his knuckles ran along her cheek and jawbone. "As bitterly ironic as that statement is, yes, we're going home."

Chapter 5

Emma awoke when the truck rolled to a stop. Her head felt as if someone had stuffed it full of sawdust. She sat up and stared out at the white world outside the truck. Gusts of snow buffeted the vehicle and through the haze of white she saw the outline of trees in the darkness around them.

"We'll have to walk from here."

A deep voice drew her attention. Her vision had cleared enough for her to see him. Pitch-black hair and eyebrows brought out the emerald green in his hazel eyes. With the snow reflecting the partial moon's light through the windows as if it were almost daylight, the effect defined his cheekbones, while the overnight beard coating his jaw hollowed his features in sharp, vivid clarity.

Caine. She remembered his name now. He was more primal and hauntingly attractive than the dim nightclub light had given him credit for. God, whatever drug those kidnappers had used to knock her out earlier really had sent her mind off to la-la land for her to have had such a hard time remembering him.

"Caine."

"You remember." He touched her cheek, and the tingle from his touch was surprisingly warm, considering she could already see plumes of frost from their breath as the truck's cab quickly cooled down.

He literally sucked the air from her lungs when he looked at her the way he did—like he would've done anything, touched her everywhere and then some, to make her remember him. Her smile wobbled. "Just bits and pieces." But her peace suddenly evaporated as her past worries came back to her full force. "My aunt! Did you see an older lady in that place where they kept me?"

Caine frowned. "No, I didn't." He cupped her jaw, his expression intense. "You were my priority. I've sent friends back to the building, though, and if your aunt is there, they will get her to safety."

Emma vaguely remembered a phone call he'd made earlier. "Can you call and see if they found her?"

Caine shook his head and released her to slide his cell phone into his jacket pocket. His coat appeared to have mostly dried. "I tried to check my messages earlier, but the storm has apparently knocked out the cell tower's reception."

"Wait! I have my cell." Emma dug into her front pocket and pulled out her cell phone. It fell apart the moment it was free of her jeans. "Damn." She tossed the ruined cell to the floor and frowned at him, feeling utterly useless. *Please let Aunt Mary be okay.*

When a strong gust of wind whistled around the truck, rocking the vehicle with its ferocity, Emma glanced out the window and shivered. "Where are we?" She racked her brain, trying to remember. "Did I give you directions to my house?"

"Your home isn't safe. I went there after you were taken from the club. I found—" He paused and his jaw flexed. "We have to get you to a safe place."

What was he about to say? Emma grabbed his hand. "Is something wrong with my house? Did it burn down or something?" Caine clasped her hand, locking his fingers with hers. The electric buzz between them seemed even stronger now.

Heavy thumps of snow thudded on the roof and hood of the truck, falling from the trees above them. "No. Your house is fine." Squeezing her hand, he continued. "We need to get out of my truck before more snow falls and blocks the doors. Come on."

She held fast to his hand before he could pull away. "Why are you helping me?"

His expression hardened briefly. "That's a good question…" He glanced down at their clasped hands, then ran his thumb across her palm. The spark and sizzle that followed his finger's wake made her breath catch. The sensation was seductively erotic. His gaze snapped to hers, piercing sharp. "We'll talk later."

When he pulled away, his expression had turned guarded once more. "What's wrong?" she asked.

Caine opened the door and climbed out. Facing her, he held his hand out for her, his tone curt. "I'll expect full honesty, Emma. Safety first, answers later."

Emma shrugged into her coat. As she buttoned it, she wondered what in the world Caine was talking about. He appeared displeased about something. Was he upset she didn't tell him why she was at the club? She had no idea she was going to be kidnapped, for Pete's sake! "Yes, of course," she said as she started to put her hand in his.

Instead of grabbing her hand, he shoved his glove on her left hand, then motioned for her right. Emma scooted forward and while she waited for him to put the other glove on her, she watched the falling snow coat his black hair, turning it salt and pepper.

Now that she was fully gloved, he'd let go of one hand and she expected him to let go of the other. Instead, he leaned down a bit and jerked her forward.

Emma let out a slight yelp when she found herself lying facedown across his shoulder. "What are you doing?" Her voice was muffled against his thigh-length black coat.

He shut the door and locked the vehicle, then jammed the keys into his front pocket. Shifting her body a bit on his shoulder, he said, "I can get you there much faster if I carry you."

"I seriously doubt that." Emma snorted and reached up to tuck her coat tighter around her hips to keep out the snow. "I might be several inches shorter than you, but my legs work just fine." A heavy hand came down on her butt. "Ow! What was that for?"

Caine glanced her way and slid on a pair of sunglasses. "I suggest you cover your eyes. The snow's going to sting them otherwise."

The snow was coming down in fat, soft flakes. A gust of wind made it blow softly into her face. "I think I'll survive."

"Ready?" Caine grabbed hold of her butt underneath her coat.

Despite the cold, her face burned at his possessive, intimate hold. "Hey!" She stiffened and smacked his thigh. "Paws off!"

Caine grunted. "When I grab your butt for real, Emma, you'll know it." As if for effect, his fingers spread wide across her rear and he caressed her butt cheek, before he gave it a firm, "this is all mine" squeeze.

Despite her flaming cheeks, Emma's breasts tingled and her stomach clenched in response. "Caine!"

He laughed. "Time to go."

Before she could say a word, they were flying through the woods. *Damn, he can run fast. Maybe he's an athlete,* Emma thought, then realized with swift shock that she knew nothing about this man, other than the fact he'd rescued her and her brain refused to work whenever he was near. Then again, circumstances being what they were, they'd started off in the strangest of situations. She couldn't explain why she trusted him, but she did. Implicitly.

During Caine's rapid uphill trek, snow fell on them twice from the heavily laden trees above, and now her coat and the back of her pants were soaked. She began to shiver all over. Her teeth chattered and her lips had probably changed to a lovely shade of "popsicle" blue. The wind had really picked up as he ran. She was frozen to the point of numbness. "How much longer? I'm so tired."

Caine's grip tightened around her. He never broke his stride as he ordered in a sharp tone, "Stay awake, Emma. We're almost there."

A few minutes later, when her eyes had begun to droop once more, Caine's fast pace slowed. Then he stopped and set her down on her feet.

Emma was shivering so hard, she could barely keep her eyes open. Caine's warm fingers touched her cheeks. Tilting her chin up, his gaze searched her face and his tone turned rough with concern. "Hey, stay with me. We'll be inside in a second."

They were standing on the porch of a cabin-style house. The roof above gave them some relief from the gusting wind and blowing snow, while Caine's intoxicating smell melted her stomach and his tingling touch encouraged her frozen skin back to life.

Without a second thought, Emma pressed his hot hands to her face, then turned her mouth toward one of his palms. Kissing the warm surface, she closed her eyes and relished in his glorious heat. "Wh-why aren't your ha-hands freezing? I want *your* metabolism."

A low growl rumbled from his throat before the hand she was kissing slid into her hair. His fingers pressed against the back of her neck and he cupped her jaw in a possessive hold, his thumb turning her face upward.

Emma's breath caught when Caine leaned close. An invisible electric current hummed between them, its magnetic pull irresistibly strong. Up close, she realized with giddy delight that Caine's bottom lip was fuller than the top—the man had such kissable lips. That sexy mouth was less than an inch away from hers and she was so ready to feel their sizzle once more. Her gaze locked with his fierce hazel one, and her stomach sucked inward as she waited for him to close the small distance between them; to warm her from head to toe.

Caine's fingers flexed a couple times against the base of her skull before he took a step back. "Let's go inside and get warmed up."

The gruff edge in his voice confused her. A second ago he'd been about to kiss her. She'd swear he was. Wrapping her arms around her shivering body, she followed him into the cabin.

After Caine shut the door behind them, Emma stamped her feet to keep warm. She didn't think it was possible, but the house was even colder than outside. Caine turned on a couple of electric lanterns he'd pulled from under a cabinet in the kitchen, then walked over and handed her one. As he set the other lantern on the kitchen counter, she held hers up to see the rest of the cabin.

To her immediate left was a sofa, chairs and a huge polished tree stump that doubled for a coffee table. There were two doors to each side of the main room, which she assumed led to bedrooms and probably a bathroom. A kitchenette took up the nearest corner to her right and a bed took up the far right corner of the main room. Emma's gaze locked with longing on the stone fireplace in the far left corner. Her entire body shivered, rocking the lantern she held up. "Pl-please tell me you have wood out back somewhere." Billows of frosty breath floated in front of her, making her even more aware of the depth of the chill in the house.

"This house depends solely on heat from the fireplace." Caine blew on his hands and rubbed them together, mumbling, "Even my body temperature is dropping from the prolonged exposure."

Emma shook her head when he walked over to stand near her. It was the first she'd seen him react to the cold. *Sheesh, did the guy think he was immune?*

He glanced at her, his gaze serious. "Someone followed us for a while. It may have been them. I'm pretty sure I lost them in the storm, but I don't want to take a chance. Once the snow stops falling, the smoke from a fire could alert them to our location. There's a space heater that will provide a small amount of heat for us."

Emma realized she didn't even know where their *location* was. She shivered uncontrollably. "Wh-where are we?"

"We're in the Shawangunk Mountains." Caine's jaw tensed. "I have a feeling the people who took you won't give up looking for you so easily."

Emma's throat closed and she blinked several times to keep tears from surfacing. "I'm so scared, Caine. They took my aunt and—" her voice began to quiver "—I don't know what they want from me."

Caine put his hands on her shoulders and frowned. "You didn't know the people who took you?"

Emma shook her head in frantic jerks. "No! I have no idea who they were or why they took a sample of my blood. Maybe they wanted to check my blood type and see if I was compatible so they could steal a kidney or something." Her eyes widened. "Your friend, the man you sent to that address…he won't call the police, will he? They took my aunt and told me 'no police.'"

Caine began to unbutton her coat with rapid movements. "No, he won't call the police."

A blast of cold air hit Emma in the chest the moment he opened her coat, and she tried to step away. "What are you doing? I'm freezing!"

He held firm to her coat, his dark gaze snapping to hers. "Your clothes are as wet as mine. The first thing we need to do is get out of them."

She smacked at his hands when he tried to push her jacket off her shoulders. "The first thing we need is heat before any of these clothes come off my body."

His lips thinned but he turned away from her and walked over to open a door in the kitchen area. When he came back carrying a small heater no bigger than a shoe box, she snorted in disbelief. "Th-that's it?"

Caine set the heater on the floor near a twin-size bed, plugged it in, then turned it on. As he walked away toward one of the bedrooms, he called over his shoulder, "Set the lantern down and finish getting undressed."

Emma stared transfixed at the single bed he'd set the heater beside. "Where are you going to sleep?" she called after him. Approaching the bed, she set the lantern on the nightstand next to it.

Caine reappeared with a stack of blankets in his arms. Setting them on the end of the bed, he stepped in front of her, his expression serious. "*We're* sleeping in this bed. Your metabolism apparently can't hold heat, so I'm your best shot at getting warm and staying that way."

"There must be other beds," Emma started to say when he slid his hand under her hair and cupped the back of her neck. The blast of heat emanating from his palm and fingers sent glorious shivers down her spine. It wasn't as hot as she remembered, but damn the man had an effective way of making his point.

His smile held a touch of arrogance as he traced his thumb along her neck, leaving steamy lightning trails behind. "Take off your clothes, Emma."

Heat shot up her cheeks at the idea of undressing in front of him. "Can I have one of those blankets, please?"

Caine released her and grabbed a blanket. His dark eyebrow elevated when he handed her the navy thermal cover. "Better?"

Emma quickly nodded and gripped the thick blanket. "You, uh…are going to turn around, right?"

Chuckling, Caine moved to the end of the bed and turned away, stripping out of his jacket. When he lifted his shirt over

his head, revealing rippling muscles along his back, Emma
swallowed a gulp. His hands shifted to his jeans and paused.
"I don't hear you making any progress."

Emma swiftly turned around and kicked off her shoes,
then took a deep breath before she began to peel off her own
wet clothes. Holding the blanket around her became an impossible task, especially with her fingers refusing to work in
the cold air. Abandoning the blanket, she unbuttoned and
began to shrug out of the tight wet jeans. Grunting in frustration, she had to wiggle and tug in a weird dance of hopping
feet and chattering teeth before she finally freed her legs from
the soggy material.

"That was *interesting*."

Caine's amused tone jerked her to attention. Emma had all
but forgotten about him in her effort to be free of the suffocating frigid jeans. Standing there in her bra, underwear and
socks, she quickly grabbed the blanket from the floor and
wrapped it around her shoulders. Facing him, she narrowed
her gaze. "That wasn't meant for your entertainment."

He approached, his expression serious. Emma noticed that
he'd tied a blanket low on his hips, leaving his gorgeous upper
body on full display. Broad shoulders gave way to a narrow
waist, but it was the trail of dark hair that started at his sculpted
abs and disappeared past the blanket's edge that drew her
gaze. God, he was built.

Taut stomach muscles flexed as he grabbed up her clothes
from the floor and then held out his hand. "All of them."

Emma frowned, but moved to stand in front of the space
heater while she peeled off the rest. The moment Caine
walked away with their clothes, she called after him, "My
aunt's meds are in the coat pocket." Shaking the last bit of

snow out of her damp hair, she wrapped the blanket tight around her body before diving under the thin quilt and sheet on the twin bed.

Even wrapped in the thermal blanket and underneath the quilt and sheet, she shook as much as the house did with the howling wind battering its walls from all sides. A door slammed and a dryer started up a few seconds before Caine stepped back into the main room and set her aunt's medicine container on the kitchen table.

She watched him through slitted eyes and chattering teeth as he covered the twin bed with five layers of blankets. The extra blankets didn't really warm her, but the heavy weight made her eyelids slowly close. *I could just fall asleep and the cold wouldn't bother me anymore.*

It didn't even faze her when the bed dipped. *Caine was getting in. That's nice.* Her mind floated on a different plane, meandering down a path of cool darkness, seeking the sleep her body seemed to need.

"Emma, no!"

Caine's sharp tone made her eyelids flutter, but they wouldn't open. His hand touched her shoulder and she shrugged it away, murmuring, "Just let me sleep."

"Son of a bitch!" When he began to tug hard on the blanket she'd wrapped around herself, Emma's heart jerked and this time her eyes flew open. She gripped the blanket. "What are you doing? Let go!"

Caine didn't even look at her. His expression held fierce determination as he continued to unwrap her body. "Your body temperature has dropped too much. You must get warm quickly."

She flinched at the anger in his voice. Caine's gaze locked

with hers and his jaw muscle began to jump. "You know I can provide the warmth your body needs, Emma."

He was right. Closing her eyes, she slowly nodded and let him unwrap the thermal blanket completely from her body. When warm hands clasped her waist and her back was yanked fully against a warm, hard chest, Emma couldn't help the sigh of pleasure that escaped her lips.

Pulling the covers back over them, Caine spooned her entire body with his, from the top of her shoulders to the back of her thighs. He even entwined his muscular legs with hers, sliding his warm feet along her lower calves and feet.

For several minutes Emma just shivered from the contrast in his body temperature and hers before she began to glory in the warmth that enveloped her. Caine leaned close and breathed hard against her neck. She tensed until she realized he was using his breath to warm her. Only then did she relax against him.

Caine felt the difference instantly when Emma's body fully yielded. He'd been scared when he came into the room to find her already dozing. The moment he touched her and her body temperature was so low, fear drove him. He didn't give a damn if she'd refused to give him permission. He'd have ripped the blanket off her anyway and dealt with her affronted anger later. She wasn't going to die on him.

In the short time he'd known her, Emma had become someone special, someone he wished hadn't turned out to be a panther. She claimed not to know who kidnapped her, and instinctively he believed she was telling the truth, but what other secrets did she hide? She'd yet to admit she was something other than human. And why did the other panthers kidnap her and take her blood? The man who'd shoved his way through the truck window was too strong to be human. He had to be panther.

Tons of questions flooded his mind as he wrapped his arms around Emma and tucked one hand underneath her armpit, then slid his other hand between her legs—the two areas he'd been trained in search and rescue to warm first to prevent hypothermia. When Emma didn't question what he was doing and her eyelids began to droop, Caine's chest tightened. He needed to keep her awake, at least until her body temperature was back to normal. "I saw schoolbooks at your house. Do you go to NYU? That's a heck of a commute for you from Greenwood Lake."

Emma gave a tired laugh. "No, I have to take care of my aunt. She's gotten to the point where she can't drive as well as she used to. I didn't like to have to cut her off, but I finally insisted on driving her to various doctor appointments, running errands for her and such. I'm too busy to be a full-time student. I'm in a part-time satellite program with the community college."

That's a lot of responsibility for someone so young. Caine stared at her with respect. "What's wrong with your aunt?"

Emma sighed. "Age and I guess a family predisposition for ailments. My mom died young. I don't remember her at all. My aunt has a heart condition." Her body tensed. "God, I hope she's all right."

Caine regretted reminding her about her aunt's predicament. "If she was there, Landon will take care of her, Emma. Don't worry."

They lay there for a good twenty minutes before he saw a bit of color start to return to her cheeks. After what she'd told him, Caine understood why Emma had seemed mature and confident for her age. Taking care of an elderly aunt, she'd had to grow up fairly quickly. Once again, he realized just how much he appreciated the past support of his pack. Sadness knotted his throat now that he'd pretty much cut himself off from the Lupreda and faced life alone.

The skin along Emma's thigh was soft under his fingers and her earthy smell was driving his wolf nuts, making him want to howl. Caine couldn't resist. He leaned close and inhaled deeply before he let his breath flow over her neck and down her back to warm her. Fierce pride welled within him to feel her skin warming under his touch. "What are you studying?"

"Marketing. Having some college training under my belt should help me get a better-paying job. Instead of using my aunt's savings for school, I can contribute to her retirement. I hope to switch to the university at some point if I can convince my aunt to move closer to town."

He could tell she was still worrying about her aunt. "As soon as this storm subsides, my cell's reception should return and I'll give Landon a call." Sensing her anxiety, Caine released his tight hold on her body and sat up and leaned on his elbow to press his lips to her bare shoulder. "I'll find out for you. I promise."

"Thanks." Sighing, she arched her spine, then clasped the covers to her chest and rolled onto her back to meet his gaze in the dim light. "What about you? You've risked your life to save mine and I hardly know you. What do you do when you're not saving girls who've been kidnapped?"

I was Second in my Lupreda wolf pack. "I used to be a tour guide for the Shawangunk Mountains, and on the side, I led search-and-rescue teams if a hiker got lost. Now that I'm in town, I deliver packages among other small jobs here and there."

She let out a surprised laugh. "All that hiking must be what kept you fit. I assumed you were a professional athlete or trainer or something. You ran through the snow as if it wasn't in your way. I know *I* couldn't have kept up with you."

I know that's not true, my little panther. "It's time for the truth, Emma." Caine's voice turned serious as he slid his knuckles down her cheek. Now that her skin wasn't frozen, the tingling started the moment his fingers touched hers.

Emma gasped and pressed her face closer to his hand, surprising the hell out of him that she seemed to crave the humming sensations between them. "I've told you everything already. While I was out in the woods looking for our cat, Casper, early this morning, someone took my aunt. The note they left behind at my house told me to come back to the club tonight and to not call the police. That's why I had initially thought the note was from you, because I'd never been to Squeeze before last night, and you were the only person I'd spoken to while I was there."

"What else?"

Her eyes widened. "There *is* nothing else. You seem to want an answer I can't give you. I told you I don't know who they were, why they kidnapped me or why they wanted a sample of my blood."

Why did they take a sample of her blood? Caine wondered while he trailed his fingers down her throat.

He wanted to shake her for not telling him everything, yet at the same time he ached to explore every part of her. From her beautiful dark head to her frozen toes, he wanted to run his hands all over her skin, to warm her everywhere until she writhed and moaned and spread her legs, pleading for him to touch her in every intimate, sweet place on her body.

He'd revel in her moist heat and in the intimate act of sliding his fingers deep inside her, of pleasing her and stroking her body to orgasm. His groin heated and his erection hardened instantly as the fantasy played in his head. Nothing would be more erotically satisfying than revving Emma up and hearing her beg him to take her, to claim her body and soul—nothing more…than the act itself.

As the spark of electricity charged higher between them, he felt her swallow beneath his fingers and his entire body tensed in need. The more they physically connected, the more sensitized his skin became, making the electric sensations between them highly arousing. Caressing Emma had quickly turned into an addiction. As easily as breathing, it had become a necessity to touch her, to feel their connection every chance he got.

"And this electricity between us?" he said in gruff voice. "Why do you think we're like two live wires when we touch?" He waited for her to speak, hoping she trusted him enough to tell him the truth.

Emma tensed and lowered her gaze, then rolled onto her side away from him, whispering, "I don't know."

Why had she turned away? He'd heard the uncertainty in her voice. Caine instinctively reached out to comfort her, but caught himself and fisted his hand above her hip. He couldn't believe just how much he'd grown to care for this woman in such a short time—a woman whose DNA alone should give him reason not to trust her.

When he'd scented her at the café, an involuntary predatory awareness splintered through his mind and senses, quickly followed by an intuitive need to dominate. But her scent, combined with their unique physical connection, had ignited his predatory awareness of her, shifting his natural domination instincts to a strong physical need to stake his claim and protect. Every time he looked at Emma, Caine felt savagely territorial over her, to the point that…if it came down to it, he'd go up against his own brethren in order to keep her from harm.

Anger weighed heavily on his chest that she'd burrowed so deep under his skin, twisting his mind and disrupting his steadfast loyalties. He clenched his jaw so hard his teeth hurt. Why was she pretending to be human? Did she not smell his musk? Scent how much he wanted her? He was supposed to be her deadly enemy, yet the way she'd looked at him earlier, her beautiful golden eyes reflecting vulnerability and trust, made his chest burn like hot coals had been raked across it. Why wouldn't she trust him enough to tell him the truth?

When Emma's shoulders began to shake again, Caine realized he'd pulled his warmth away from her too soon. He quickly gathered her chilled frame against his chest and wrapped his arms tight around her. "Rest now. I'll keep you warm."

Emma's slight frame began to relax in his arms and when her body temperature leveled off, she murmured, "Thank you," right before her breathing finally evened out in sleep.

The lantern closest to them finally flickered, then died, dousing their area in darkness. Caine brushed his lips lightly against her temple and thought about the kiss they'd shared on the dance floor that evening. Her avid participation had been damned convincing. But the fact she'd turned away from him just now made him wonder…had his chance meeting with Emma in the club the night before really been a random encounter? She'd have nothing to gain by using him. He was no longer with the pack. Then again, maybe she didn't know that.

Caine's gut tightened at the distrustful thoughts that slammed through his mind. He'd wanted Emma to tell him what she was on her own without him confronting her and forcing her hand. He'd proven he would protect her, but that apparently hadn't been enough to convince her to tell him everything and admit who and what she really was.

The fact remained, she was Velius. Even now, her black hair reflected the truth. Spread across the white pillow, her hair sparkled as if covered with flecks of iridescent glitter. Caine's mind warred with his heart.

She whispered his name in her sleep and his grip on her tightened as his gaze shifted to the log walls around them. The cabin had been assigned to the zerkers before their deaths a few months ago. It would become his permanent home the day he discovered he could no longer shift back from Musk to human form. As he stared, the logged surface appeared to slowly move inward, closing in on him.

Caine closed his eyes against an inevitable future and focused on Emma. Inhaling her earthy scent, he hoped she'd been sincere about her fear of the panthers who'd kidnapped her. In the brewing conflict between the Velius and Lupreda, he had to know for certain that Emma's loyalties weren't firmly ensconced with the panthers—that she hadn't played a part in the Velius' torturous murders of the three Lupreda zerkers in an effort to start a war between the vampires and the werewolves.

When she woke up, he would get the answers he needed. One way or the other.

Chapter 6

Something smelled strong and delicious. Food. And it smelled like chicken. Emma inhaled deeply and the sensation of steam touching her nose made her eyes fly open. Her gaze swept the muscles along Caine's shoulders and his bare chest as he pulled the oversized coffee cup away from her face and sat down on the bed bedside her.

"Your stomach kept growling while you slept. This is the best I could come up with."

When she quickly checked to see that he'd pulled on a pair of jeans, his lips quirked upward in the dim light. "Disappointed? Here, take this. It should stave off the hunger pains until I can go out and hunt for something to eat." He glanced back toward the main window where streaks of light shone through the crack in the closed curtains. "It stopped snowing a little over an hour ago."

The room was still cold, but nowhere near as frigid as it was earlier. Emma sat up and held the covers around her chest with one hand, while she took the mug with the other. "Thank you." Her words came out in a low, husky rasp, and she instantly put the warm mug to her lips. When she leaned forward to take a sip, her hair fell in her face.

Before she could blow it out of the way, Caine reached over and tucked the errant strands behind her left ear. His fingers lingered on her skin for a couple of seconds and she shivered at the humming sensation arcing between them. Lowering his hand, he watched her take another swallow. His gaze held a mix of desire and avid interest, making the steaming chicken broth the most provocative meal she'd ever had.

While Emma was busy gulping down the broth, she had an excuse to remain silent, which meant she wouldn't possibly make an embarrassing faux pas and ruin the charged moment between them like she had before she'd fallen asleep.

When Caine ran his fingers down her throat earlier, sending sparks ricocheting throughout her body, and then asked why she thought there was such an electric charge between them, she'd frozen up. She'd wanted to say something worldly and sexy, but she didn't have a clue how to go about that.

And the truth was, she honestly didn't know what was going on between them. Only that the amazing pull felt seductive and irresistible. Whenever he cupped his hand around her neck, electricity vibrated between them, but it was more than that. She literally couldn't move. It was both scary and incredibly erotic that he had that kind of power over her, because instinctively, even though he came across as an intense, dominant man, she knew he'd never use his control to hurt her.

Now that she wasn't shivering uncontrollably and her loud

stomach had calmed to a random low gurgle, her confidence was bolstered. Setting the cup on the nightstand, Emma bit her lower lip.

Caine cupped her cheek and turned her face toward him. "What's wrong? Are you feeling okay?"

Emma sighed into his palm, then met his concerned gaze. "I've never been very good at small talk or making friends. I wouldn't have gone to the club on my own the other night, but there was just something about your smell when you came into the café that day that I couldn't let go. It felt familiar and comforting."

Caine's eyebrows shot up. "*My* smell seemed comforting to you?"

She nodded and her cheeks heated with embarrassment. "I know it sounds crazy, but I just wanted to get a glimpse of your face—to see if I'd met you somewhere before. I planned to run in, assuage my curiosity and leave. And then you were there, standing beside me wearing 'women' as a second set of clothes and offering to buy me a drink."

Caine chuckled as he ran his thumb along her lip in a gentle caress. "I saw you watching me on the dance floor." He moved his fingers in slow reverence along her skin, as if he couldn't resist touching her. "But when you refused my offer to buy your beer and then slammed me all in one shot, I had to get to know you better."

Emma shook her head. "I wasn't trying to play hard to get." Shrugging, she continued. "I always speak my mind. It's a character flaw, but there you have it."

Caine moved closer until his thigh brushed against hers. Sliding his fingers into her hair, he locked gazes with her. "Honesty is very important in a relationship."

Pulse racing, Emma's eyes widened and she gripped the covers against her chest. "We have a relationshi—"

Caine's warm mouth covered hers, cutting off her question. She laughed at the sizzling pop that zinged between them, but Caine nipped at her bottom lip and Emma gasped in excitement, opening her mouth to his intense kiss. A low growl rumbled in his chest as he traced his tongue alongside hers. Her insides melted at the sexy, primal sound. Emma teased him with slow swipes of her tongue before she pressed quick kisses against the corner of his mouth and along his jawline.

"You're everything I want," he murmured at the same time big warm hands cupped her face. When he tilted her head and slanted his lips across hers in a harder, deeper kiss, the intensity sent shocking heat splintering through her system. Her entire body lit on fire, the flames singeing every intimate place at once.

Emma groaned when her sex began to throb deep inside her in a near-painful physical ache. Holding the covers against her chest, she used her other hand to clutch him closer, inhaling his fresh outdoors scent. Primal and musky, and full of sensual promise, his smell surrounded her in a blanket of arousing seduction.

"Your smell is… I can't describe how good you smell to me. It makes me feel so free." Emma's heart thumped and her breasts tingled in response to his strong essence inundating her senses. Sliding her fingers into his thick dark hair, she was shocked to hear herself moan as she pulled him closer.

"I have a pretty good idea," Caine grated out and pressed hot, electric kisses across her jaw. Easing back, he met her gaze. "What do you smell?"

Emma couldn't believe how much his aggressive smell

called to her inner temptress, melting away her insecurities and inhibitions. She might not have much sexual experience, but when it came this man, pure instinctual desire drove her actions beyond her own conscious thoughts or understanding. Closing her eyes briefly, she inhaled. "You smell musky and exotic, masculine and…unique. I could pick you out of a crowd by your scent alone."

His fingers traced her jaw. "The musk you smell is heightened interest, Emma." He leaned close and pushed her hair out of the way to press a kiss behind her ear. "Tell me what you hear," he whispered.

Her breathing turned erratic and her heart ramped up at the things he was making her feel. She closed her eyes once more and listened. The rapid whoosh, whoosh, whoosh of her pulse rushed in her head. She heard his heart beating steady with a slow upward tick. Jerking back, she met his gaze with wide eyes. "You have a powerful heartbeat. I can hear it rising."

He touched her chin, his smile darkly feral. "That's excitement." Placing his hands on the bed on either side of her, he shifted his weight very close as if he were going to kiss her neck. "What do you feel?" He moved his chin to within an inch of her shoulder, then slid it along her collarbone. Not touching but close enough that they'd connect if she moved forward the slightest bit.

His magnetism pulled at her, but more than that, she felt his heat. Glorious, primal heat ran along her skin, warming it. "I feel how hot your skin is, even though you're not touching me," she said in a breathless voice.

Caine's penetrating gaze snapped to hers. "That's lust and desire. I want you."

His declaration slammed her hard in the stomach, making

her feel light-headed. Emma opened her mouth to speak, but nothing came out.

What does all this tell you about me? About us? he demanded, suddenly serious.

Emma blinked. She had just heard him speak in her mind. It wasn't some drug-induced imagining when he'd rescued her. How was that possible? Her pulse raced and she searched his gaze for some clue as to what he wanted her to say. She had a feeling that whatever words she spoke next would be very important. "That you're different."

His expression hardened. "*We're* different. You and I. Tell me, damn it!"

The ferocity in his expression scared her, not because she was afraid, but because she thought he was going to push her away. She tried to blink back the tears of frustration that burned behind her eyelids and answered him as honestly as she could. "You're unique, and we have a connection that's undeniably mind-blowing, but…" Tears began to roll down her cheeks anyway. "I don't know what you want from me!"

Caine's hand encircled her neck. He'd moved so fast, she didn't have time to react other than to wrap her fingers around his wrist. His firm hold locked her in place as his thumb slid along her throat, stopping at the hollow where her pulse thumped a staccato beat.

His steady gaze held both frustration and desire. Emma remained still. She didn't take a breath. If he wanted, he could apply pressure to that spot and cut off her air. Permanently.

Survival instincts demanded she push his hand away, but she refused to act. Instead, she listened to her heart. Her hand slipped away from his wrist and she closed her eyes, tilting her head back.

What do I want? The raw hunger tapped into her primal senses. He was on a ragged edge, barely hanging on, despite his langour. She forced herself to remain calm as his thumb rubbed lightly on her pulse. *For now…this.*

Emma gasped when his lips replaced his thumb. He nipped at her collarbone, then kissed a hot trail along her chest, branding her skin with tingling, fiery kisses. She bit her lip to keep from moaning. His warm mouth felt so good on her skin. Placing her hands on the bed behind her, she arched her back and murmured his name.

Large hands encircled her waist through the covers, cinching tight. "Never whisper your desires, Emma. Always demand them!"

Emma was shaking inside with the need to feel his lips and hands caressing her skin. Her body felt like it was on fire. Tilting her head forward, she met Caine's gaze. His fingers flexed against her waist and his musk grew stronger. The evocative scent made her skin prickle and her breasts tingle in response.

Caine slid the sheet down until only her nipples were covered. His hungry gaze lowered to her chest, then lifted back to her face. "Once we start, our primal natures *will* take over. Are you prepared for that?"

Emma gave a nervous laugh. She was afraid to tell him she'd never been with another man. What if the thought of her inexperience was a major turnoff? "I'm as prepared as I'll ever be. I want to feel the electricity sparking between us. Everywhere."

Caine's warm hands moved up the sides of her rib cage at the same time he lowered his dark head to press his lips to the curve of her breast. Electricity zinged through her as he slid his lips down her cleavage, his movements slow, reverent and achingly tantalizing.

Cool air brushed her nipples as the sheet slipped away, baring her breasts. The sensitive tips puckered and her stomach fluttered when she felt his warm breath bathing her responsive skin. He slid the sheet the rest of the way down her waist and said in her mind, *You're beautiful and...all mine,* right before he ran his tongue around a hard pink tip.

Emma's sex began to throb from his intimate attention. She crossed her legs to keep from crying out and demanding he make the thrumming ache go away. She arched closer and moaned low in her throat.

His hot breath rushed over her nipple once, twice, a third time to the point she thought she might go insane. And then his lips grasped the aching pink tip tight. Emma cried out and dug her fingers into his hair, clutching him close. The spark sent tremors all the way down her limbs. When he began to suck in long drawing pulls, she moaned and gripped his shoulder, digging into the muscle. "More," she begged.

He grunted his approval and his thumbs pressed on the sides of her breasts as he moved to her other nipple and gave it the same provocative treatment. *You taste so good, I could kiss your breasts for hours,* he murmured in her mind.

When he nipped at her nipple, Emma mewled in her throat. *You're purring.*

Of course she sounded like she was purring. The man made her hum on many levels. Emma folded her legs to the side and arched her back. Pressing forward, she lifted up on her knees and wrapped her arms around his neck.

Caine grabbed hold of her arms, and before she knew what was happening, he had her flat on her back with her hands pulled over her head. "Slow down, my little wildcat. Let me love on you the way you were meant to be appreciated."

Emma thought she'd done something wrong, but she couldn't control the urges clamoring inside her. She squirmed under his hold. "I feel like I'm going to crawl right out of my skin if something doesn't happen soon."

His dark gaze narrowed, then turned downright sinful. "Things are going to get out of control between us soon enough. Your scent is incredibly hard to resist. Let's try and take it slow for a bit. Hmm?"

Emma panted as he released her hands and pushed the covers completely back. Oddly, she wasn't embarrassed at all while his hot gaze swept her naked body. Instead, she wanted to touch him as intimately as he had her, to see him free of clothes and trace her fingers across his warm skin and hard muscles.

When he bent to place a kiss on her shoulder, she ran her hand along his biceps. "Aren't you going to take off your pants?"

"Not yet," he said in a rough tone and set his hands on the bed on either side of her, pressing another kiss between her breasts.

Curling her fingers inward, Emma ran her nails down his chest. "I want to see you."

A low growl erupted from his throat and he grabbed hold of her hand. His nostrils flared and he gritted out, "You're not making it easy for me to remain calm."

She raised her eyebrow and ran her other hand down his arm, enjoying the tingling sparks. "I want you to feel what I do. All over."

He gripped her other wrist and pressed it to the bed. "I'm having a very hard time not taking you now. Stop pushing me or what you're going to get is a man who's too far over the edge to go back."

Caine glanced down at his chest and she followed his gaze.

Five red furrows had begun to well with droplets of blood. Emma pulled free of his hold, her shaky hand moving to investigate his wounds. "Dear God, did I do that?"

Caine grabbed her hand and lifted it to his lips, kissing her knuckles. "I'll be fine, but you're making it difficult for me to maintain my cool. Let me enjoy your reaction first for a bit before we move forward."

Emma bit her lip and nodded. She felt horrible for what she'd inadvertently done to Caine's chest. He smiled and ran his knuckles down her belly. "You have a body of sheer beauty, Emma. It was made to be worshipped…every single inch of you."

His compliment flooded her cheeks with heat, but when his fingers reached the bit of hair between her legs, her gaze locked with his and she held her breath. She'd never ached to be touched as much as she did at that moment.

Caine leaned close and grazed her jaw with a kiss at the same time his fingers slid between her legs. Slow, assured… teasing. Emma arched her back and rocked her hips. Anything to assuage the aching need deep inside her.

"Your primal smell is driving me insane. I want to taste every part of you, to suck and nip at your sweet body until you're screaming for me to make you come." He looked at her and his eyes were a lighter green. "And then you'll beg me to do it to you all over again."

Emma began to pant and she arched her back once more before she finally gripped his wrist to stop his teasing. She'd grown wetter with each passing swipe of his fingers along her sex. He moved so close but didn't touch her where she wanted—no, needed—him to. "Touch me. I can't stand it anymore."

The dark look in his eyes made her heart hammer as he slid his finger along her damp folds, then plunged it deep inside her. Emma yelped at the surprising pain and Caine's hand froze inside her. Cupping his palm against her mound, his eyebrows drew downward. "Are you okay?"

Emma winced, then nodded.

"You're so tight and…" Caine closed his eyes, his entire body tensing. His gaze jerked back to hers. "Why didn't you tell me you were a virgin?"

She bit her lip. "I thought it might be a turnoff to you."

"That couldn't be further from the truth—" he started to growl in a harsh tone.

Emma was surprised when he withdrew his hand from her body and leaned forward to bury his nose along the column of her neck. His voice was ragged with emotion as he gripped her inner thigh. "Say the word and I'll stop if you want me to, but damn it to hell, Emma, the last thing I want to do right now is to move away from you."

Emma desperately wanted him to stroke her back to the heightened arousal she'd felt seconds ago. Caine's heartfelt request and the need in his voice only made her want him more. She cupped his face so he would have to look at her. "I want whatever this amazing connection is between us. Very much. Never doubt it."

Her golden eyes shimmered in the dim morning light with honest passion, stealing his breath. For several seconds, Caine just stared. She completely enthralled him. As he rubbed his thumb along her inner thigh, her skin felt so soft and feminine, a knot formed in his throat, locking the words inside. The complete trust Emma gave over humbled him, obliterating his doubts as to her motives. Her attraction was as sincere and heartfelt as his. When their secrets finally came to light, they would face them together. That's all that mattered.

As if she knew he had a hard time voicing his thoughts, she gave a shy smile and ran her fingers across his shoulder. "Say something in my mind. I like the closeness."

Emma, I—

A deafening crash slammed the cabin's front door open, nearly ripping it off its hinges. Emma screamed and Caine whirled around to see three men standing outside the door. One of them took a step through the doorway and fury engulfed him. The need to protect Emma sent him leaping across the twenty-five-foot distance in one single bound. As he sailed through the air, his wereclaws unsheathed while his spine and rib cage began to pop.

Without a second thought, Caine instinctively called forth his Musk form, welcoming the enlarged chest and the searing pain as his jaws started to elongate. When he landed, he hadn't yet fully shifted to a werewolf, but that didn't stop him from instantly attacking the first man who dared to invade his home.

The short stocky man flew backward through the opened doorway with one swipe from Caine's deadly claws. Caine snorted in satisfaction at the blood dripping from his fingers, then started to stalk through the door after the intruders when a dark-haired man of medium height stepped from a hidden spot outside the door and rammed his fist into Caine's chest.

His surprisingly powerful hit sent Caine flying backward to land with a heavy thump on the wood floor. Caine heard Emma call his name in the background as he howled his rage. He recognized the man who'd attacked him as the guy Caine wouldn't let exit out the club's back door last night. Snapping to his feet, he started to go after the guy when the bastard lifted a crossbow-style handgun toward him and pulled the trigger with a snarl. "Down, dog."

Something zinged through the air. The impact threw Caine several steps back and pain exploded in his left shoulder right before a similar jolt slammed into his right arm. Caine roared his rage and tried to yank the silver arrows out of his chest and arm, but the flange on the ends suddenly spun, slicing his hands. Blood spewed from his hands and wounds while the metal shafts drilled deeper into his flesh.

Growling, he fell to his knees in sheer agony, running his claws down his skin, anything to dislodge them. When the flange tips stopped spinning, then curled inward and imbedded themselves into his muscles, the silver began to poison his body with vicious, deadly purpose. Caine fell back against the end of the twin bed, breathing with heavy painful snarls as the silver forced his body to revert back to his human form.

"Damn, he's a tough sonofabitch." A man with thinning blond hair stepped beside the man who'd shot Caine, his own weapon held out, ready to shoot. "It took only one shot each to take down the other bastards."

They're the ones who killed the zerkers. I'll rip them to shreds. Caine snarled and tensed his body, preparing to fight. Despite the pain making him see double, he pushed his shoulders off the bed and fear shot across the blond man's face at the same time his hand tensed on his weapon.

A dark shadow appeared over Caine a split second before a panther landed in a crouch on all fours. Its paw planted on the floor between his feet, while its bulky body blocked Caine from the shooter's line of sight. The animal twitched its long tail and let out a deafening, high-pitched roar, full of anger and warning, daring the men not to get any closer.

Emma! *How had she shifted without an injection?* Caine wondered. *Had she been shot with one while he was fighting?* His worry for her spiked. She was definitely challenging the men, despite the weapons they held. Caine grabbed her tail and yanked her backward slightly. "No!" he growled.

A third man stepped to the leader's other side and raised a different gun toward Emma, a look of worry flashing through his eyes. But the dark-haired man in the center waved him back. Closing his eyes, the leader inhaled deeply, then said in a reverent whisper, "Listen to the sheer beauty. It has been so long since we could unfurl and give a battle cry out in the open like this."

The man beside him tensed. "Her roar will alert the Lupreda to our presence, Malac."

Malac opened his eyes. Lust and covetous desire reflected in their brown depths as he stared at Emma in her panther form. "We'll be gone before they can reach us," he said to the blond man once Emma quieted. Her rib cage heaved as she snorted out warning clicks and snarls through her bared fangs.

The leader lifted his hand toward her. "If you come with us, we'll let him live."

The panther lowered her head. A deep growl rumbled in her throat, while her claws flexed against the wood floor and her long black tail twitched in Caine's hand. Caine squeezed. "No, Emma!"

Malac tsked. "Debating your chances? Remember, I still have the old woman."

The panther's head came up in a fast jerk and the growl in her throat rose to menacing levels. Pulling free of Caine's hold, she turned toward him. Her beautiful yellow eyes reflected sadness as she lowered her mouth to his shoulder.

Caine shuddered when she used her teeth to pull out the silver bolt. Before he could speak, she'd removed the other one from his arm, as well, dropping it with a heavy thunk on the floor. He gripped her ear as she laved at his wounds with her warm tongue. "Don't do this."

"We leave now!" the man demanded behind them.

Emma turned toward Malac and gave an annoyed snort before she returned her attention to Caine and ran her whiskers along his cheek. *Don't go, Emma! I can't protect you if you go with them.* Caine touched her head and started to slide his hand down her neck. She grunted out a little growl and quickly pulled out of his hold before his touch could lock her in place.

Emma walked with a stealthy gracefulness toward the men, but when the blond man raised his gun toward Caine, she bared her teeth and moved with lightning speed, slicing his wrist with a swipe of her extended claws.

The man yelled and held his hand over his gushing wounds, looking to Malac. The leader shrugged and shook his head. "You should know better, Scott." His gaze shifted to Emma as he squatted to pick up the gun the man had dropped. "It's only a tranquilizer gun. The one we'd planned to use on you."

"Emma, no!" Caine's entire body shook from the fever the silver spikes left behind.

When Malac raised the tranquilizer gun toward him, Emma hissed, but she didn't attack. Caine roared at his body to ignore the nausea and pain. *Move, damnit.* He began to slide across the floor, willing his muscles to respond…to react. He'd shifted only a couple of feet when a sharp pain jabbed him in the chest.

I will come for you, Caine vowed in Emma's mind as he struggled to stay conscious through the heavy tranquilizer. The last thing he remembered was Emma lifting up on her hind legs to scoop her aunt's medicine container from the table with her jaws.

Chapter 7

After they ran through the woods for about a mile, the men pointed their guns at Emma and told her to jump into the back of what appeared to be a moving truck. She heard radio squawks as they closed the doors on her and locked them. "We've got her. We're heading home."

Emma's legs began to tremble and all the bravado, fear and adrenaline that had kept her moving through the woods fled her body. She released the pill container onto the truck floor, collapsing onto her belly with a heavy thump as her mind raced with chaotic thoughts.

Emma stared in shock at her fur-covered arms—paws—stretched out in front of her. Not only could she see in the total absence of light, but she blinked several times as she flexed her fingers and her panther claws extended. *I'm having a nightmare. I'll wake up soon,* she told herself as she set her chin on her trembling arms and closed her eyes.

The truck started up underneath her, its loud rumble refusing to let her block out everything that had happened. She'd shifted. To a panther. God, I'm not human, but I felt human. Why had her aunt lied to her, raising her as a human and never telling her of her true nature? Did her aunt not know what she was? Or was her aunt a panther, too? So many questions flooded her mind, making her tense with worry that the one person she trusted above all others might've lied to her all her life.

And Caine…her heart sank with worry for him. She hoped she'd saved him. What was he? When he'd started to shift to some kind of half-man, half-creature form, she bit back a cry of shock, but nothing scared her as much as those men shooting at him and disabling him with their strange, deadly silver arrows. She'd both cried and seethed when she saw him sitting there, wounded but still snarling and ready to fight them, even once he'd shifted back to his human form.

Instinctively, she knew the men were there for her. Maybe it was because of the way Caine had fought, refusing to go down. When he fell to the floor, something inside her snapped. Anger and worry had curled in her stomach as she watched the violent scene unfold in front of her. Guilt rode her spine, sending ripples up and down it. Maybe her hackles were actually raising and because she was unaware of her true primal nature, she didn't recognize the sensation for what it was—her body readying itself to shift.

Instantly.

She didn't feel a thing, not a twinge. It was so surreal. One moment she was shaking on the bed, fearful for Caine and furious at the men, and the next she was diving out of it to protect Caine, to yell at the men to stop. Then her body felt like she'd slipped into the skin she'd been born to wear, even if shifting like that had scared the hell out of her.

Hearing herself roar stunned and frightened her, but once her panther's battle howl came out, all her primal instincts took over. She would've taken out any man who went near Caine without a single ounce of regret. No matter what truths she was sure she'd discover about herself and Caine, he'd saved her when she needed him and she would do the same for him. She owed him that much, regardless of the beasts that lay underneath their human skin.

Caine knew, she realized suddenly as she thought back to what he'd said. *"We're different. You and I. Tell me, damn it!"* He'd been trying to get her to tell him that, as if she knew what she was and even what he was. Shaking her head, she snorted. God, she had no freaking idea!

The truck's back door opened and the leader, Malac, hopped in. When she saw he was alone, the need to rip him to shreds for taking her aunt, hurting Caine and kidnapping her rose within her. A low roooowwwl rumbled in her throat.

"Music to my ears," he said in a calm tone before he sat with his back against the wall diagonally across from her. "We're going to chat while we drive home." Placing his elbows on his knees, he leaned back in a relaxed pose as the truck began to move.

Emma didn't miss the gun he held casually in his hand. She narrowed her eyes and opened her mouth a little to let free her threatening snarl.

"We've been searching for you for a very long time."

When he looked directly at her, she saw his eyes for the first time in the dark. Even though they were brown, they glowed like Caine had said hers did. He was a panther, too. Why couldn't she catch his scent like she did Caine's musky one? And why didn't he shift earlier when Caine had gone after him?

She stared him down. *You're not the man who kidnapped me from the club. Tell me why you've been looking for me.* She wished she had Caine's ability to speak in the bastard's mind, but as much as she would've loved the ability to rail at him, there was no way in hell she was letting go of this panther form. It was her best defense. She didn't blink as she waited for him to continue.

He tilted his head to the side, contemplating her. "Your roars in the cabin…they sounded beautiful but stiff, like you've never done them before."

Emma tensed. She didn't want the man to know that she'd just discovered what she was…what she could do. She could hardly believe it herself. Right now he seemed to know a hell of a lot more about her panther half than she did. She didn't like being at a disadvantage.

He inhaled and nodded, understanding dawning on his narrow face. "Ah, that old woman kept you in the dark."

When Emma didn't react, his gaze narrowed. "You are Velius, Emma. A panther, like me and the others. Don't believe the lies I'm sure they tried to tell you about me, however indirectly."

Who might've told her lies about him? Was he referring to the people who kidnapped her from the club? Weren't they all from the same group? And that word…Velius? Why did that sound familiar to her? She racked her brain trying to remember where she'd heard the term before.

"We were created by the Lupreda, ones like that nasty dog you just defended back there."

Emma gave a low growl. She didn't like the contempt in his voice when he talked about Caine.

He clenched a fist on his knee. "He's your enemy! Meant to hunt you down and tear you apart. That's all you are to him. His kind created you for prey!"

No! He didn't hunt me. Instead, he protected me from the likes of you and the others who kidnapped me. Emma quieted and tilted her head to let him think she was beginning to listen to him. She needed as much information as possible if she had any hope of escaping.

Malac gestured toward her. "Don't you see? You're special and that's why he took you. To keep you from us. From your own kind. To keep us weak," he finished with a snarl of disgust.

Emma's ears perked. What made *her* so special? And how were the Velius weak? It suddenly struck her where she'd heard the term Velius before. Caine was on the phone talking to his friend Landon when she was half out of her mind from the drugs. He'd said something like, "If you want the Velius, they're here," before he gave an address. Why did Landon want the Velius? Caine had saved her, so why had he sent Landon after the other panthers? Were they—the Lupreda—trying to destroy her panther race? Was the man right? Did Caine save her because she was special? Whatever "special" meant.

"We need to reinforce our army. And you're the key, Emma."

Malac's comment drew her out of her musings. An army? Were they at war? Where in the world had the Lupreda and Velius come from? And how did the humans not seem to know they existed? And, damn it, *how* was she the key? She grunted to encourage him.

Malac gave her a calculating smile. "I'm the Velius' leader, but my rule will be fully solidified now that I have you. Unlike the rest of us, you're the only one who can shift at will. If you mate with a Velius, chances are that the offspring will be able to shift like you, without the need for an injection. That would give our army a definite advantage when fighting the vampires and werewolves."

Ah, that's why he didn't shift when Caine went after him! But an army against vampires and werewolves? He was psychotic on all counts. She couldn't produce enough children for an army! And something like that would take decades. Not to mention the most important fact—He. Was. Not. Touching. Her. Emma began to growl, low at first but the growl of outrage steadily grew.

Malac scowled. "You act like you have a choice in the matter. You don't. I'm taking you to our facility where our doctor will check you out and make sure you're physically fine and then we'll proceed with my plans." His frown slowly curved into a deadly smile. "The Lupreda may have engineered us to mature very quickly so they could have quick replacements for the ones they killed, but in the end, our rapid reproduction will be to our advantage this time around. Any offspring of yours will be physically mature by age four and ready to wage a war."

Emma snorted and shook her head back and forth. Age four? Going to war? He *was* insane. She could only guess he was referring to the Lupreda when he spoke of werewolves, since he'd called Caine a dog and she'd seen him start to morph, but what of the vampires? They existed only in history books, a bloodthirsty race who'd attacked humans. Wait, there was that article in the paper a few months ago about vampires returning. Was it true? Were the vampires never really extinct? And if so, Malac wanted to wage a full-on war against these two other powerful species? He was a power-hungry nutcase.

Pulling something out of his pocket, Malac popped the lid on a pill bottle and scattered the contents on the floor between them. "Soon there will be no more need for these." His upper lip curled in disdain as white pills pinged everywhere.

They looked like the same vitamin pills she'd taken all her life. Emma's gaze snapped to his and she stood on her feet to slowly push one of the pills over with her nose. When she batted at it with her paw, he gave a harsh laugh.

"Those are how you've stayed hidden for so long. If you didn't know you were a panther, what did the old woman tell you that you were taking?"

Another lie. Why, Aunt Mary?

He waved his hand and continued in a dismissive tone. "It doesn't matter. The pills mask our scent, keeping us hidden from the vampires' and werewolves' detection. But when that bitch stole you away, the pills worked too well. *We* couldn't find you either."

Stomping on one of the pills with his shoe, he ground it into the truck floor with relish, showing just how much he resented having to take them. "An unfortunate side effect for an immature panther like you was that the medicine slowed down your maturity." He met her steady gaze. "Which is why, unlike many of us who were already mature before we started taking the pills, you grew up at a similar pace to that of a human child and not as fast as a panther should've matured."

Now what he said earlier made a bit more sense. *By four her offspring would be fully matured and ready to fight—the panthers have one hell of a metabolism!* He was still crazy. She didn't want to wage war. She didn't want to mate with him or any other Velius for that matter. She wouldn't. Emma backed up and began to growl, the rumbling in her throat elevated with her rising anger. She wasn't going to be any-body's chess piece to move to whatever strategic advantage they thought she could provide them.

Malac narrowed his gaze and held the gun toward her. "You would choose the hard way. At least you'll produce strong, willful panthers. Just don't think you'll ever rule me," he said right before he pulled the trigger.

The tranquilizer stung her shoulder, embedding deep into her skin. She roared and leapt toward him, but he rolled out of the way of her claw's swipe and slammed his fist against her snout the moment he came to a crouched position. Pain exploded across her jaw and she saw bright flashes behind her eyes as she flew back and slammed against the truck's wall. Infuriated, she started to jump up and attack once more, but her legs wobbled. The strong tranquilizer was already doing its job. Toppling to her side, Emma's panther roar slowly changed to a human moan. "No!" she said in a fading voice before she lost consciousness.

Caine wondered if he'd been thrown from the roof of a building. His eyes were heavy and his chest and body ached like a son of a bitch.

"Wake up!"

Who the hell was slapping him in the face? His eyes jerked open at the same time he snarled and grabbed the bastard's arm, ready to snap the bone in two.

Landon grasped Caine's forearm and said in a deadly tone, "Are you ready to find out who would win in a wrestling match, wolf?"

"Are you?" Caine shot back, even though he felt weak as hell.

Snorts of amusement drew Caine's attention to the group

of Lupreda who were standing behind Landon's crouched form. As soon as he smelled the panther's lingering earthy scent, everything came back to him.

"Emma!" Caine instantly tried to sit up and fell back to the floor. Dizziness blurred his vision for a second, while buzzing filled his ears. Damn it to hell, his brain was swelling inside his skull.

Landon put a hand on his chest. "Lay there for a minute until you get your bearings. The tranquilizer dart we pulled out of you is going to take a bit to wear off. Your body's already fighting its effects."

Glancing at the wood floor around Caine and then over his gouged chest, Landon frowned. "There aren't any weapons around, but I see the blood and your wounds are healing slower than usual." His gaze narrowed. "Silver?"

Caine nodded and sat up, grunting through the wooziness in his head. "The bastards must've taken the spikes they used on me. It was some kind of arrow that, once it finds its target, embeds itself deep in the tissue. If it weren't for Emma pulling them out, I'd be dead by now."

"If it weren't for Emma, they would never have dared to come on our land," Landon said.

Caine's gaze narrowed. "They're the ones who ambushed the zerkers. They bragged about how it took only one of their silver bolts to take down each of the 'others.'"

Landon's jaw clenched before he straightened and folded his arms across his chest. "She's *still* Velius."

Caine stood and tied the blanket someone had thrown over him around his waist. Clenching his fists by his sides, he grated out, "Emma's obviously valuable enough for them to take the risk and come back here. She didn't go with them willingly. The only reason she went was because they have her aunt."

Glancing from Landon to Kaitlyn, he continued. "Because they still have her aunt, I take it you were too late when you went to the address I gave you."

Kaitlyn nodded. "The place was stripped bare by the time we got there."

"Several humans left residual smells behind, including the human who took Emma from the club," Laird said, sliding his hand through his auburn hair.

"We didn't detect Emma's aunt's scent. I don't think she was ever there," Landon finished.

Caine tensed. *Emma's aunt wasn't there?* Frowning, he rubbed his overnight beard. "I'm beginning to wonder if there aren't two groups after Emma. A human stole her from the club, but the leader of the ones who came here, Malac, he's panther. I slammed into him back at the club. He was pissed as hell. You'd think if he *was* with the people who'd successfully taken her, he'd have snuck out of the club without drawing attention to himself."

"It's possible. Then again, he could've been trying to distract you to let them get away with her." Landon gestured toward him. "Get dressed. We're going home to regroup."

Lowering his hand to his side, Caine curled his fingers inward until his knuckles popped. He didn't want to think what they might be doing to Emma. There was no mistaking the lustful, possessive sweep of Malac's gaze over Emma's sleek panther form or the scent of testosterone rising in the man when she'd moved past him to retrieve her aunt's pills. "I'm going after them. I won't rest until I find her."

"This team has been going all night with no sleep."

Landon's green eyes slitted. "You'll rest. At home. With your pack."

Landon's steady stare was hard to resist, like he'd wrapped an invisible chain around Caine's chest and yanked. Hard. Caine rolled his head from one shoulder to the other and gritted his teeth, fighting his physical response to the Alpha's powerful influence. Landon's low growl made the chain cinch tight, closing off his air, burning his lungs. Any other time he'd be able to fight it, but the silver had weakened his body too much for him to challenge Landon's dominance right now. "Fine," he gritted out.

When Landon grunted in satisfaction and turned to walk away, Caine's own alpha nature roared from deep inside, fighting like a junkyard dog, despite his weakened state. "I'll stay for an hour and then I'm heading back to town," he grated out.

Emma's shoulder ached a little as someone shined a penlight in her eye. She instantly shoved the light away and jerked back from the person, nearly toppling off the table she was on. Her heart raced at the near miss as the petite woman, with glasses and pale shoulder-length blond hair, grabbed her wrist and steadied her.

"Take it easy," she said in a calm voice. "I'm all done now." Releasing Emma, she backed away and picked up a clipboard from the counter. Squinting, she pushed her glasses up on her nose and began to jot down a few notes.

Emma breathed in an out of her nose, trying to calm her nerves. She quickly glanced down to see she was on an examining table and wearing nothing more than a thin hospital gown with tiny blue flowers.

Her gaze jerked to the woman, noting her crisp white

coat and the name Doctor Thurman embroidered on the pocket. Malac had said he was going to have her checked out. Emma scanned the tiny exam room, her heart racing. On the counter, a vial of blood sat on top of other paperwork. Rubber gloves turned inside out and a couple other personal instruments were lying in a metal pan. Emma ground her teeth and panic knotted her throat. "What have you done to me?"

The woman glanced up from the chart, her green eyes sympathetic. "I didn't do anything to you other than check that you weren't violated."

"*You* violated me!" Emma quickly sat up and swung her legs down the side of the table, her cheeks flaming with indignant heat. "How dare you!"

The woman's gaze darted to the door and her voice lowered. "I insisted on doing your physical instead of Doctor Thurman."

Emma's eyes snapped to the name on her coat. "You *are* Doctor Thurman."

"The other Doctor Thurman is my father. Would you rather a male have done your exam?"

Before Emma could respond, the door opened and Malac stepped into the room. He put his hand out and the woman instantly handed him the clipboard, saying, "She's perfectly healthy."

He flipped the first page over and his dark gaze narrowed. "Did he touch her?"

The doctor shook her head and her tone held a tinge of warning. "She's a virgin."

He raised a dark eyebrow and a pleased, calculating smile creased his narrow face. "An interesting development I hadn't expected." Snapping the page closed, he handed the clipboard back to the doctor and addressed Emma. "Eat and then you'll be allowed to see the old woman to know she's still alive."

"The 'old' woman is my aunt, and she'd better be in good health or I'll claw your eyes out," Emma hissed.

Malac chuckled, but amusement didn't reflect in his brown eyes. "So protective. You really believe she's your aunt, don't you? What other lies did the old bat tell you? You do realize she's human, right?"

Now I know.

When the only answer he got from Emma was her growling stomach, his chuckle turned to a full-out laugh before he sobered. "This is rich. Your reunion would be interesting to observe. Too bad I have business to deal with."

The tips of her fingers tingled, curled tight underneath the examining table. Emma realized her claws were ready to unsheathe, while an angry growl rumbled in her chest. It was so much easier now to feel the panther lying in wait under her skin. This time she wasn't afraid or scared. She welcomed her panther's strength. Apparently, all it had taken to bring out her primal side was seeing someone she cared about threatened.

Malac ignored her hostile sounds and spoke to someone in the hall. "Once she's eaten, escort her down to the old lady. Give her five and then bring her to my quarters."

"What about my aunt's medicine?" Emma snarled after him when he started to leave.

He turned back to her, his expression suddenly serious. "It'll be up to you whether or not she gets her meds."

The moment he turned away and walked out of the room, Emma was off the table, intending to go after the manipulative bastard. But a big man with light brown hair tied back in a severe ponytail stepped in front of her, blocking her way.

She realized he was human, like the doctor, because he *had* a scent. "Eat, then we'll go," he said in a curt tone.

Emma glanced at the gun strapped to his side, then narrowed her gaze after Malac's slim form walking down the hall.

"You need to eat." The blond woman held out a plate that had been wrapped in aluminum foil on a far counter. An apple sat next to a ham-and-cheese sandwich.

Even though her stomach rumbled, Emma didn't want to waste time. She shook her head. "I want to see my aunt."

The woman shoved the plate toward her. "You won't be allowed to see her if you don't eat."

Glaring at her, Emma jerked the plate from her hand and sat back down on the exam table. It took her less than five minutes to devour the food. The stem was the only bit of food left on the plate.

"Let's go." The guard grabbed her upper arm and escorted her out. Emma's bootie-covered feet shuffled quietly, while his shoes made heavy tapping sounds on the hall's gleaming white floors. She squinted at the fluorescent lights shining brightly on the stark white walls. Behind them, at one end of the hall, a young blond-haired man stood with a pulser gun in his hand, obviously on guard. Everything about the space felt sterile and pristine—like a lab. Except for the presence of the guard and pulser guns. They made it feel like a military facility.

A man with shoulder-length dark hair exited the elevator at the opposite end of the hall and walked toward them. As he passed, the diamond stud in his ear caught Emma's attention. Her gaze caught his for a brief second. The coldness in his deep green eyes surprised her. He was too young to appear so detached. She noted the gun strapped to his hip and tried to catch his scent, but couldn't. He had to be another panther.

He appeared to be of similar age to the young sentry down the hall. No more than seventeen or eighteen.

They reached the end of the hall and went through a door on the left which led to a stairwell. Emma's heart raced while they walked down two flights of stairs to the ground floor. They turned down a long, carpeted hall with several doors lining the right side, reminding her of a hotel.

When they stopped in front of the third door on their right, the guy swept his card through the reader and pushed her inside, saying in a gruff tone, "You have five minutes."

Her aunt turned from staring out the barred windows. "Emma!" she called, holding out her arms. She was still wearing her nightgown and slippers, but they'd at least allowed her to slip into her coat when they kidnapped her, Emma realized when she saw the gray wool overcoat lying on the bed.

"Aunt Mary!" Emma hugged the only family she'd ever known as tight as she could. "I was so worried." Emma cupped her aunt's pudgy cheeks and leaned back to look at her. "How are you feeling?"

Mary's wrinkled fingers ran gently across her hair, then touched her gown. "Where are your clothes, child? Are *you* okay?" Her expression hardened and her blue eyes slitted. "Have they hurt you?"

Emma gripped her aunt's hands to stop her fidgeting. "Are you feeling okay? How's your heart?"

Mary pulled her close and whispered, "Don't worry about me. The young female doctor has been checking my vitals." Leaning back, she gave Emma a smile meant to eliminate her worry. "Really, I'm okay. Where are your clothes?"

Emma knew she didn't have time to go into everything that

happened to her so far, so she went for blunt honesty. "I know what I am now." When Mary started to speak, she shook her head. "Don't worry, I'm not angry with you for keeping the truth from me all these years. We'll talk about your reasons later. I just wanted you to know I'm going to do everything I can to get us out of here."

Mary's worried expression softened and tears filled her eyes. "I did it to protect you and because I love you as if you were my own."

Tears spilled down Emma's cheeks and her heart ached for their situation. She hugged Mary tight. Trust was a little hard for her right now, but she cared very much for this woman who raised her all her life. "It's okay. You don't have to expla—"

"No, I want to tell you so you'll understand…in case I don't make it."

Emma's heart jerked. "Don't talk like that. We're going to get out of here. It doesn't matter to me that you're human and I'm panther. You'll always be my family."

Mary sniffled and pushed Emma's hair away from her face with a gentle caress. "Hush and just listen. My brother and I didn't have a normal life growing up."

Emma listened intently. Mary had only mentioned her estranged brother once in passing, but she'd never told Emma why they didn't speak anymore.

Mary's lips compressed into a hard line, then she continued. "Our parents had a nasty divorce. Throughout our childhood, Roland and I were shuffled back and forth between them for years. Mom and Dad each did and said horrible things, trying to turn us against the other parent, which actually made Roland and me closer. We had only each other, and as kids, we promised ourselves that we'd never have children of our own so they wouldn't have to go through what we did with our parents.

"When Roland met Jade, everything changed. I could see his devotion to her right off the bat. No matter our promises about not having children of our own, this young woman instantly became like a daughter to my brother. Only, she wasn't human."

Emma's heart thumped. "Jade was Velius?"

Mary nodded. "My brother helped Jade by creating the medicine that masks the panthers' scent from their natural enemies. I joined their group to be by Roland's side and just like my brother—" the old woman cupped Emma's chin, her smile full of love "—I quickly grew attached to a little girl in the Velius pride. The day before I decided to take you away was the last time I spoke to my brother." Her smile faded and she gave a self-deprecating laugh. "I suppose it's life's ironic justice that Roland and I had become so hopelessly devoted to our 'children's' happiness, to the point our dedication has kept us apart all this time. You see, if he had ever learned where I'd taken you, he would've brought you back to make Jade happy."

"Why would you take me away?" Emma asked, her mind racing in confusion.

Mary's lip curled in contempt. "Malac had splintered off from Jade's group, taking young Hawkeye with him. I was very unhappy about that, but when I later learned that Hawkeye had run away, I knew something had to be done. Even though Jade acted as your guardian and her intentions toward you seemed honorable, because you were special, I knew you'd always be at risk of becoming a pawn in Jade's and Malac's constant power struggle, just like poor Hawkeye. I wouldn't allow that. I wanted you to grow up without strife, to have a happy childhood—at least the best I could provide for you." She touched Emma's cheek. "You're a bit older than I led you to believe, but as far as I was concerned, your life started the day I took you with me."

Emma stared in shock. "How old am I?"

"The medicine slowed your maturity considerably. You're twenty-six."

Emma didn't really remember any other life than that with her aunt, though she felt sorry for Hawkeye having to live with Malac. She'd have run away, too. Tucking all of the truths raining down on her into the back of her mind for future contemplation, Emma gave an apologetic half smile. "I ran out of my pills and forgot to mention I needed a refill. I think that's how the Velius finally tracked me down." When her aunt nodded her understanding, Emma plunged on, needing to know the whole truth. "Malac told me I was created. Does that mean I never had a mother?"

Mary nodded, her smile sympathic. "I'm the closest thing to a mother you've had."

Emma's head spun with all the new information, yet finding out there were two groups of panthers answered a few questions, while triggering a vague, nagging memory in her brain. She squeezed her eyes shut for a second, trying to process everything. Then the memory suddenly flooded her mind. She gripped her aunt's hands and pulled her over to sit down on the bed. "Has anyone ever called you Margaret? Is that your real name?"

Mary chuckled. "Roland always calls me that, even when everyone else calls me Mary. How did you know about Margaret?"

Emma was excited to share some news of Mary's brother.

"I believe I spoke to him. I was waking up from being drugged, so I never saw his face, but I heard him ask me about Margaret. He was worried for you. He's the one who took me from the club last night." *And the female talking to Roland about me had to have been Jade!*

Mary's blue eyes lit with hope. "Then he knows they have you! They'll come for us!"

Emma shook her head. "It's a little more complicated than that. He doesn't know Malac has taken me, but I'm sure others are searching for me."

Worry pulled at Mary's soft features. "What others?"

"I met a man. Malac says he's Lupreda—" Emma started to tell her about Caine when the door opened.

The guard walked into the room. "Time's up. Let's go."

He stalked over and grabbed Emma's arm, pulling her to her feet. Mary gripped Emma's hand tight, her brow creased with worry. "You can't trust that man you met. Don't trust anyone other than my brother or Jade. No one else has your best interests at heart, Emma."

Chapter 8

Mary's parting words kept echoing in Emma's head as the guard hauled her to the end of the hall, then used his key card to open an elevator to her right. Once they were inside, the man pushed the button and they rode the elevator to the third floor.

Whom could she trust? Everyone seemed to want something from her. First, Roland and this unknown Jade had kidnapped her, and now, of course, Malac.

But what about Caine? Did he also have an ulterior motive? Was their attraction just another lie to get something he wanted from her? To keep her from her people? Her people? She didn't even know what that meant! Mary might love her, but she was human. Emma had never felt more alone or scared. Her heart raced when the elevator pinged and the silver doors slid open.

"Come in, Emma," Malac called from somewhere in the

room. Piano music played off to the right; it was a classical piece. Straight ahead was a huge mural painting of New York City's skyline on the far wall directly across from the elevator entrance.

When a cool breeze blew up her gown, making her skin prickle, she said to the guard, "Don't I at least get to change clothes or something first?"

His answer was to shove her onto the thick Persian rug right outside the elevator and punch the elevator button. As the doors slid noiselessly closed, Emma dug her toes into the soft carpet and turned to see Malac sitting at the piano, his fingers running across the keys flawlessly.

"Ah, there you are." The music suddenly stopped and he stood, grabbing his glass of wine off the top of the grand piano sitting all the way across the three-thousand-square-foot space.

As he passed through the sunken living room area, decorated with an oversized couch covered with opulent pillows in similar earth tones to the area rug under her feet in the foyer area, her stomach tensed. Malac was a wiry, slightly built man, but what his smaller frame lacked, his eyes more than made up for in terms of sheer power and determination. The penetrating way he looked at her as he approached could only be described as cold and calculating. She could almost see his diabolical mind working through the numbers, considering all the strategic angles…how best to use her to his ultimate advantage.

From the way he'd decorated his living quarters to the clothes he wore—a black silk shirt, dark gray slacks and custom leather dress shoes—it was clear Malac liked to surround himself with the finer things in life. Emma didn't doubt for one minute that that skyline painting on the wall to her left held some deeper significance for him…something far sinister than a general appreciation of the city. Malac was maniacally ambitious.

Sheesh, I'm reading all kinds of things into this creep. All she knew for sure was the man made her skin crawl and he definitely had a God complex. She resisted a shiver of revulsion when he stopped a few feet away from her.

"Now that you've seen that the old woman is alive and well, we're going to talk."

"My aunt needs her meds," Emma stated.

"Still clinging to that human?" Malac tsked and walked over to a side bar where he poured himself some more wine. "Want some?" he asked as he took a sip and faced her.

Emma clenched her fists. "I will not be a part of this 'war' insanity you mentioned in the truck. Nor am I mating with you or any other Velius."

Malac leaned casually back against the bar. "My team of scientists and doctors assure me that they can successfully extract your eggs, fertilize them and implant them in surrogate mothers." His dark gaze swept appreciatively down her bare legs, then back up to her face. Closing his eyes briefly, his nostrils flared. "I smell the change in your musky scent. You're heading toward your fertile cycle. Before we extract your eggs to build this army, *my* offspring will come the old-fashioned way, conceived and carried by my mate."

He was going to violate her, then make her his broodmare? Horrified shock slammed through Emma in waves of fury and fear. A chill swept down her spine and bile rose to her throat as her disgust built. "You won't get within an inch of me and neither will your doctors!" she snapped.

Setting his wineglass on the bar top, he turned an unconcerned gaze her way. "And what about your 'aunt'? Doctor

Thurman informs me that she'll need her meds very soon for her health to remain stable."

God, Aunt Mary. You've given up so much for me.

When she didn't answer, his smile held an icy ruthlessness that sent a jolt of fear splintering through her. "You *will* cooperate."

Emma stood there in that thin hospital gown, feeling the most vulnerable she'd ever been in her life. If she said yes, in two seconds he'd have the damn flimsy thing torn off her body. If she said no, Mary might die and she would be responsible.

She glanced around the open living space for an escape path. A huge glass window, farther down the same wall as the mural, led to some kind of concrete patio partially covered in snow. It dropped to nowhere as far as she could see from her vantage point. The elevator to her right needed a key, so she couldn't leave that way.

Every fiber in her being screamed out against the choice she was having to make…and she thought of Caine. How she wanted her first time—her only time—to be with him. Was he sincere in his feelings for her? She desperately wanted to believe he was real. *I will come for you*, was the last thing he'd said to her. In that, she believed.

His strength, while fighting his wounds and the tranquilizer, reminded her that she wasn't completely helpless. "Fine." She yanked the front of the gown, and the snaps popped open. Cool air hit her spine and she slid her arms out of the gown to let it flutter to the floor. Standing naked in front of him, she tilted up her chin. "You want me?"

Malac's white teeth flashed in victory. "Faster by the second," he murmured, his gaze slitting with lust as he began to unbutton his shirt with quick flicks of his wrist.

Emma kept her expression calm while her insides quaked. She curled her finger inward in a come-hither movement. "Then you're going to have to work for it."

When he took a step toward her, she turned and fell toward the floor at the same time she let all her anger for her aunt's current situation, for the impending loss of her own innocence—both mentally and physically—and for what Malac had done to Caine well up inside her. All the strong emotions merged into a brewing storm, fast and furious—ready to unleash its wrath.

Her panther form hit the floor on all fours. She turned to face him, her roar shaking the pictures hanging on the walls and rattling his glass of wine on the bar.

"Shift back!" he snarled, his face distorting in fury.

Emma blew air through her nostrils, then swiped her paw across the wood floor, purposefully digging gouges. Like a bull preparing to charge, she planned to make sure he didn't come away from their altercation unscathed.

Sweat coated his forehead. He quickly flipped open a gold engraved box on the bar top. "You'll pay for this," he gritted out over her panther roar.

When her bellow slowed to a steady growl, Emma smelled the beginnings of fear edge his scent, pungent and sharp. She'd almost forgotten he couldn't shift at will. Now, she was the predator and he was the prey. He was still stronger than a human man, but the fact remained that she was a force to be reckoned with in this form, and with no tranquilizer gun at his disposal, he was as trapped as she'd been a minute ago. The air hit her canines with sweet biting sharpness as she smiled and slowly walked toward the bar, her muscles flexing sleekly with each step she took.

He jammed some kind of short needle into his neck and closed his eyes with a hiss as if he'd just shot himself up with his favorite drug. When his eyes snapped open, his pupils had dilated to the same size as his dark irises. It was like staring into a soulless being.

He gave her a pleased smile. "Taking you this way will be harder and bloodier, but I'm up for the challenge. It's probably the best way to show you that my panther rules you just as much as the man does."

His threat brought her survival instincts out full force. Emma curled her upper lip back, bearing her teeth once more. She dug her front claws into the wood flooring, then crouched on her back legs, ready to pounce before he shifted to panther form.

She'd learned Malac's tactics the last time she'd tangled with him. This time she didn't leap for his face; instead, she lunged forward and used her strong paws to grab his legs, pulling him to the floor.

He fell over onto his side, hitting the floor with a hard thud. As her claws dug deep, ripping his calf muscles, his yell of pain deepened to a vicious growling roar. Emma didn't have time to dodge his blow before his powerful front paw swiped at her shoulder, shredding skin as he sent her flying through the air.

She hit the back of the couch and her momentum toppled the heavy piece of furniture. Fire raged across her shoulder where he'd wounded her. She panted and quickly rolled off the couch's plush cushions onto her paws. The smell of her own blood filled her nostrils while she crouched and twitched her ears back and forth, listening for Malac's approach.

Before she heard him coming, Malac soared over the couch and knocked her hard, sending her skidding on her side across the floor. She slammed into the legs of a console table and a vase shattered, spewing flowers, water and ceramic bits all around her.

Malac let out a triumphant rrrrooowl and slowly stalked toward her, his head bent low, his growl promising retribution. His panther body was bigger than hers, easily outweighing her by sixty pounds, but he was still slim in stature, just like his human form. His slightly larger size gave him brute strength, but it probably also slowed him down in agility.

If she could just get on her feet, she might be able to evade him. Emma tried to scramble to her feet, but the water and pottery bits made her paws slide out from underneath her. She slipped back to the floor, banging her chin hard.

Panic closed her throat, keeping her from roaring the way she wanted to. Instead, the sound that came out of her throat was a low, warning rumble.

When Malac reached her side, his roar slowed to an almost evil-sounding snarl as he reached out with his forepaw and batted her body out of the mess underneath her and into the middle of the floor.

Emma spun with his forceful blow and dizziness rattled her mind for a second before she could get her bearings. The moment her head cleared, she jumped up, only to feel Malac's heavy weight slam over her back.

The dominant position sent fear spiraling through her belly. She tried to scramble out from underneath him, but he bit down on her neck. Hard.

Emma howled in pain and her legs began to shake when his hot breath rushed out his nose in a growling grunt. She jerked forward slightly when his hips pushed against hers. As his musky scent elevated several levels, she couldn't mistake what his vise hold meant.

She tried to jerk free, but he deepened his bite, sending pain shooting down her neck. Despite her fear, she hissed and tucked her tail underneath her in an act of rebellion.

He snarled his anger at her defiance, then jammed his right forepaw on top of hers, digging his claws deep.

At the same time Emma let out a yowl of pain, something big burst through the huge picture window across the room. Glass flew everywhere as an enormous panther barreled straight for them.

Malac barely had time to release her before the other panther rammed his huge head into Malac's side.

Emma heard ribs crack right before Malac careened all the way across the room. He collided with an oversized wooden trunk against the far wall, the piece of furniture exploding on impact. Lying among broken planks and splinters of wood, Malac shook his head to clear it, then jumped to his paws with a roar of fury.

The panther who'd attacked Malac stood there. Waiting. The only indication he was on high alert was the slight twitch at the end of his long tail.

Emma backed up when Malac bared his canines and claws and leapt across the room toward the taller, broader panther, who probably outweighed him by at least forty pounds.

As Malac's form began to descend in the air, in a motion that defied his bulky size, the panther moved with grace, rolling forward to land underneath Malac where he hammered his back paws into Malac's underbelly.

Malac's body bowed from the impact before vaulting across the entire room's expanse to land with a sickly thud against the grand piano. Eerie notes played as he slithered across the keyboard. The bench fell to its side before he landed with a solid thump on the floor, lying completely still.

Emma turned frightened eyes to the panther who now approached her with sure-footed steps. Not once did he make a sound. No growl or roar of fury erupted from him while he'd attacked Malac. He'd just taken out the bastard as if he were a weak-limbed rag doll, full of fluffy stuffing.

When the panther reached her, he lowered his head and pushed at her shoulder.

Emma stumbled back, unsure what he was telling her. He did it again, this time more forcefully and she realized he was trying to direct her toward the window.

She shook her head. She wasn't leaving without her aunt. The lights on the elevator began to move. She waited, watching them. Once the elevator finally reached the floor and the doors slid open, she'd force her way in, taking out whoever was in her way.

When she tried to sidestep him, the panther's low warning growl surprised her. She dodged, then attempted to dive past him, but he was much faster than she expected. Before she knew what had happened, he'd grabbed her wounded scruff with his teeth, then hurled her across the room toward the window.

Emma landed on her side, sliding across the floor. She quickly rolled to her feet and started to charge toward him, but bits of glass had embedded in her paw pads. As she yelped and tried to shake the glass from her paws, she was surprised to see him run toward her, then turn onto his side and skid across the floor in front of her.

He stood up and shook the bits of glass from his fur, then looked at her and jerked his head toward the window with a commanding grunt. He'd just cleared a path for her to the window and he wasn't going to let her go in any other direction.

Emma was torn. She didn't want to leave Mary behind, but this panther wasn't giving her a choice. The elevator dinged, and three men stepped out holding pulser guns. Damn it, they weren't giving her a choice, either.

One man yelled and pulser fire zoomed past Emma, jolting her into action. She ran a few steps and vaulted toward the window. Something pinched her side as she crossed the windowsill, but she didn't pause once she'd landed on her feet on the concrete patio—which turned out to be a flat roof. Following her rescuer's lead, who'd landed beside her, they took off in a fast run. Pulser fire singed the snow-covered cement around them as she headed toward the edge. Emma's heart jumped to her throat when the panther in front of her bunched his long powerful legs and easily cleared the six-foot distance to land on the flat roof of an adjacent building.

She came to a skidding stop, sending snow scattering over the building's edge.

The panther impatiently pawed at the cement under his feet, then let out a bellow, commanding her to follow.

Pulser bursts zipped past her ear, elevating her heart rate several notches. Emma backed up several feet, then sucked in a deep breath before bolting forward. Her heart nearly stopped as she took the flying leap between the buildings. When her paws landed on the roof, the shock sent jabs of pain shooting up her legs, making them as useless as rubber. She came to a jolting stop for a second, trying to regain strength.

The panther nudged her with his snout and a low purr of encouragement against her jaw, combined with his familiar scent, evoked a strong feeling of support. She took a deep breath and put one paw in front of the other in order to shrug off the pain in her shaking legs.

Emma followed him inside the building where a rock had been wedged between the rooftop door and the frame, holding it ajar. Her right side stung like someone held a match against her skin, but she pushed forward. Their paws made no sounds as they trotted down the three flights of stairs and then out another door the panther shoved open once he'd pushed down on the metal bar with his front paws.

As soon as they were free of the building, he began to run on the pavement, his sleek, large muscled body both powerful and graceful in his movements. Was that how she looked? She doubted it. Emma gave a self-deprecating snort as she clumsily tried to match his smooth gait. She at least kept up with his pace for a good five blocks while they weaved through what appeared to be a snow-covered, run-down industrial area of town.

She didn't have time to look at street signs, they were moving so fast. The panther seemed to know where he was going. The way she was starting to feel—run-down and weak, her side stitching and throbbing with each pounding brush of her paws across the snow-covered pavement—she hoped he didn't suddenly take off or she'd be lost forever in the maze of buildings and streets around them.

Only, her body had decided it had had enough, even if her mind screamed for her to continue. Emma's rapid run slowed to a trot, and she finally managed to mewl a tired growl before she stopped and fell over onto her left side. As she lay on the freezing asphalt, her nose deciphering car oil and gas aromas under the heavy layer of snow, her ribs heaved up and down with each wheezing breath.

Emma's racing pulse spiked when her vision began to fade in and out. She couldn't pass out. Not now.

A dark-haired man with deep green eyes came into view. His forehead creased with worry and he leaned over her to run his hand across her shoulder. "What's wrong—" he started to say, then swore under his breath. His high cheekbones hollowed with his swift intake of breath when his palm reached something sticky wet on her side.

Bright red blood coated his hand. "Why didn't you tell me you were hurt?" he said in a harsh tone.

Emma grunted her annoyance. How could he give her a hard time about speaking up? It's not like she could at the moment. But if she were in human form...

As if he knew what she was thinking, he ordered, "Don't shift!" while he moved behind her. One big hand slid under her hips and another under her shoulder. "You've lost too much blood as it is. Your human form couldn't handle a wound like this."

She whimpered as he lifted her. Cradling her body against his broad chest, he whispered against her ear, "Hang on. We're almost to my truck."

A few minutes later, he rounded a building and stopped behind a truck. Emma let out a tiny yowl when he shifted her so he could open the covered tailgate.

Sliding her body gently onto the truck bed, he said, "The hard cover above you should keep off the wind. I'm going to slide you forward a little bit so I can talk to you through the cab window."

Emma could only moan her approval. Her eyes rolled in her head and she was having a hard time staying awake, the pain hurt so much. As he pushed her forward, she bumped into rolls of paper. She blinked and tried to focus. Maps. Tons of maps were all around her. One had unrolled near her nose and she saw trails among mountain ranges and trees; they had all been intricately hand-drawn.

He'd disappeared for a second and then he was climbing into the truck bed beside her. She lifted her head at the sound of material ripping. Bare-chested, he sat on his knees in a pair of faded jeans and no shoes, ripping open a T-shirt at the seam. He must've grabbed the jeans and T-shirt from the front of the truck.

Moving at a rapid pace, he cinched the T-shirt tight around her waist, covering her wound. After he jumped out of the truck, he put his hand on her hip and murmured, "That's all I can do for now, Emral."

Emral? The name stirred something familiar deep within her. She knew this man…somehow. The truck started and Emma closed her eyes, trying to remember.

The vehicle began to move and a window slid open at the same time he barked in a gruff voice, "Stay conscious!"

Yeah, yeah, she thought even as his commanding tone jerked her eyes wide open. It was an involuntary response, but one she felt must've happened often in her past for her body to instantly react like it did.

"You don't remember me, do you?" he called through the window.

Emma sighed, wishing she could talk.

"I couldn't let Malac do it to you—I had to save you from the same fate," he ground out. "I promised you I'd always protect you. When I found out Mary had taken you and even Malac didn't know how to find you, I thought you were safe, but I always kept tabs…" He flipped on what sounded like a radio. Airwave static filled the air, then angry squawks came through.

"That traitorous bastard has taken her. Find Hawkeye, no matter the cost," Malac's enraged voice shot through the truck's cab.

"Do you want us to take him alive? His DNA—"

"I don't give a damn about him," Malac snarled. "Kill him on sight, but I *want her back.*"

So this was Hawkeye. But why did he call her Emral? Her name was Emma. The hitching pain in her side kept her from thinking about anything for very long. Her stomach knotted and the burning wound on her side seemed to grow even hotter while the pain throbbed incessantly.

They swerved around a corner and she rolled into some of the maps. Emma moaned. "You okay—" he started to ask through the window, then hissed, "Sonofabitch." Two seconds later, she heard a cell phone being dialed.

"I need the address for Landon Rourke Private Investigations in New York City."

Emma's ears perked up. Landon was the name Caine had mentioned.

"That'll do."

When he snapped closed his cell phone, he gunned the engine and the truck shot forward. Several minutes passed, or was it a half hour—she'd lost track of time as her eyes opened and closed—before the truck rolled to a stop?

The tailgate opened and Hawkeye slid her out of the truck, lifting her into his arms. All she could tell was that they were in some kind of alley. "Let's hope he has this place on an alarm," Hawkeye mumbled. Emma jerked when he lifted his foot and rammed it into a door, splintering it off the hinges.

He carried her inside a storage room and through another door to lay her on the carpet. A desk, a rolling chair and a lateral filing cabinet was all she could see from her vantage point on the floor while he scribbled something on the desk.

An annoying beeping sound invaded her mind as he went down on his knee and ran his hand across her forehead and over her ears. An alarm was going off. "You're bleeding too much. For obvious reasons, I can't take you to the hospital." He glanced toward the front door and her gaze followed his. Landon Rourke Private Investigations, she read the backward words on the glass as Hawkeye finished, "This man saved us once. He might be Lupreda, but he's proven he has a conscience. Right now, he's the only one I trust."

He stood up and Emma made whimpering clicks. She didn't want to be left alone. Crouching beside her once more, he ran his hand over her pelt. "I'll be watching from a distance to make sure he takes care of you."

With a sigh of relief, Emma quieted and closed her eyes.

"Stay conscious," he reminded her in an authoritative tone not to be ignored.

When her eyes flew open, he was already gone.

Chapter 9

Caine jerked his gaze to the rearview mirror. Something heavy had landed in the back of his truck. Landon knocked on the glass behind him, then made a thumbing motion to the side of the road.

Gritting his teeth, Caine gripped the steering wheel tight and for several seconds considered swerving to the side, just to knock the Alpha on his ass. He was so pissed at Landon for waiting an hour and a half to wake him, he could feel his Musk form howling to be free, itching for a fight. The tips of his fingers tingled, his wereclaws scratching just below the surface.

When Landon pounded a dent in the roof above his head, he finally pulled his truck to the side of the interstate. Laird drove up behind him in Landon's truck with Kaitlyn in the seat beside him. Roman stood in the bed of their truck, his hair windblown to hell, grinning like a fool at the icy wonderland around him. The idiot.

Why had Landon chased him down? He was almost to the city at this point. He sure as hell wasn't going back to Lupreda land.

Before he could say a word, Landon had jumped down and climbed into the passenger seat. "I told you not to leave without me," Landon snarled.

"And I told you to wake me in an hour," Caine challenged, pulling the truck back onto the road.

Landon's low growl was interrupted by his cell phone's ring. Grabbing the phone from his belt, he flipped it open and read the text message.

"Hell and damnation," he mumbled, then hung up and called another number.

"What is it?" Caine's shoulders tensed.

"My office has been broken into again," Landon said before he spoke into the phone. "Gabriel, I got an automatic call. Can you pull up the monitoring system and tell me what body temperature the sensors are registering?"

Caine heard Gabriel's rumble across the line. "One hundred and three, Landon. Definitely not human, unless the human's sick as a dog." Gabriel snorted at his own joke, then quickly sobered. "You want me to cut the backup call to the police?"

"Cut it," Landon said in a brisk tone before he closed the cell and addressed Caine. "Gotta be Velius. Let's see how fast this souped-up rig of yours can go."

When he gunned the truck, Laird honked and followed suit. Caine glanced in his rearview mirror to see Roman now hanging out the passenger window, shaking his fist and yelling, "Yeah, baby! Go!"

Caine shook his head. "We can't take him anywhere."

"At least he's a talented nut," Landon grunted, then glanced his way. "If we can catch one of them there, we'll do whatever it takes to find out where they've taken Emma."

Landon had just given Caine his full support, surprising the hell out of him. Caine gripped the steering wheel hard and dipped his head in a curt nod, swallowing the lump of appreciation in his throat.

"You will follow my lead. Understood?" Landon ordered when they entered the outskirts of the city.

Every fiber in Caine's body howled in protest. He knew Landon was trying to control the situation so Caine wouldn't use his Musk form. He didn't like it, but right now Landon had the advantage—a lead on finding the panthers. And Emma.

Setting his jaw, Caine stared straight ahead. "Got it."

The moment he stepped out of his truck, Caine smelled Emma's earthy scent and blood. A lot of blood. Panic knotted his stomach. He started to take off for the front door, but Landon was by his side in a millisecond, grasping his arm.

"My lead," the Alpha reminded him as Laird, Roman and Kaitlyn joined them. Releasing Caine, Landon jerked his chin toward the front of the building. "Laird, you and Roman make sure to shield Kaitlyn as you approach from the front. Caine and I are going around back."

Laird nodded his understanding and Kaitlyn pulled her gun, rolling her eyes and mumbling about overprotective wolves.

Narrowing his gaze on Caine, Landon said, "We go in together."

Tension rode Caine's spine, raising the hairs on the back of his neck. He gritted his teeth but dipped his head in agreement.

Landon and Caine headed to the side of the building and rounded to the alley behind it in mere seconds. When he saw the condition of his back door, Landon growled, clenching his fists. "Let's go."

Caine prepared for a fight as he walked into the back room, but no one was around. He and Landon made their way to the front room. The moment he stepped through the doorway, he saw the blood-soaked T-shirt wrapped around Emma's bloody wound. She was breathing with such shallow pants and her pulse sounded slower than it should; his heart nearly stopped. He rushed forward and fell to his knees by her side.

Running his hand over her snout and then down the soft fur along her shoulder, he was so racked with fear she wouldn't survive that his words came out in a guttural grunt. "Emma, it's Caine. I'm here. Stay awake for me, sweetheart."

She whimpered and her forepaw jerked slightly, giving him hope that she recognized him.

"I have the panther's scent." Caine looked up at Landon. "I'm going to rip the bastard who did this to her apart one limb at a time."

"I think you've got it all wrong." Landon approached and with a grim expression turned the piece of paper he held around so Caine could read it.

Save Emral!

Caine frowned. "Who's Emral?"

Landon glanced down at Emma. "*She's* Emral, or Emerald rather. The Lupreda who created these panthers named them after gemstones—Jade, Emerald, Hawkseye, Malachite, Jasper, and so on."

Caine snarled at the note, mentally plotting his vengeance. "It doesn't mean the panther I'm scenting wasn't responsible."

Landon went down on one knee beside Emma and spoke to her. "It's Landon Rourke. I recognize your scents now that I smell Hawkeye's, too. Did he bring you here?"

Emma turned toward Landon's voice and nodded before letting her head roll back to the floor.

Caine had so many questions, but right now Emma's dire condition needed to be addressed. He bent down to run his tongue along a wound on her shoulder and was surprised when it didn't instantly start to heal.

He jerked his gaze to Landon. The Alpha was shaking his head, his jaw set in a hard line. "Apparently our saliva doesn't heal them like it can humans and our own kind."

Caine pressed his hand over the largest wound on Emma's side. "She'll bleed out if we don't do something soon."

Kaitlyn stepped forward to stand beside her mate who was still crouched beside Emma. "Obviously we can't take her to a hospital and because there aren't any doctors among the Lupreda…" She placed her hand on Landon's shoulder and continued. "I have a suggestion. You told me about the vampire leader's sister saving his human mate, Ariel. Do you think his sister might be able to help Emma?"

"A vampire?" Caine growled low in his throat.

"This might be our only option. None of the Lupreda have ever needed someone with medical knowledge." Landon stood and retrieved his cell phone from his belt. Flipping open the cell, he reached into his jeans' front pocket and held his hand toward Caine. "I'll make the call to Jachin after you agree."

Emma had started to bleed again. The warm blood seeped under his fingers, soaking the makeshift bandage. Jerking his gaze to Landon, Caine saw the lone silver chain curled innocuously in the palm of the Alpha's hand.

Returning his line of sight to Emma, Caine couldn't believe Landon would blackmail him like this. Anger and resentment boiled in his chest, building steam. He couldn't lose her. Grinding his teeth, he snarled, "Just do it."

Landon dropped the chain around Caine's neck, then started dialing.

After a few seconds, Caine's keen hearing picked up Jachin's voice across the line. "Rourke. Haven't heard from you in a while."

"I'm calling in my marker for helping you take over leadership of the Sanguinas," Landon said in a matter-of-fact tone.

Shocked, Caine jerked his gaze back to Landon.

Jachin remained silent for a second. "Must be pretty important for you to ask for a debt owed so soon."

The Alpha returned Caine's steady stare and continued in a calm tone. "It's a matter of life and death."

"Whose?"

"I'll tell you everything when you get here. Can you bring your sister to the city? We need her medical expertise."

While Jachin responded on the other end, Kaitlyn put her hand on Landon's arm. Then Landon nodded and went on. "Fine. Meet us at my mate Kaitlyn's house after dark."

After Landon gave Jachin directions to the suburbs and hung up, Caine shook his head. He couldn't believe Landon had just played the pack's most important chess piece for his sake—a wolf no longer with the pack—yet his worry for Emma overrode the varied emotions of guilt, shock and deep appreciation tightening his chest. "We can't risk moving her. She's losing blood."

Landon squatted next to Emma and put his hand on her

head. "The last time I saw you, you were just a cub, so tiny you fit in the palm of my hand." Glancing up at Caine, his green gaze hardened. "If you want her to live, we have to move her."

Caine set his jaw, then pulled off his T-shirt to begin re-binding her wound.

The moment he heard a car pull into Kaitlyn's driveway, Caine tensed. Kaitlyn had put him in a guest bedroom, and he'd sat there for two hours with his back against the head-board, holding Emma on the bed between his legs, her head propped on his thigh. While time had ticked past, Caine realized those two hours were far more agonizing than his own experience a few months ago, waiting to see if he'd shift back to human form from his Musk one. In comparison, that was nothing. He could not lose Emma.

As voices filtered up from the hall downstairs, he stroked her head and the soft fur down her neck for the thousandth time and whispered, "They're here. Hold on just a little longer, Emma."

Emma had stopped responding to his encouraging words fifteen minutes before, tearing him up inside. She was conscious but barely.

Landon and Kaitlyn appeared in the doorway, followed by a tall, dark-haired man, an equally tall and broad-chested blond man and a petite woman with fine features and long black hair. The woman immediately pushed her way past everyone and approached the bed, a look of concern in her blue eyes.

"She's a shapeshifter, yes?" she asked Caine. Kneeling beside the bed, she ran her hand gingerly over Emma's fur.

Caine tensed when her vampire scent slammed into him. It took every ounce of willpower in his body not to rip the woman's hand away from Emma—his distrust in vampires was too ingrained. Gritting his teeth, he jerked his gaze to Landon's.

As Landon nodded his permission, the woman spoke again. "I'm Mira, what's her name?"

Caine's grip on Emma tightened. "Her name is Emma and yes, she's a shapeshifter. She's lost a lot of blood. We've been unable to heal her wounds."

"You said you'd explain when we got here." The dark-haired man gave Landon a sharp look. "Now would be a good time."

Mira spoke to the blond man. "Talek, please bring all my supplies from the car, quickly." As Talek left the room, she cast her gaze to the dark-haired man who'd come in with her. "Take it into the hall if you want to talk, Jachin."

"I believe the second part of the prophecy referred to the Lupreda," Landon said as he and Jachin stepped outside the room.

Caine listened while he watched every move the female vampire made. Landon appeared to trust them, but damn, it was hard for him.

"The first part of the prophecy was fulfilled by Ariel and the second part is about us, but it—"

"Has something to do with that panther lying in there, doesn't it?" Jachin cut off Landon in a grating tone.

Caine felt Landon's Alpha anger rise and Kaitlyn must have, too, because she walked into the hall and stepped between the men. "No fighting or I'm kicking you both out of my house."

Jachin glanced down at Kaitlyn, then met Landon's gaze. "Only you would pick someone as stubborn as you for a mate."

Landon laughed outright. "Hello, pot."

"So glad I can help put you two back on common ground."

Kaitlyn snorted at them before she walked into the room and approached the bed. "I'm Kaitlyn. Can I get you anything, Mira?"

Mira twisted her hair up in a knot on her head. "Do you have something we can put under her? There's going to be a lot of blood and fluids when I start to clean the wound." Before Kaitlyn turned to get the items, Mira listed a few more things she needed.

Caine tuned in to Landon and Jachin as his Alpha spoke of the prophecy. "It's not our proudest moment by far, but some of the Lupreda used the abandoned lab to create their own prey to hunt. The Velius."

"While you were still under our rule?" The annoyance in Jachin's tone made Caine smile.

Smugness laced Landon's response. "We were far smarter and more stealthy than the Sanguinas ever gave us credit for."

"And you condoned this?" Jachin challenged.

Landon's testosterone levels elevated. "Hell no, I didn't. When I found out, I destroyed the lab and set the few panthers free." Snorting his annoyance, Landon continued. "I didn't expect them to rally and try to start a war between the vampires and werewolves."

"Ah, so the panthers are the ones who killed your zerkers."

"Yes," Landon ground out.

Jachin glanced through the doorway at Caine and Emma. "Yet, you're trying to save this one. Why?"

Landon met Caine's gaze briefly. "Because I think the panthers are part of the prophecy, as well."

Kaitlyn walked up carrying blankets and what appeared to be plastic trash bags. As she passed the men, she addressed Jachin. "I'd like to hear this prophecy. Landon mentioned it to me but not in detail."

Landon and Jachin followed Kaitlyn inside the room, and once Talek returned and handed Mira her supplies, Jachin told them the full prophecy.

A human will speak of our demise.
Her purity and intelligence will help us survive.
A mate she becomes to the leader of vampires
Joining our races, fulfilling our ultimate desire.

The hunted becomes the hunter, no longer the prey.
An enemy in your midst is less dark and more gray.
Examine your failures and there you will find
The answer to all your questions in time.

A leader is needed, you know this is true
Look not to one, but two.
A lesson was the goal you sought
You too must learn from what you taught

Layers of deception must be unveiled
For three to become one and peace to prevail.

"It fits," Caine mused once Jachin finished relaying the full prophecy. He'd heard it before, but now with all the context of what had happened in the past six months, his mind pieced it together. "The part about the human was obviously about Ariel writing her book about vampires and then Jachin and Ariel becoming mates. The 'hunted becomes the hunter, no longer the prey' part refers to the Lupreda creating the Velius to hunt. And 'an enemy in your midst is less dark and more gray'…that would describe Emma, but I can't say that's true of the other panthers we've tangled with so far."

"'Examine your failures…' I made sure the Lupreda failed with their panthers project," Landon finished.

"We'll figure it all out eventually," Mira murmured, her focus on the panther as she pulled out a scalpel.

Caine quickly dropped his ponderings about the rest of the prophecy when Mira moved close to Emma with the sharp instrument. Protective instincts flared and he grabbed the female vampire's wrist, giving a low growl.

Talek was by Mira's side and gripping Caine's shoulder in a crushing hold. "Release her or I'll break every bone in your body, wolf."

Caine's growl intensified. His fingers tightened around Mira's arm as he met Talek's angry gaze. The tension in the room spiked until Emma gave a low mewl and lifted her paw. Placing it over Caine's hand on Mira's wrist, she tugged.

Caine met Emma's pained yellow gaze and sheer worry filled him. Letting his hand slip from Mira's wrist, he grated out, "Don't hurt her any more than she's already been injured."

Mira nodded to Talek and he released Caine with a grunt and a warning glare. As the healer began to cut away the T-shirts binding Emma's wound, she spoke to her in a soothing voice. "Emma, I need you to shift back to your human form so I can see exactly how deep your wounds go."

"She should've shifted back by now," Landon said. "The drugs the Lupreda used to make them shift only lasted a couple hours."

"They could've developed a longer sustaining drug," Kaitlyn suggested.

Emma whimpered and her eyes fluttered open and closed as she shook her head. Caine's heart seized with panic when Mira's concerned blue gaze locked with his. "I can't help her if she doesn't shift. I'm not familiar with panther anatomy. Talk to her. See if it's some kind of mental block." Standing up, she backed away from the bed to give them privacy.

"They can't control their shifting," Landon said when Mira moved to stand beside her brother.

While Caine slid out from underneath Emma, Kaitlyn walked up with a lightweight blanket. Handing it to him, she said, "All you can do is try. We'll be in the hall when you're ready."

Caine took the blanket and nodded his appreciation while everyone filed out. Once he spread the cover over Emma, he went down on his knees on the floor and ran his palm over her head and along her neck and shoulders in a rhythmic, soothing motion. "Emma…" Caine choked on his worry. He tried to act calm, even though his gut felt as if it were jamming up his throat. He couldn't lose her nor could he let her know just how bad off she was.

Instead he spoke in her mind, giving them true privacy. *I didn't get to tell you how much you mean to me before Malac took you. I hope you felt it in my touch.* His fingers shook as they traveled along her pelt and met bloodied, matted fur. Caine worked hard to focus. *I don't give a damn that you're a panther and I'm a wolf. I want you…us very much. If I can overcome decades of hatred for the vampires, enough to let Mira help you, know that it's only because I care very much what happens to you.*

Emma released a heavy sigh and she instantly shifted back to human form. Caine blinked at the lightning speed of her shifting. He'd never seen anything like it. Even shifting to his full Musk form took at least thirty seconds.

"You really didn't know I could control my shifting, did you?" she said in a tired voice.

Caine was surprised to see her smile slightly before her eyes fluttered closed as she lost consciousness.

Chapter 10

"Mira!" Caine yelled, his heart thumping in fear for Emma.

The vampire was by his side in an instant, saying in a commanding tone, "Go to the other side of the bed if you want to be near her."

Caine swallowed the retort that came to his lips and did as the healer commanded. Emma looked so pale and the claw marks marring the soft skin across her neck, her shoulder and down her collarbone made him see red. His Musk form howled for vengeance just below the surface.

Clasping Emma's limp hand, Caine laced his fingers with hers and held on tight, blinking back the moisture blurring his eyes. He refused to look at the gaping wound on her side or he'd lose it completely. Seeing the damage to her fragile human body tore him up even more inside, leaving him raw and shaken. He plotted the many ways he would repay the favor to Malac before he killed him.

Mira began pulling tubes out of her bag, then beckoned Jachin over and asked him to roll up his sleeve. Caine's entire frame tightened with suspicion. "What are you doing?"

Her blue gaze met his. "Your friend has lost too much blood. We must replace it or she will die. While I'm sewing her wound closed, my brother's blood will help her heal."

Caine gritted his teeth and began to roll up his own sleeve. "I'll give Emma the blood she needs."

"Landon said you couldn't heal her wounds," Mira reminded him.

Caine's jaw flexed. "My saliva couldn't heal her wound, but if it's blood she needs, I want her to have mine."

Mira set her lips in a firm line, then nodded.

Jachin moved out of the way and Caine retrieved a chair, setting it next to the bed.

Caine heard Jachin speaking in a low tone to Landon while Mira connected Caine to Emma via the tubing. "Did you hear the panther before she passed out? She said she can shift at will."

"She and the other panther were just cubs when they were released. Their abilities hadn't been tested yet, but if it's true that she can control her shifting, she'd be a valuable asset to the panthers."

An asset worth fighting over, Caine realized, staring at Emma's pale face. He stood at Mira's urging to let gravity help the blood flow from his body to Emma's. Caine stared at Emma's wan features and mentally yelled for his blood to flow faster. *Help her heal, damn you!*

Mira began to sew Emma's gaping wound closed, first on the inside and then moving to her outer skin with rapid speed and precision. Caine's heart squeezed tighter and tighter as time crept by. It felt like an eternity. He watched his deep red blood flow to Emma and realized if it took every last drop of blood in his body to save this woman, he'd give it to her without a moment's hesitation—the young panther had her whole life ahead of her, while his human life could end the next time he shifted to Musk form.

Mira smiled up at him from her seated position on the bed. Snipping the thread, she set down the scissors and held two fingers around Emma's wrist, checking her pulse. "The wound is already healing ahead of my stitching and her heart rate is leveling off. Your blood was exactly what she needed."

Caine's gaze jerked to Emma's wounds. They were closing and light pink scars were forming in their wake. Color had begun to spread across her cheeks.

Emotional relief tightened his chest. After Mira removed the needle and tubing from his and Emma's arms, he helped her take the plastic out from underneath Emma. When they were done, he put his hand out. "I can't thank you enough for your help."

Holding up her bloodied hands, Mira's smile was apologetic. "I'd shake your hand, but mine are a bit messy at the moment." She nodded to Emma. "Sit with her. I have a feeling she'll be waking up in a bit and she'll want you with her."

Caine watched the woman walk out of the room with a regal, assured bearing.

"Mira?" Talek jumped up from the sofa the moment she passed by the office.

Mira expelled an inward sigh. Somewhere along the way, Talek had assigned himself as her personal bodyguard, and her brother fully supported such nonsense. Damn Jachin's hide. She didn't need a babysitter. "I'm fine, Talek," Mira said. "Just need some air."

"And Emma?" Kaitlyn asked once Talek zoomed past Mira to open the front door for her.

Mira smiled at the attractive redhead, liking the woman's straightforward approach. "She hasn't awoken yet, but her heartbeat's strong. She'll be okay."

When Talek tried to follow her outside, Mira shook her head. "I'd like to be alone."

Talek set his jaw and stubborn concern hardened his strong features.

"I'll be fine," Mira assured him.

His gaze dropped to her blood-covered hands. "Don't you want to wash up first?"

She shook her head. "Back in a few minutes."

With a look of doubt, Talek gave her a curt nod and slowly pulled the door shut, leaving her alone on the porch that spanned the entire front of the house.

Mira sighed and rolled her head from one shoulder to the other to relieve the tension that had built inside her as she dealt with suspicious Lupreda and operated on Emma. She moved to the edge of the porch and leaned over the railing to stare into the unusually clear night sky above her. No more snow was coming. Stars twinkled all around her, and one seemed suddenly brighter than the others until she realized it was moving.

A shooting star! Mira stared in wonder, wishing she believed in fanciful dreams enough to make a wish upon the star. But she didn't. Glancing at her bloodstained hands, she stared at the signs of both life and death coating her palms and fingers and thought about how easily it would be to let herself slip away from this life, like she'd wanted to do while saving Ariel. All she had to do was stop taking blood from her clan members. Eventually she'd fade away.

A sound in the woods drew her attention. She glanced into the darkness and saw a tall, black-haired man standing on the edge of the woods. Stark naked, his broad-shouldered body formed a perfect muscular V down to his trim waist. Mira blinked and gripped the railing to remain calm. She knew he wasn't human and she doubted he was Lupreda, either. Her gaze locked with his steady one at the same time she caught his earthy, primal scent on the light wind blowing around the house. He smelled like the blood on her hands.

His black eyebrows slashed downward. "Her heartbeat is steady. Did you save her?"

Mira nodded. "With Caine's help. Yes, we saved her."

Not a flicker of emotion crossed his face. Instead, he bowed his head in acknowledgment and immediately turned, falling toward the ground. Before his human hands hit the leaf-covered underbrush, he'd shifted to a sleek black panther, then took off into the forest.

Wondering about the man's swift retreat, Mira stared into the dense woods for several minutes before she finally walked back inside the house. Talek stood once more and she waved him back, addressing Landon. "I just saw another panther."

Landon jumped up from the office chair he'd been sitting in behind the desk. His green gaze narrowed. "Where?"

Mira waved to the front door she'd pushed closed with her foot. "He emerged from the woods and asked if I had saved Emma. When I told him she would be okay, he shifted back to his panther form and ran off."

Landon's tense stance relaxed and he rubbed the back of his neck as he came around from behind the desk. "Damnit, I want to talk to him. Hawkeye could provide some much-needed answers."

*He didn't seem to want to interact…with anyone. I under-
stand that feeling sometimes.* "Maybe Emma can help when
she wakes. I'm going to wash up and then check on my
patient," Mira said.

Emma awoke to the scent of honeysuckle and the sensation of soothing warmth gliding over her body. The softness
disappeared, followed by the sound of water falling into a container. Then the wonderful heat was back, stealing over her
skin. It felt so good, she peered through half-closed eyes to
see Caine leaning over her with a sponge, his black hair falling
across her brow creased in concentration.

Her heart melted when she realized Caine was bathing her
body. Her side was a little sore, but other than that, Emma felt
rejuvenated. For a split second she wondered if everything had
been a dream, if she was still in the cabin with Caine.

But when he looked up and his hazel eyes were shot with
streaks of light green, she remembered everything that had
happened to her—from Malac kidnapping her, his crazy plans
for the Velius, her near-rape and Hawkeye saving her, to the
memory of a beautiful vampire doctor trying to save her life
as she bled out from a gaping wound that could've killed her.

"You knew what I was, yet you rescued me. Why?" she
asked in a whisper.

Caine dropped the sponge in the water, then ran his warm
hand up her belly, creating a sparking, heated path in its wake.
He cupped his hand over her heart, the edge of his fingers
resting just below her breast. "I didn't know what you were
when I met you in the club, but the electricity between us…
was and still is…undeniable."

His brow furrowed as he ran his thumb along the inside

curve of her breast. "When I went to your house and learned what you were, that you've been hiding yourself with those damned pills, I felt as if someone had ripped me in two. I hated how betrayed I felt." His gaze snapped to hers. "But what I hated worse was that it didn't matter—that I still felt the same way about you, regardless of what you were."

Emma's eyes watered with tears. She gripped his hand and brought it to her lips. Kissing his palm with reverence, she kept her gaze locked on his as hot tears streaked down her temples. "This is what you were trying to get me to tell you in the cabin, wasn't it? That I knew what you were and that I was a panther."

She shook her head slowly and she gulped back a sob. "All my life I've been told I had a vitamin deficiency and that's why I had to take a daily pill. When Malac took me, he told me the pills' true purpose was to mask my panther scent—and that the medicine was what kept him from finding me all these years. He has such horrible plans, Caine. He wants me to be his broodmare, to produce a legion of panther offspring who can shift at will."

Fury swept across Caine's face and his eyes stormed, turning even greener. Worry filled her when he began to growl deep in his throat. Pushing aside her fear, Emma touched his stubbled jaw and continued in a trembling voice. "I only discovered what I was when I shifted to protect you. Please, please believe me."

Caine touched her hair where her tears had left damp trails. He vibrated all over with tension. "Did. He. Touch. You?" he bit out through clenched teeth.

His slowly spoken words scared her. Emma worried if she told him what almost happened to her, he might go after Malac alone. She didn't want anything to happen to him.

Mira walked into the room, distracting her from answering right away, which was apparently too long for Caine.

He let out a growl and punched his hand straight through the bed's headboard. "I'll shred him to pieces. I'm going to—"

"Hawkeye saved me in time, Caine!" Emma panicked and quickly sat up, pulling the covers against her chest, speaking as fast as she could. "Malac…didn't get a chance to do anything—"

"What is it?" Landon came barreling into the room, his expression alert, wereclaws on full display. Jachin and Talek were directly behind him, fangs and vampire talons extended. Laird and the blond man from the club quickly followed, looking equally intense. Kailtyn stepped into the room behind them. Everyone was on alert. Ready to battle.

Mira stood frozen in the center of the room, while her brother and Talek glanced at her for acknowledgment that she was okay. Tension arched through the air, and the men glared back and forth between each other, testosterone rising. The fierce looks on the vampires' and werewolves' faces made Emma's heart pound with anxiety. Did their hatred run so deep?

The sudden ringing of a cell phone sliced through the thick adrenaline hanging in the air between the different species.

Caine's chest heaved and his eyes glazed as his fists opened and closed reflexively. Landon growled at Caine, "Answer the damn thing before a fight breaks out."

Caine pulled his cell phone from his pocket and looked at the caller ID. His gaze snapped to Landon's. "It's the Velius bastards who kidnapped Emma from the club."

He flipped open the cell phone and tilted it so Emma could hear a woman speaking. "Hello…I'm assuming this is the

Lupreda who took Emral from us. Because you used Roland's number to find us, I'm returning the favor. My name is Jade."

Caine's eyes instantly narrowed. "This is Caine. What do you want, Jade?"

"To talk."

Jade? Emma's heart thumped. She pulled her knees underneath her and gripped his hand. Once Caine muted the phone, she said, "Jade's not with Malac. Before Hawkeye rescued me from Malac, my aunt told me the panthers splintered into two factions a while back. She said I could trust Jade, that she wouldn't mean me harm."

Caine's jaw tightened, suspicion in his hazel gaze. "They kidnapped you!"

Emma ran her hand through her messy hair. "I—I'm beginning to think they did it to keep Malac from finding me first." Expelling her pent-up breath, she continued. "It's a long story."

"Caine?" Jade called. "Are you there?"

Caine unmuted the phone. "Yeah."

"I think we should discuss this in person."

"Discuss what? The fact I'm going to tear every single one of you apart for drugging and kidnapping Emma? Your man tried to kill us," Caine gritted out, his gaze snapping to Emma.

"He was trying to protect Emral," Jade said, concern in her voice. "Can I talk to her?"

Caine gripped the phone tight. As he laced his fingers with Emma's, she could see the complete distrust on his face. "No, and her name is Emma."

The woman on the other end of the line sighed. "This is why I think it's best that we meet in person. And because they're there with you, we'd like the Lupreda and Sanguinas representatives to come with you and Emra—Emma."

Caine tensed and glanced toward the curtain-covered window. "How'd you know they are with me?"

"Hawkeye told me when he called to say Emma was safe."

Caine narrowed his gaze and Landon dipped his head to acknowledge that Hawkeye had been around, then the Alpha and Jachin exchanged meaningful looks. Tense shoulders relaxed and wereclaws, talons and fangs retracted. Returning his gaze to Caine, Landon gave him a curt nod and mouthed the word, "Trap."

"We'll meet, but we choose the place," Caine said.

"Fair enough," the woman replied in an appeased tone. "Call me back with the location and the time."

The moment Caine snapped the cell phone closed, Kaitlyn stepped forward. "All right, everyone, please go to the living room. We obviously need to talk, but Emma must get cleaned up and put on some clothes first. She can meet us downstairs when she's ready."

Once everyone but Caine left, Kaitlyn looked at him and raised her eyebrow.

"You expect me to leave?"

Emma almost smiled at the surprise in his voice. Kaitlyn put her hands on her hips and sighed. "Yes, you, too. Emma needs some time to herself."

Caine's fingers tightened around Emma's. "But she might need help—"

"And that's why *I'll* be here if she needs anything."

"I'll be fine." Emma squeezed Caine's hand, then untangled her fingers from his. "But she's right. I'd like to take a shower and put on some clothes." Letting her gaze slide over his bare chest, she chuckled. "Maybe they can find a shirt for you to wear, too."

Caine glanced down at his naked torso and snorted. Leaning over, he kissed her forehead, then whispered in her ear, "I'll be right downstairs if you need me."

Emma nodded and pushed at his hard chest, her heart pounding at the muscles underneath her fingers. "Go on. I'll be fine."

The moment Caine walked out of the room, Kaitlyn shut the door. Facing Emma, she shook her head and mumbled, "Lupredas and their strong protective streaks," as she walked over to the chest of drawers near the closet and rifled through them.

Once she'd pulled out a few articles of clothing, Kaitlyn carried them over to the bed and sat down with the bundle in her arms, her expression sympathetic. "I know you're probably feeling a bit outnumbered, surrounded by a bunch of werewolves and vampires."

The truth was Emma was completely torn. She trusted and cared for Caine, but she didn't want the werewolves to attack Jade and her people. "I am a bit confused at the moment."

"These clothes should be close enough to your size." Kaitlyn handed her the bundle, then smiled. "I grew up living a human life for twenty-four years. I didn't know that my father had been bitten by a werewolf before I was born and that as his offspring I carried Lupreda blood in my veins." She gave an ironic chuckle. "At least not until I met Landon. My point is, I totally understand how you feel, because I was in your position not too long ago."

"I might be a panther," Emma said, her voice trembling, "but I was also raised thinking I was human all my life. I only discovered what I was when Malac took me, but the fact remains, I *am* Velius. I don't want to go to this meeting with a plan to ambush those of my own race. It's not right. My aunt said Jade can be trusted. I have to give her the benefit of the doubt. She might be able to help me rescue my aunt. I passed out before I could get a feel for the area of town where Malac resides…and Jade may know."

Kaitlyn squeezed Emma's hand. "When you come downstairs, you can help fill in the missing pieces. Then we'll discuss all the options."

"I don't believe Jade would harm me," Emma insisted.

"That may be true, Emma, but the panthers have had no problem murdering three Lupreda zerkers and in doing so—"

"Zerkers?"

Kaitlyn nodded. "Lupreda who are permanently caught between human and wolf form."

Emma's brow furrowed. "Are you talking about a werewolf?"

"Yes, the Lupreda call it their Musk form. The Lupreda discovered too late that only mature wolves can handle shifting in and out of their Musk form. Once those three Lupreda went zerker—unable to shift back to human form—the wolves declared that no Lupreda can use their Musk form until they've fully matured. The Lupreda are bound to their wolf form during the three nights of a full moon. That they can't control, but the older ones can call forth their Musk form at will any other time."

Emma thought about the fight she'd witnessed between Malac and Caine. "When Malac shot Caine, Caine was shifting to what must've been his Musk form. That arrow forced him to shift back to human form at the same time it seemed to literally destroy his strength. What was in that weapon?"

"Thank goodness for small favors," Kaitlyn mumbled,

piquing Emma's curiosity, but she continued on, distracting Emma from the question she wanted to ask. "When the vampires first created the Lupreda, they used silver collars to keep them from shifting to their wolf form until the vampires were ready to hunt them. Over time the werewolves developed a deadly allergy to silver. So silver around their neck keeps them from shifting from their human form and if infused in their system, the metal can kill Lupreda.

"Apparently the Velius have figured that out and are using those silver arrows on the Lupreda to their complete advantage. They kidnapped the zerkers, then left their burned bodies in strategic places meant to incite a war between the vampires and wolves. It probably would've worked, too, if Jachin and Landon hadn't been on speaking terms."

"Um, the Lupreda and Sanguinas still seem wary and distrustful of each other," Emma said with a frown.

Kaitlyn sighed her agreement. "They have decades of hatred to overcome, Emma, and the panthers' devious and murderous acts aren't making that any easier."

"That was Malac's doing," Emma interjected, finally piecing together the conversation between Caine and Malac in the cabin. "He admitted his role in killing some of the Lupreda to Caine before he kidnapped me."

"It might just be Malac, but all the panthers have been masking their scents, and until their motivations are clearly understood, Landon and Jachin have to look out for the best interests of their pack and clan. Their truce is tenuous enough."

When Emma tensed, Kaitlyn tilted her head, an encouraging look in her hazel-blue eyes. "No matter whether you're panther, werewolf, vampire or human…it's always in your best interest to be prepared for anything. Wouldn't you agree?"

The woman had a valid point. Emma was going purely by what her aunt told her about Jade. The female panther could've changed over the past twenty years. Malac was definitely insane, and even if Jade might not want to hurt Emma—as she claimed—her intentions toward the Lupreda and Sanguinas could be completely different. Emma didn't want to put Caine, his pack or the vampires who'd helped her in jeopardy. She nodded mutely while her stomach churned in turmoil.

Kaitlyn smiled. "Good. As long as you're willing to consider a contingency plan, we can make sure those testosterone junkies downstairs hold their primal instincts in check."

Emotions welled within Emma. The thought of going against a race she barely knew, yet one she was very much a part of, weighed heavily on her chest. She impulsively hugged Kaitlyn. "Thank you for understanding."

Landon's mate hugged her and leaned back with a wink. "We women have to stick together to keep these alpha men in line. Do you think you can get a shower on your own? There's plenty of extra supplies in the linen closet."

Emma gripped the blanket and stood up from the bed. She felt a little woozy for a second, but her mind quickly cleared. "I'll be fine. Fill everyone in on what we've discussed and I'll be down as soon as I'm presentable."

The moment Emma entered the living room, all conversation stopped. Everyone stared at her, making her feel like a bug under a microscope. She resisted the urge to fluff her damp hair, but couldn't quite stop herself from biting her lower lip.

Caine jumped up from the wingback chair he'd been sprawled across sideways and was by her side before she dug her teeth too deep into her lip. He looked sexy as hell in a thin, black V-neck sweater. Clasping her hand, he pulled it to his mouth and kissed her knuckles. "Hey, beautiful," he said in a soft tone and finished in her mind, *Are you feeling okay?*

Emma blinked away the emotion that swept her heart when his deep voice, full of worry, entered her mind. His intense hazel gaze held hers for several seconds until she realized he was waiting for a response. She gave him a tremulous smile and nodded. "Thanks to you and—" Emma swept her gaze to Mira sitting on the formal couch between Talek and Jachin "—Mira. I can't thank you both enough for all you've done."

Mira inclined her head and smiled. "If Landon felt strongly enough about you to ask for our help, that was enough for us."

Caine released Emma's fingers and settled his hand against the small of her back as her wide gaze locked on Landon. He was leaning against the side of the other wingback chair Kaitlyn was sitting in. "Why *did* you help me?"

"Apparently, I'm not the only pack member who does crazy things," a man with longish blond hair snorted from his position near the window.

"Shut up, Roman!" Laird elbowed the blond in the arm.

Landon's gaze held Caine's as he addressed her. "Caine is the pack's Second. He cares for you. That's why I helped."

Caine was Second to the Alpha? Emma glanced at Caine to see him shaking his head. Banked tension vibrated in his edgy tone. "I'm no longer Second."

Landon instantly straightened from his relaxed pose. "The hell you aren't—"

"Emma, why don't you tell us why you think Jade can be trusted. We want to help you and your aunt if we can, but we need to know everything you do before we meet with the other Velius," Kaitlyn said.

Emma had seen the anger flash across Landon's face when Caine said he wasn't the Second. She wondered what that was all about, but was thankful Kaitlyn had intervened. They needed to stay focused, not fight. Time was ticking and she hoped that Jade could help her find and rescue her aunt. Nodding to Kaitlyn, she began with the story Mary told her about the panthers splintering off and the fact Malac took Hawkeye when he left and she stayed with Jade. She told them about Mary and her brother Roland's history, how Roland created the pills that masked the panthers' scent and how Mary hadn't seen her brother since she took Emma to hide her from all the panthers. "She didn't trust that they wouldn't begin to fight over me."

"Because you can shift at will?" Landon asked.

Emma nodded.

"Malac is certifiable. I have no doubt he's the one behind for trying to start a war between the vampires and the were-wolves. *He* wants to go to war with both your races, but he needed me to help make that happen."

"The sonofabitch wants her ability to shift at will," Caine snarled.

Emma curled her lip in a derisive snort. "He wanted to take my eggs so he could create an entire army of shape-shifting Velius."

A growl emanated from Caine and his hands fell to his sides, clenched in tight fists. "His death will be very painful."

Caine's dark tone sent a chill across Emma's skin, making her glad he was on her side.

Landon narrowed his gaze. "If Malac had gotten what he wanted from Emma, combined with the Velius' swift maturity rate, he feasibly *could've* produced a formidable army in a few years. As to whether or not they'd be shape-shifters…" He shrugged.

When Landon trailed off, it suddenly occurred to Emma what Hawkeye had alluded to; Malac had already done something similar to him—or tried to. *"I didn't want you to suffer the same fate."* She closed her eyes and her heart ached for the little boy who'd been forced to live with Malac. The memories came flooding back to her. Of how Hawkeye had always watched over her, worried about her.

Glancing up at Landon, she said, "Now I know why Caine's smell intrigued me when I first met him—because, even though I didn't remember your saving Hawkeye and me when we were cubs, your Lupreda smell has lingered with me."

When Caine's expression went blank, Emma realized he'd taken what she'd said the wrong way. The devastated look in his eyes slammed her in the stomach. She wanted to grab hold of his hand and reconnect with him, but she forced herself to focus. "Where do you want to meet with Jade?"

Jachin's dark blue eyes stared at her. "You don't know what Jade's true intentions are. We have to plan for the worst." He glanced at Landon. "Especially because she wants us there."

"But she could just want to talk," Emma insisted, feeling desperate. "Can't we meet somewhere in public, where we can discuss without worry of a surprise attack? I don't know how to get in touch with Hawkeye. Jade may be my only connection to finding my aunt. I have to help her!"

Caine soothed her before she could get too worked up. "We'll find your aunt, Emma."

"We could tell them to meet us at Jamie's Pub," Landon said, rubbing his hand along his stubbled jaw.

Jachin nodded slowly. "It's crowded and loud enough to cover whatever we might discuss."

"Not to mention…it's dark in there." Landon's lips tilted in a feral smile.

Kaitlyn looked at her mate and understanding lit in her eyes. "That could be advantageous."

Emma frowned. "Why would dim lighting be to our advantage?"

Caine looked down at her. "The pills the panthers are taking to mask their scent leave behind a glittery, iridescent residue on anything they touch. They're unaware that Kaitlyn and Landon have the ability to see this substance, which could clue us in as to how many panthers are present among the crowd."

"Taking their element of surprise down considerably." Jachin nodded, a dangerous smile on his angular face.

Kaitlyn stood. "Come in my office across the hall. We can look up the city maps and check for places around Jamie's they might try to hide."

Jachin unfolded his tall frame from the couch. His long black coat fell past his knees in a quiet whisper of leather as he pulled his cell phone from his pocket. "I'll call my Sanguinas Sweeper unit. Instead of hunting for rogue vampires, tonight they'll be our backup."

As everyone brushed past her standing in the living room doorway, Emma felt a rush of panic that Caine had moved to walk away without a word to her. "Caine, wait!" she called. Turning to the blond Lupreda, who was about to leave the room, she quickly grabbed his hand, and said in a hushed voice, "It's Roman, right?"

Roman's gaze locked with Caine's, then a brilliant, sexy smile tilted his lips. "At your service, Emma. I guess this is a formal introduction."

Emma felt Caine's tension behind her. The spiked wave of heat and testosterone was that powerful. Her pulse skittered as she squeezed Roman's hand and asked, "What do you feel?"

Roman didn't even miss a beat. "Horny."

Caine's snarl of fury made the tiny hairs on Emma's neck stand on end. Before she lost her nerve, she held fast to Roman's hand at the same time she quickly turned and grabbed Caine's fisted one. The moment her hand touched Caine's, his fingers unfurled and clasped hers tight in a crushing, possessive hold. Electricity flew, whirling so fast and furious between them that it knocked Emma slightly off-kilter. All this happened in milliseconds, yet she had to practically tear her gaze from Caine's to address Roman once more. "What about now—"

"Sonofabitch!" Roman instantly jerked his hand from hers, his brow furrowing. "What the— What was that?" His confused dark brown gaze darted between them as he opened and closed his hand. "Are you trying to electrocute me?"

"You didn't feel that when Emma shook your hand?" Caine's words were measured.

Roman's blond eyebrows elevated. "Hell, no! Only when—" His eyes lit up and he reached for her hand once more, a sly grin tilting his lips. "Let's try that again—"

At the same time Caine's muscular arm curled around Emma, pulling her against his hard chest, his palm slammed into Roman's chest, sending him back against the doorjamb with enough force to shake the whole house. "Back off, wolf!"

Chapter 11

Emma had never felt so protected and wanted. It thrilled her to her toes. "I'm sorry," she whispered to Roman. She felt a bit guilty for involving Roman, but he'd seemed good-natured enough, and she didn't think any other way would've proven her point as effectively to Caine.

"Is there a problem?" Landon's hard voice sounded from the office doorway.

"Why don't you go do some recon with the others," Caine said to his packmate in a less forceful tone. "I need a minute."

Roman rubbed his chest and snorted. "You two need more than a minute. A room would be better."

"Go!" Caine barked, sounding ready to snap off the other werewolf's head.

The moment Roman walked away, Caine hauled Emma into the living room and set her back against the wall. Caging her in with his hands on the wall beside her, his black eyebrows slashed downward as he growled in a low voice, "That was a hell of a risk you just took!"

Emma met his intemperate hazel gaze with determination. "You took what I said about your Lupreda scent the wrong way. I saw it in your eyes. You'd closed up and were already shutting me out."

"If Roman had felt that same charge when you first touched him, his wolf would've instantly challenged me for you, Emma. You just riled his rocks, sweetheart. What happens between us is *that* intensely sexual."

Heat shot up her cheeks at his comment. "Are you saying I just—"

"Sent a jolt that bypassed his brain and went straight to his cock."

Emma closed her eyes and groaned with embarrassment, but her breath quickly caught when she felt Caine's musky heat, hot and thick, envelope her as he leaned close and whispered near her ear, "Is it any wonder why I can't stop touching you every chance I get?"

As if to prove his point, his warm hands slid under her cardigan and tank top and up her sides, sending electric shimmers in their wake. His fingers gripped her rib cage in a fierce hold and he yanked her against his hard chest. Emma barely had time to take a breath before his lips covered hers.

From the moment his lips slanted across hers, Caine staked his claim, tasting her instantly as he spoke in her mind. *I've never been so scared in my life when I thought you might die.* His tongue delved deep, sliding along hers in a provocative, possessive dance. His seductive intensity demanded her participation and Emma was more than willing to accommodate him.

"After everything that's happened, having you there—fighting *for* me, and not *over* me—was the only thing that kept me from giving up," she confessed and encircled her arms around his neck, locking him tight against her. Emma never wanted to let him go.

Caine's arms locked around her and he planted a kiss along her jawline. "No matter what happens tonight, know that I'll always be there to protect you."

Tears burned the back of Emma's eyes when she thought of the tension she'd seen in the bedroom earlier between the vampires and the werewolves. The history and distrust between their races went deep, as did the history between the werewolves and the panthers. Would their differences eventually come between Caine and her, too? Her arms cinched tighter. She wasn't going to let that happen to them.

"Caine, we're ready to call Jade back whenever you are," Kaitlyn called from the office.

Emma sat in Caine's truck, her stomach knotted so tight she felt like she might throw up the food Kaitlyn had forced her to eat before they left. "You must eat, Emma. You look way too pale."

She looked pale because she was worried about her aunt. Plus, she didn't know if the meeting they were getting ready to leave for would end in an all-out war between the panthers, vampires and werewolves. Where would that leave her and Caine?

Landon leaned his elbow on the driver-side door as he spoke to Caine. "We'll meet you there."

While Landon talked, Caine started to lift the silver chain over his head.

Landon grabbed his wrist, his tone harsh. "We made a deal."

Caine's jaw worked for a second before he gritted out, "We don't know what we're walking into. Emma's life could be in danger."

"It's not worth the risk. I've got your back. I'll keep Emma safe."

Lowering the chain back on his neck, fury emanated from Caine. "She's mine to protect."

Landon glanced Emma's way and the curt edge in his tone softened. "Exactly why it's not worth the risk."

When Landon walked off and slid into the car with Jachin and his Sweeper unit—who'd shown up only minutes before, allowing Talek to take Mira home—Emma asked, "What was that about?"

Caine started the engine and stared straight ahead, his face impassive. "Nothing."

As he pulled away from the curb outside Kaitlyn's house, Emma's gaze drifted to his necklace. Kaitlyn had told her that silver kept the Lupreda from shifting. It wasn't quite a full moon tonight, but Landon's mate had also said the Lupreda did have control over their Musk forms—at least the older ones did. Which meant they could shift whenever they wanted as long as they weren't hampered by the silver.

"Are you too young to shift to your Musk form?" Emma asked.

Caine's hazel gaze glinted sharp and dangerous in the darkness between them. "Do I look like a young pup to you?"

He looked on edge, but Emma wasn't about to let him intimidate her. "What you 'look' is angry. Kaitlyn told me the Velius killed some of the Lupreda—zerkers she'd called them. If you're not too young, why did Landon make that deal with you about wearing the necklace before he called Jachin to help me?"

Caine turned a corner faster than necessary. The truck's tires skidded in the slushy snow, then caught on the pavement, squealing in protest. His fingers gripped the steering wheel tight, while a vein thumped along his temple. Emma's chest weighed heavy with worry. "Why doesn't Landon want you to shift?"

"Because I'm the last of them, Emma!" Caine shouted. Jamming his hand through his dark hair, he continued in a calmer voice. "I'm the only one left of my generation who hasn't gone zerker. The pack learned from our mistakes."

Silence, thick with tension, descended in the truck and several seconds ticked past. Emma chewed her bottom lip, trying to understand. "He doesn't want you to shift because it could be permanent the next time?"

His narrowed gaze sliced her way. "I'd be neither human nor wolf, forever." Staring at the road once more, he continued, his words cold and grating. "No one wants that. We called them zerkers for a reason. Not being able to shift back eventually screwed with their minds. They became dangerous, their urges more primal, their reactions unpredictable. That's why they didn't live with the pack. They used to live in the cabin we stayed in."

Tears threatened and Emma's throat burned with the effort to hold back a sob, but she had to know the rest. "The cabin… But you called it *your* home."

"It'll be my home when I finally go zerker," he said, his words flat and final.

Reaching out, she dug her fingers into the corded muscles that ran along his forearm. "If going zerker would force you to stay away from me, then keep your promise to Landon. Never take the damn necklace off—"

"I'll do whatever it takes to keep you safe." He cut her off with a low rasping growl.

"You can protect me just fine. You've proven that already. I'm not worth losing your humanity over." Panic swelled her lungs, pushing the air out of them until she could barely catch her breath. "I don't want to lose you," she finished in a whisper.

Caine quickly grabbed her hand and pressed his warm lips against it. The roughness of his five o'clock shadow, combined with his tingling kiss, skittered along her skin, sending tingles scattering down her arm. "I'm here, Emma. Don't worry."

Emma laced her fingers with his, gripping his hand tightly. "I want to believe you're listening to me, but I know you're too stubborn. You'll do what you want to regardless of my wishes."

Once Caine slowed his truck and parked it along the side of the road, his hazel gaze met hers. "I'll grant your every wish if I can, but your safety comes above my own."

Emma shut her eyes and tears squeezed past the corners. Caine's fingertips brushed away a tear and she opened her eyes to see his hungry gaze on her face. "I'm on shaky ground as it as, Emma." His low, tortured voice slid over her like a velvet caress, while his fingers cupped her face, tilting her chin so she had to look at him. "It would rip me apart if anything happened to you."

How could she argue with that without sounding ungrateful? Appreciation and respect combated with guilt and anger at their situation. Emma pressed a kiss on his palm, then cupped the warmth against her cheek. "I've never felt more blessed than to have met you." She spoke from the heart, even as she wondered what the outcome of this meeting would bring.

Would seeing her among her people highlight their differences in his mind? She knew he felt protective of her, but would Caine's loyalties to his pack and his own kind eventually pull him away from her, making him want to be with a Lupreda woman instead? Her chest ached at the thought. A knock on Caine's window made Emma's heart jerk. Caine's hand fell away when Landon thumbed for them to accompany their group inside the pub.

The moment Emma slid out of the truck, Caine wrapped his arm around her and pulled her close as they walked along the sidewalk. Dark shadows hid in nearby alleys, filled with day-old trash and dirty snow. Bums, stray dogs and cats foraged in and around the Dumpsters, looking for scraps. If a Velius jumped out of the alley in its panther form now, would Caine be able to inflict enough damage with his wereclaws and superhuman strength to protect Emma?

He gritted his teeth and tensed in anger and resentment at the truth. Hell, no! Without his Musk form, he'd always feel as if he weren't giving his all, using everything within himself to defend the woman he cared deeply about. Landon and his brethren wouldn't always be around to help defend her, nor would Caine let anyone fight his battles for him. Ever. Was it fair to shackle Emma with a man who couldn't defend her as he should? No, yet he curled his lip in a snarl at the idea of any other man touching her.

By the time they neared the pub, Caine's testosterone levels had elevated considerably. He was ready to take down anyone, in any form necessary. Several more Lupreda converged with their small group, and Caine didn't miss their rumbles of discontent. Some of the weres curled their lips in a low growl at the members of Jachin's Sweeper unit who'd accompanied them from their vehicles.

"Enough," Landon snapped. The dozen Lupreda before him quieted and instantly splintered off, disappearing into the darkness to take the positions Landon had given them via his cell before they'd left Kaitlyn's house. Once the Sweeper unit of six men dispersed to take up their own sentry duties on the rooftops and at the building corners, Landon, Kaitlyn and Jachin entered the pub, followed by Caine and Emma.

Only a few steps into the crowded, dim pub, Kaitlyn looked at Landon. Placing four fingers at the corner of her eye, she signaled that she saw four Velius in the place, then she nodded to a man in a baseball hat and a woman with short dark hair sitting alone at a table in the far corner of the room. Caine inhaled in the direction of the table and instantly recognized the human man's scent as the one who'd taken Emma from the club. The other four panthers must be positioned elsewhere in the room on guard duty.

Steeling himself, Caine's hand cinched tighter around Emma's rib cage. Just because Kaitlyn saw only four Velius with iridescent sparkles on them in the crowd didn't mean there weren't other humans helping the panthers. He mentally cursed the "unknown variables" of the situation and followed Landon, Kaitlyn and Jachin's lead toward the back of the bar. As they weaved around the various tables, filled with patrons watching the latest game and talking, drinking and laughing among themselves, Caine scanned the room for all possible exit points in case they had to get out of there fast.

The moment he smelled Roman and Laird's presence in the room several feet behind him, some tension eased from his shoulders. Knowing the weres would merge into the crowd to keep a general watch helped him move to an "aware and focused" mode from his "jacked-up and ready-to-battle" one.

They'd just reached the table where the man and woman sat when the man pulled off his baseball cap and ran a hand through his spiky graying hair.

"Sonofabitch!" Jachin froze and stared at the man. "I thought you were dead."

The man, now free of the beard Caine remembered seeing on him in the club, smirked. "That was the whole point, Jachin."

Seeing Mary's same facial expressions on the man's face, Emma knew she was staring at her aunt's brother. She gripped the back of a wooden chair and glanced at Jachin. "You know Roland?"

A muscle twitched in the vampire's jaw. "Yes, but I knew him as a surly, extortionist named Roach."

The man's steady gaze locked with Jachin's. "Who kept you alive for ten years."

"What the hell is going on?" Landon growled.

The dark-haired woman gestured to the chairs in front of the table and spoke in a calm tone. "It's good to see you again after all these years, Landon. Why don't you have a seat and we'll talk."

"We prefer to stand," Caine snarled. He didn't like this new surprise—the Velius' connection to the vampires.

The woman glanced toward the crowd. "You're drawing attention to us by standing."

"And growling," the man added with a snort.

"Start talking," Jachin demanded through clenched teeth. Yanking a chair out from under the table, he sat down and pinned his gaze on Roland. "You have one minute before I rip out your throat. I don't give a damn who's watching."

"And here I thought you might've missed me just a tiny bit these past six months," Roland said in a light tone.

"Forty-five seconds," Jachin shot back, curling his lip briefly to show that his fangs were fully extended.

Emma couldn't stand the tension crackling across the table. Pulling from Caine's tight hold, she sat down in a chair beside Jachin and put her hand on the vampire's tight fist sitting on the table. "Let's hear what Roland has to say before you tear him apart."

Heaving a heavy sigh, Roland said, "Actually, despite our barbs, I've only had Jachin's best interests at heart."

"By gouging me for ten years? Making me think you were dead? Leaving me without food?" Jachin challenged.

Roland gestured toward him. "You had Ariel. She was the answer to your prophecy."

Jachin's gaze slitted. "You never believed in the prophecy."

Roland pointed to him. "Ah, but *you* did…and that's all that mattered. We thought we were going to have to convince you there was a better way for the vampires, but then you told me about the prophecy and you were so convinced…your survival became very important to us."

"None of this is making any sense." Landon's voice was cold and hard as he moved to stand to Emma's left.

"Start from the beginning, Roland." Emma spoke quickly, hoping to tamp down the rage she felt emanating from the vampire and werewolf leaders on either side of her.

Roland looked at Jade and the female panther inclined her head to acknowledge Emma's request. "It's good to see you again, Emma. I wish the circumstances were less—" she glanced at the group of people surrounding Emma "—intense."

"You drugged and kidnapped her! What do you expect?" Caine stood directly behind Emma, placing a hand on her shoulder.

Jade stiffened in a defensive posture. "We were trying to get her out of there quickly. Emma ran out of her pills and had called Roland's number, trying to fill the prescription. We knew something had to have gone wrong with Mary if Emma was calling us, thinking we were a pharmacy and that it was only a matter of time before Malac or one of his team scented her. We tracked her cell phone to the club."

"What does all this have to do with the Velius' involvement with the vampires?" Emma asked, feeling Jachin's fury winding tighter and tighter beside her.

"The Sanguinas have everything to do with it, Emma," Jade said in a quiet voice, her gaze snapping nervously between Landon and Jachin as the two men exchanged a look.

Before anyone could say a word, Jade continued, speaking at a rapid pace. "After Landon freed us, we were few in number compared to the vampires and the werewolves. We barely kept it together, trying to survive while hiding from the vampires who ravaged the city each night. Then I met Roland." Patting Roland's shoulder, she plunged on. "With his background in chemistry, he helped us devise a plan that would make the humans' blood unpalatable for vampires, therefore freeing the humans from the vampires' vengeance."

Jachin snarled and slammed his fist on the table, sending a hairline crack all the way across the wood's surface. "You tried to wipe out my race!"

Emma glanced around the pub, thankful the patrons were so into the game that no one noticed Jachin's outburst.

"I *told* you the Lupreda weren't responsible." Landon cut his gaze over to Jachin. His casual comment belied the tension that had vaulted within him. Emma knew he wasn't as calm as he let on, because Kaitlyn clasped her mate's left hand and Caine's hold on her shoulder had tightened.

Roland shook his head, seemingly unfazed by Jachin's anger and oblivious to Landon's reaction. "We had to take drastic measures. Too many innocent humans were dying while the Sanguinas' numbers were inching upward."

"Many of us were moving toward peace." Jachin's low tone held a defensive edge.

"But the majority of the Sanguinas weren't and humans were still being slaughtered. How many people had to die before the vampires realized this wasn't the way? How long would it have gone on?" Roland countered. "Our goal was to slow down the Sanguinas, not destroy them. But your race was stubborn and many vampires succumbed to the effects of the tainted blood before the clan finally withdrew from human society. When you came along ten years ago, we realized our ultimate goal might finally be accomplished."

"What goal was that?" Jachin bit out, his temper simmering.

Sympathy filled Roland's gaze. "You were outcast, Jachin. You were barely hanging on, and we saw an opportunity. It was risky, yes. You could've killed me when I purposefully put myself in your path so you'd attack me. But it was the only way I figured that you would accept my offer to provide the blood you needed—if you thought the only reason I came up with the idea of a partnership was because I was desperate and didn't want to die."

"You didn't make it easy for me."

Roland snorted at Jachin's surly tone. "I knew that whatever I said or did, you'd take the opposite stance. You hated humans *that* much. If I simply gave you the blood, you'd throw it aside out of distrust. But if you had to work hard for it…" He trailed off and his eyebrows elevated. "The same was true for your belief in the prophecy. My comments to dissuade you from believing were because I knew you'd only dig your heels in deeper, holding on to your prophecy's promise even more."

"Don't try to bullshit me, Roac—Roland. You never gave a damn about the prophecy."

Roland's shrug was unapologetic. "Whether the prophecy was true or not didn't matter to us in the beginning, but *your* belief in it did. Every time you spoke of it, I heard 'desire for peace' in your voice, saw it in your eyes. That's ultimately what the Velius sought. Peace. And that's the reason I helped them treat the water system to turn the humans' blood poisonous to vampires all those years ago."

"You had no way of knowing that things would unfold the way they did—that Ariel would write a fictional book about vampires, that Jachin would discover Ariel's blood was pure or that he'd want to take her for his mate and become the new leader of the Sanguinas." Landon sliced his hand through the air between Jachin and him. "And there's no way in hell you'd know that he'd forge a truce with me."

"That's true," Jade jumped in with a nod. "But Jachin followed his own heart and did what he felt was right and that included his interactions with you. As far as we were concerned, the Lupreda weren't a threat to the human population. Only the vampires were."

"You *had* to hate us." Suspicion laced Landon's comment.

Jade shook her head. "No, I didn't, because you freed us, Landon." Sighing, she continued. "But Malac never could let go of his hatred. We splintered off in our beliefs a long time ago. The only reason he stayed in check for as long as he did was the fact we manufactured the pills and he didn't know how to replicate them. If he went after the vampires or the werewolves, we would have cut him off from his pill supply. He would've been exposed and very easy to hunt down."

"We've had the upper hand with him all these years, until recently." Roland curled his lip in disgust. "Malac had always had underworld dealings with the Mafia, but his connections grew stronger and he formed his own team of scientists. A few months ago, he stole my formula." The man's gaze locked on Jachin. "The attack in my house—on me—was real, Jachin. The only difference was that I realized it was probably in your best interest to let you think I was gone. You'd eventually discover Ariel's generation didn't have tainted blood. We'd stopped treating the water fairly early on, but ironically the older humans' blood stayed poisoned, while the younger ones' blood seemed to be able to adapt and resist the treatment, eventually eradicating its effects on their blood. I knew your goals for peace would set you on the right path from there."

At the look of disbelief in Jachin's eyes, Roland snorted. "It was all over the news that Ariel Swanson who'd written a book about vampires had been kidnapped. I knew how obsessed you were. I was fairly certain you were responsible."

"Malac was aware of your belief in the prophecy, too, Jachin," Jade said. "And when you kidnapped Ariel, the prophecy appeared to be coming true. That's when he broke into Roland's home. He wanted that formula and his freedom from us, so he could inflict as much damage as possible to both the Sanguinas and the Lupreda without any repercussions."

"He wants an all-out war, not just skulking-behind-the-scenes-wrecking-havoc scenarios." Emma finally broke her silence.

When Jade stared at her in shock, Emma quickly told her of the plans Malac had for the future of the Velius—at least how he saw it.

Jade's forehead pinched with fury. "He was going to take your eggs?"

Emma nodded. "Malac's insane. He has to be stopped." Turning to Roland, she conveyed the rest of what she knew. "He has your sister, Margaret, and he's keeping her a prisoner to blackmail me into cooperating with his plans. The only reason I agreed to come and meet you tonight was because Mary said I could trust you. Tell us where Malac's place is so we can get my aunt out of there."

Roland shook his head. "We don't know where he is. He's always kept himself well hidden."

Emma's brow furrowed in frustration. "I was wounded and the snow covering everything kept me from seeing landmarks the way I might've when Hawkeye helped me escape the facility, but…he should know. If we can contact Hawkeye, he'll tell us how to find Malac."

Roland's lips thinned. "We tried a trace, but Hawkeye called us from a pay phone. He doesn't trust us. Why do you think he brought you to the Lupreda instead of us?"

Emma's gaze narrowed. "Why *doesn't* he trust you?"

"Because we let Malac take him when he splintered off from us all those years ago. Hawkeye's never forgiven us," Roland said with a sigh.

"Then why did he bother to call you at all?"

"He called to let us know that the Sanguinas and the Lupreda were with you and that they had helped you. He said if we believed in the prophecy at all, now might be a good time to finally reveal ourselves," Roland grunted, then mumbled, "Damned arrogant panther."

"You didn't come tonight because you wanted to be with us, Emma? To be with your pride?" Jade had been quiet through Emma and Roland's exchange. Emma shifted her attention to the female panther. Disillusionment filled the woman's expression. Her green eyes glistened with unshed tears, yanking on Emma's conscience.

"I—I'm here about my aunt." Emma straightened her shoulders and Caine's hold tightened on her. "She's my priority right now. How can you two sit there so casually when her life is in danger?" Her gaze jerked to Roland. "She's your sister, for God's sake!"

"Aw, man!" Several men in the bar began yelling at the referee on TV, who apparently had the nerve to make a bad call.

Pain and sorrow reflected in Roland's eyes when he turned them back to her from watching the fans. "I *am* worried. I got a call from Malac earlier today. He assumed Hawkeye brought you back to us. Malac wants to trade my sister for you— manipulative sonofabitch! He won't let anything happen to her or his advantage is lost."

Emma's chest tightened and her breathing came in pants. "Aunt Mary is not some bargaining chip to be shuffled back and forth. She's a human being with a frail heart, arthritis and—"

"And she gave up her life so you could have one!" Roland's harsh words cut her off, notching her guilt up considerably. "An hour ago, I got a whispered call from a female doctor who's in Malac's facility. Unfortunately, I couldn't trace the call because she hung up too quickly, but she wanted me to know she's been slipping Mary the meds she needs. I'm worried about my sister, too, Emma, but do you really think, after giving up twenty-plus years of her life for you, that *she'd* want you to walk right into some trap that Malac has set without careful planning? You know as well as I do that he's not going to give my sister up—you said so yourself, she's his only leverage with *you.* He's planning something. I guarantee it. With his own group of panthers and his Mafia people, he outnumbers us at least five to one."

"Not anymore, he doesn't," Caine said.

Emma glanced up at Caine, to see his sharp and ruthless gaze locked on Roland.

Were the Lupreda offering their help? She jerked her attention to the Alpha, who placed his hand on the table and leaned forward. "You've got our support. When and where does Malac want to make the exchange?"

"Tomorrow night on the west side of town. He said he'd call with the specifics tomorrow morning," Jade said.

"He *would* pick tomorrow," Caine snarled.

"What's wrong with tomorrow?" Emma asked. The sooner the better as far as she was concerned.

"It's the first night of the full moon, Emma," Kaitlyn supplied with a concerned look at Landon.

"The moon's pull will force the Lupreda to their wolf forms tomorrow night. We won't be able to shift to our Musk forms to use to our advantage at all," Caine gritted out, his face turning dark.

"But Malac doesn't know I'm with the Lupreda. He thinks I'm with Jade," Emma argued.

"He knows I won't give up looking for you. It's the perfect time to make an exchange. He expects me to stay close to home while I'm bound to my wolf form," Caine said.

"The bastard definitely has something planned," Jachin cut in. "The Sanguinas will offer their support, as well. There's enough distrust between our races as it is. This prowling menace needs to be eliminated."

"We don't want to go to war with our own kind," Jade argued, sadness making her voice quaver. "There are so few of us as it is. Many of the Velius are just confused, unsure who to follow."

Emma's heart wrenched for the panthers. They seemed so divided and torn by Malac's vengeful aspirations. "Malac won't stop until he's destroyed everyone involved, including you."

When Jade's eyes widened and she began to shake her head in denial, Emma nodded. "It's true. He told me he planned to rule the Velius. *All* Velius. No matter what it took." Nibbling her bottom lip, she thought about how things might unfold tomorrow evening. "There might be a way. During our meeting with Malac—"

"He doesn't intend for it to be a sit-down discussion, Emma," Caine warned.

She nodded to acknowledge Caine's comment, then returned her focus on Jade. "If, during the battle with Malac, we can get to him and take him down, the others may then follow your lead instead."

"My lead?" Jade laughed, her green eyes glinting in the dim light, full of amusement.

The bar crowd suddenly uproared. The game was almost over. Some yelled at the referee, while others cheered him on.

"Emma, *you're* our leader," the Velius woman continued. "You and Hawkeye can shift at will. That gives you the highest rank, the most respect and the most responsibility for our panther pride. *You* two are our leaders. We've waited a long time for you. Now that you're back with us, you can convince Hawkeye to rally the panthers under Malac to his lead. He can help bring our divided pride back together by taking his rightful place at your side."

"But you've led the panthers just fine all these years," Emma insisted, while twinges of panic began to swell in her chest. *This is wrong. I'm no leader.*

Jade shook her head. "I'm not as respected as you might think or I wouldn't have lost some panthers to Malac. Don't you understand? Your 'pure-blood' leadership is needed. You and Hawkeye are the key to not only merging our groups, but also to helping us build a 'pure' pride of panthers."

With each word that slipped from Jade's lips, Caine's fingers cinched tighter and tighter on Emma's shoulder. He wasn't hurting her, but the tense pressure was there. Emma glanced at him. He'd lost some of the natural color in his face and his eyes held a stormy, tortured expression.

"It all comes down to the prophecy," Jachin murmured, drawing Emma's attention. The vampire's deep blue gaze was locked on Roland and Jade. "Before I left, Ariel reminded me that it involved others."

"Yes, the prophecy." Roland nodded solemnly. "After everything that's happened these last several months, we have come to believe it is true, and that the last part was about the Velius."

A leader is needed, you know this is true
Look not to one, but two.
A lesson was the goal you sought
You too must learn from what you taught

Layers of deception must be unveiled
For three to become one and peace to prevail.

While Roland recited the last part of the prophecy—that Emma remembered hearing Caine, Jachin and Landon discussing while she was injured—she'd already gone over the entire prophecy in her mind three times. *"Look not to one, but two,"* she whispered in a hushed voice.

"Yes, two. You and Hawkeye," Jade said with excitement.

"A lesson was the goal you sought. That fits with the Velius hoping to slow down the vampires, not destroy them," Roland added.

"You too must learn from what you taught." A derisive smirk lifted the corner of Jade's lip. "We've certainly had our own issues with Malac—who apparently wanted to rule *everyone.* It's ironic, I know. I'd hoped he would come around to our way of thinking once we found you, but now I know that'll never happen."

"For three to become one and peace to prevail." Roland repeated the last line of the prophecy and spread his hands wide, staring at each of them across the table. "And here you are side by side—Lupreda, Velius and Sanguinas—discussing strategy to keep the peace. I think a round of beer is in order while we discuss how I'm going to help Sanguinas and Lupreda arrive at this meeting without being detected."

Emma met Caine's gaze briefly and put her hand over his on her shoulder. Tension flowed from him in intense waves of musky heat. He'd curled his hand into a fist and strands of her long hair were tucked in a possessive hold between his fingers. The moment her skin touched his, electricity zinged between them and her stomach knotted.

Duty and desire twisted and tugged her heart in two very different directions. *This can't be happening. My race needs to propagate or risk extinction. To strengthen our pride, they want—no...expect—pure panthers from me...and I want only Caine.*

Chapter 12

"**I**'ll meet you back at the house," Landon said, tapping the open truck window next to Caine.

Caine rested his wrist on the steering wheel and stared straight ahead. "We're going to my cabin."

Emma put her hand on his thigh, hoping to dispel some of his tension. He'd stayed tightly wound the entire time they were in the pub. Caine didn't look down as he reached for her hand and gripped it tight.

"Your cab—" Landon dipped his head and stared past Caine to their clenched hands for a second before he spoke. "I'll post guards around the cabin's perimeter. Come by the house tomorrow morning so we can discuss more details about how we want to approach this meeting with Malac. By then we should know the location."

Lifting his gaze to Emma, Landon grimaced and pushed a

fist against his chest. "That pill you took didn't make you feel like there was a lump sitting in your chest?"

Roland had given them enough pills for every Lupreda and Sanguinas who planned to be involved in the meeting with Malac tomorrow, saying, *Take them now and have the others take theirs as soon as you arrive home. It'll take the pills eighteen hours to neutralize your scents. The medicine will start to leave your systems once another pill hasn't been taken within twenty-four hours of taking the last one.*

"Roland said it was safe for the Lupreda and Sanguinas to take—" Emma started to say.

"The *rest* of us took it with our beers." Kaitlyn stepped close to her mate, gazing at him with a smirk. "You're the only one who swallowed it without anything."

Caine snorted and tossed Landon a spare bottle of water from inside his truck door. Landon caught the bottle with a grunt, his gaze zeroing on his Second. "Be at the house by ten."

The Alpha and his mate walked back to their truck. Kaitlyn was talking to someone on her cell phone as they met Laird and Roman, who were waiting for them beside their vehicle. All the other Lupreda, Jachin and his Sweeper team had already left.

Caine started the truck, and as the engine rumbled to life, he gripped Emma's hand and kissed the back of it. Soon, the truck was sloshing through the dirty, partially plowed snow, eating up the miles back to the mountains. There was so much Emma wanted to say, and yet she was afraid to speak. Her emotions were all jumbled. Like a ball of yarn batted by a playful cat, her insides were knotted and twisted up beyond hope of ever being straightened out again.

Caine seemed deep in thought the whole time he drove. Yet even though he didn't smile, didn't say a word, he never let go of her hand. Instead, he conveyed his feelings about them through his touch, running his thumb along her palm in slow, mesmerizing circles. Each circular swipe sent erotic tingles flowing through her, shooting to her breasts and her core, spiking her need for his touch. If he paused, even for a second, her heart dipped a little. Emma realized with a start that she'd become addicted to their electric connection, like a junkie, looking for her next rush.

By the time Caine pulled his truck up to the cabin, Emma's heart felt truly ripped in two. *How can I feel so divided? I've known Jade for even less time than I have Caine, yet I still feel deeply responsible for the Velius' future and for my aunt's well-being. They're depending on me.*

They sat for a moment in the quiet darkness of the truck's cab. When she looked at Caine, his brooding hazel-green eyes were staring back at her and her heart swelled with deep emotion. She'd come to care deeply for this man, more than she ever thought she was capable of. They would find a way to make it work.

Caine climbed out his truck door, opened the passenger door and lifted her down in his arms in mere seconds. The frigid wind whipped around them and Emma wrapped her arms around his broad shoulders, tucking her nose under his chin.

Kissing the top of her head, Caine cradled her close and carried her inside the cabin. When Caine kicked the door close behind them, they both stared in shock at the transformation the cabin had undergone.

A new rug had been added to the entire expanse of the room and the exposed wood flooring around it had been polished to a shiny sheen. The single bed was gone and a couple of end tables and lamps—which currently gave off a soft yellow glow—flanked either end of the couch. The set of furniture had been rearranged on the new carpet, making the living room look much larger. Soft jazz music played on a stereo against a far wall and a fire roared in the stone fireplace, giving the room a cozy, lived-in feel.

"Wow, talk about a transformation," Emma murmured as Caine set her on the floor.

Caine hadn't said a word. She looked over to see his throat working, his expression full of surprised, pent-up emotion.

Shrugging out of her heavy coat and the cardigan, Emma set them on the back of the couch. Gripping his biceps through his sweater, she said, "Hey, are you okay?"

"Kaitlyn," he mumbled, his attention focused on the trans-formed room.

She tried to be lighthearted. "I wish I could command a re-modeling team like your Alpha's mate apparently can. Man, what Aunt Mary and I could do with our small house."

Caine's gaze finally pulled away from the room, but before his hazel eyes locked with hers, he'd moved with lightning speed. Emma found her face pressed against his hard chest and his hand fisted in her hair. Inhaling along her jawline, as if he couldn't get enough of her scent, he rasped, "You'll have an entire pride at your beck and call very soon, sweetheart."

His comment made her tense before her body instinctively yielded to the possessive slide of his other hand down her spine. Emma folded her arms around his wide shoulders, reveling in his hard-muscled frame and the arousing feel of his erection pressing against her. Caine's belief in her as the leader of the Velius kept echoing in her head until she finally confessed, "I'm no leader. Jade—and the other Velius—they've got it all wrong."

Caine wrapped a strong arm around her waist, fitting her

body fully against his. He kissed her nose, then her chin, before moving to her jaw, leaving tiny sparks behind. "Leadership radiates from you in every action you make, Emma, whether you realize it or not," he whispered in her ear.

"Wh-what are you talking about?" She tried to pull back, to meet his gaze, but Caine held fast, refusing to let her budge. His lips slid down from her ear and along her throat, sending tantalizing fiery sparks zinging through her body.

Sliding his hand up the back of her shirt, he flattened his palm against her back. Skin to skin. "You stepped in and took over when your aunt needed interference to keep her healthy and safe, you run the show at work in the café—the workers there looked to you for direction. You kept Jachin from killing Roland on the spot, you refused to let Jade believe Malac can be redeemed—"

"I've seen—experienced—what that sadistic maniac is capable of," Emma shot back as Caine's touch continued to turn her body to butter.

His fingers cinched tight in her hair and he growled, "No more after tomorrow. No matter what, I promise you Malac won't make it out of that meeting alive!"

His vow scared her. He almost sounded like he didn't plan on surviving tomorrow night's encounter with Malac, either. Emma's heart jerked and she tried to pull back, but Caine held her against him while he nipped at her collarbone. Her heart thumped in fear, even as her body betrayed her mind, responding to his dominant aggression. "Caine, I want to talk to you. Let me go."

"I can't. Not right now," he grated out, his voice rough as his fingers dug into her rear, tilting her hips, hitching her closer. "Tonight is all we have."

True fear rippled through her, the kind that left her hollow inside. Emma gripped his shoulders and pushed back until she met his gaze. "What are you talking about?"

She saw streaks of light green in Caine's eyes before he lowered his gaze to her lips. "I might not be able to use my Musk form tomorrow night, but I *will* make that bastard pay—for you, for your aunt, for the zerkers—"

When he trailed off, Emma cupped her hands around his stubbled jaws. "Don't you dare put yourself in harm's way or go and get yourself killed. I told you, I need you. Nothing has changed!"

Caine's lips kicked up just a bit and his gaze slowly lifted to hers. The sadness in his eyes tore at her heart. "Everything has changed. Your pride needs you more, Emma. You know it. And I know it. I'm an Alpha to the core, and if it weren't for the fact I could go zerker at any time, I'd be the next Alpha of my pack." Big warm hands encircled her wrists and his black brows knitted together. "I understand duty and responsibility to those in your care…and that's why I can see it in you. I felt it in your reaction to Jade when she told you that you were their leader, expected to help carry on the pureness of your breed. I saw it in your eyes when you looked at me. I know your heart will lead you to do what's right by your pride. It's ingrained in you."

Tears burned Emma's eyes and the pressure inside her chest was almost unbearable. "How can you just let me go? My heart hurts so much I can barely breathe!"

Caine closed his eyes and planted a tender kiss on her palm. "If I were a whole man, I'd be one selfish bastard, demanding we find another way. We'd merge our races…I wouldn't give a damn—" Fire lit in his eyes when they met hers. "I'd rip any panther apart who dared touch you or think for one second you'd agree to be his mate. But I'm not a whole man, Emma. I could go zerker any day. My Musk form is *that* much a part of me. I won't tie you to me. You don't deserve that and neither does your pride."

Tears spilled down her cheeks and her voice quavered with desperation. "Did—didn't Jachin mate with a human? And isn't Kaitlyn human, as well?" Emma argued, feeling as if she were stepping into a pool of thick quicksand that was sucking her down into suffocating darkness. "Hybrids are a possibility."

Hard lines creased either side of his mouth. "Your pride needs your offspring. I can't promise you a future, which children should be a part of." Touching her chin, he ran his thumb along her bottom lip. "All I can offer you is now."

It sounded so final, Emma had been breathing so hard, she suddenly lost her ability to catch her breath. She just stared at Caine, her chest caving in on itself, her heart shattering. "I—" She wheezed, trying to catch her breath.

"Emma?" Caine tilted her chin upward, concern etched in the hard lines of his face.

"I—can't—" She tried to inhale, but her breath just wouldn't come.

"Emma!" Caine scooped her up and carried her to the couch. Sitting down, he cradled her with one strong arm while he gripped her jaw, his fingers turning her face to his. "Breathe, damn you!"

He looked so angry and all she could think of was losing him. He was her rock in all this chaos. "Can't—" She shook her head and clasped his wrist, gasping for air again.

Caine kissed her and sparks shot between them. His fingers speared through her hair at the same time his lips pressed hard against hers, forceful and dominant, just as dominant as the voice in her head. *Breathe, sweetheart!*

His intimate kiss opened up her chest and Emma inhaled through her nose as she kissed him back with all the passion, all the wrenching physical connection she could give.

When she sobbed her happiness, Caine nipped at her bottom lip, making her gasp with pleasure. He took advantage and slipped his tongue inside her moist lips, thrusting deep, tasting, taking, exploring and seducing her with every sensuous swipe, every decadent thrust and parry.

Emma melted into Caine's fierce embrace. She ran her fingers across his stubble and memorized every contour of his face with her hands before threading her fingers into his thick black hair to pull him closer. And when she did, his kiss slowed, turning seductive and enticing as his hand slid up her rib cage, his palm grazing the side of her breast.

Kissing the side of his mouth, Emma tugged at his sweater, whispering, "I can't lose you… I…can't."

Swiftly pulling off the sweater and tossing it to the floor, Caine smoothed his hand along her face, pushing back her hair. "Shh."

Emma couldn't stop touching him. She ran her hands over the muscles in his shoulders and along his arms and down his chest as he kissed her temple. "I'm here, Em." Moving his lips to her ear, his voice lowered to a husky register as he slid his thumb over her sensitive nipple. "Slow down, my little wildcat."

Emma moaned and arched her back, pressing her breast into his hand.

Caine's low laugh made goose bumps skitter across her body. But he didn't take any prisoners when he suddenly rolled her onto her back and settled his hips between her legs. Pulling her hands above her head, he locked her wrists with one hand in a vise hold.

Emma panted in anticipation, butterflies of excitement dancing in her belly as he ran his teeth along her shoulder and rocked his hips in the cradle of hers, pressing his hard cock against her sex. "Damn, I can smell your sweet musk. You're ready."

"I never stopped being ready." A desperate gust of breath rushed out with her honest words. Her sex was already throbbing, her breasts tight and swollen, and with only a thin tank top separating her breasts from Caine's hungry gaze, his enticing touch and warm mouth, her nipples were more sensitive than they'd ever been.

Emma pressed closer, enjoying the pressure of his rock-hard chest against her nipples. Pushing her back to the couch, Caine's teeth blazed a teasing trail along her neck while the intimate slide of his thumb under the curve of her breast sent arousing jolts through her body. "All I've thought about is feeling your hands on me, your nails digging deep into my skin and that sexy purr growing louder right before I make you come again and again," he said, the rough rumble of his voice vibrating against her throat.

Emma's fingertips tingled as if her hands weren't getting enough blood flow, but this time she recognized the sensation for what it was. "Then let me go so I can accommodate your wishes," she said in a husky voice, tugging against his steel clasp.

His gaze darkened and a dangerous smile tilted his lips. He cinched his hand tighter around her wrists. "Not yet, my sexy little kitten." When Caine dipped his head and bit at her nipple through her shirt, sharp desire shot through her, centering between her legs. Before she could react to the pain, his lips latched on to her nipple through the shirt, sucking hard, rolling her nipple with his tongue. Emma mewled her pleasure, rocking her hips against him while her body clenched in heated response.

Her heart rate thundered in her ears and just when she thought she couldn't take his teasing torture any longer, Caine moved to her other nipple and began the pleasure-pain all over again.

Emma panted and pressed her sex against his erection to relieve the tingling painful throb building inside her. She couldn't get close enough, anything to relieve the pressure.

When Caine groaned and shoved her hips back down to the couch with a downward thrust, his heavy weight pinning her still, the pressure felt so good, Emma whimpered.

Caine lifted his head from her breast and stared at the two wet spots his kisses had left behind on her cotton shirt. The air cooled the damp material clinging to her, making Emma shiver and her nipples stand out, hard tips begging for more. Male satisfaction flitted across Caine's face right before he leaned close and breathed out across one damp tip.

Warmth skittered across her breast, flitting through her body. Emma quaked with pent-up arousal. "I—can't take it. I'm on fire, Caine. God, do something!" she demanded, her voice pleading and frustrated at the same time.

Eyes locked with hers, Caine's thumb slid slowly down her belly and then his hand was on the waistband of her jeans. He moved so fast, Emma barely felt the yank, but all that was left of her pants and underwear was shredded denim around her thighs.

"My clothes," she gasped. Yet the moment Caine had released her hands to pull her pants off her body, Emma immediately tugged off her tank top and tossed it to the floor.

"You have an extra set in the dryer," he curtly reminded her as he trailed his fingers past the trim dark bit of hair between her legs and teased her with stimulating skin-to-skin sparks of pleasure.

Emma moaned and canted her hips, trying to encourage his deeper exploration of her body, but Caine just brushed his finger lightly along her skin, then moved back to circle the bit of sensitive flesh with her own moisture. His electric touch sent splinters of pleasure vibrating through her, making her temporarily forget everything but the hungry desire clawing inside her sex. Her body demanded to be taken and assuaged with hard powerful thrusts, to be battered with fierce, all-consuming roughness, the kind that she was sure would make her heart threaten to explode from her chest.

She was surprised when Caine didn't remove his jeans, but instead put one knee between her thighs and walked his hands up the cushions until his face aligned with hers. His sexy mouth was a breath away and her body literally vibrated, needing their connection—the pull was that strong when their skin was this close.

His earthy, musky scent invaded her senses, making her feel light-headed and thoroughly seduced. Placing her hands on his hard pectorals, she enjoyed their humming physical bond and was ready to experience every part of Caine exploring her body inside and out. "Take off your jeans."

Caine's warm hand slid between her thighs, fingers tracing upward along her inner thigh. "I'm not going to remove my pants."

Apparently he needed to be talked out of this whole "slowing things down" idea he had in his head. Emma glanced at their bodies and raised an eyebrow. "That's going to make this a little difficult, isn't it?"

Caine shook his head and his fingers sent waves of excitement scattering through her body. "I meant what I said earlier. I'm almost zerker, Emma."

He couldn't be saying… Her voice trembled. "But when we were together before you were willing—"

"That was when I thought we could live a human life in the human world, but as the Velius' leader, you'll be expected to take charge and in doing so you'll be constantly challenged by your panthers. I would naturally defend you."

"And it would only be a matter of time before your Musk form became permanent," she finished for him, feeling bereft. She would never put him at risk of going zerker for her own selfish need to keep him close.

"Your pride doesn't need offspring with the taint of zerker potential in their blood, and because I don't know if this is something I can pass on, I won't take that risk with you."

"We'll use a condom."

"Which isn't foolproof." He shook his head and the determined set of his jaw made her stomach twist and her heart sink.

Emma hammered her fist on his shoulder, sobbing her frustration. "If all we have is this brief time, you're the only man I want to share my virginity with. You're the only man I want, damn it!"

A dangerous shadow crossed Caine's face and he quickly clasped the back of her neck, his power over her obliterating Emma's ability to fight him. When her fist froze on his chest and her attention zeroed in on him, Caine leaned close, his low voice dark as sin. "You might walk out of here tomorrow technically still a virgin, but I guarantee you after tonight… you won't feel like one."

Chapter 13

Caine stared into Emma's luminous golden eyes with resolute regard, even as his body shuddered deep inside. Her black hair was spread along the couch cushions and her cheeks were still flushed in arousal. She was biting her lower lip, trying not to cry, shredding his heart. The idea of another man having sex with Emma, touching her intimately, sent his mind in a vicious tailspin. He gnashed his teeth, already hating the bastard.

But Emma deserved so much more than he could ever give her. All because of his foolish youthful need for vengeance, he'd pay for the rest of his life. Ironically, he'd spent the last decade thinking nothing was worse than going zerker. Even death paled in comparison. He was wrong.

The thought of walking away from Emma, of not sliding inside her and bonding with her the way a Lupreda wolf would, was mentally and emotionally devastating, yet he couldn't let her know how much he suffered, couldn't share that his stomach burned and his heart felt like it was being ripped from his chest. He wanted the freedom to stand outside and howl, "She's mine!" across the entire Shawangunk Ridge, to snarl at any man who looked her way. And heaven help anyone who tried to touch her—if Emma hadn't been standing between them, he'd have beaten Roman senseless for daring to touch her. The dumb ass!

Sliding his fingers down from her neck to her shoulder, Caine released Emma from his hold and felt the slight tremor in his hand as he traced his thumb along her collarbone.

Tears filled her eyes, spilling down her cheeks. "Why does your touch affect me that way? Why can you lock me in place? No one else can do that."

Caine chuckled and shook his head in wonder, skimming his fingertips across the curve of her breast. "Maybe because you completely trust me and know that I would never hurt you."

Emma glanced down as her warm fingers slid along his chest. Arousing electrical currents slammed straight to his engorged sex when she pressed on his nipples, then rubbed her nails across the tiny tips. "I think it's because of this magnetic link you and I have." Her gaze snapped back to his at the same time she dug her nails into both nipples. "It's *that* powerful."

Caine ground his teeth at the erotic sensations blasting directly up his spine. Growling, he leaned forward and captured her nipple, rolling his tongue around the pink tip as he sucked hard. Not to be outdone, he captured her other nipple with his fingers at the same time, twirling the tip before he pinched, squeezing hard.

Emma's head fell back with her excited gasp. Her grip

moved to his shoulders and she rocked her hips, moaning in pleasure. Caine took full advantage of her distraction. Releasing her nipple, he continued loving on her breast with his mouth at the same time he slid his palm down her rib cage and stomach until he found her center.

Emma bucked against his hand, her fingers digging into his shoulders. Her nails marked his skin, sending his inner wolf through the roof. Damnit to hell, he wanted to slide inside her sweet body. To fill her up and never let her go. Remembering how small she was the last time he'd touched her, Caine ran his fingers up and down her slick sex, teasing her sweet clit and touching every precious pink fold to the point of driving her as insane as he felt. Emma's fingers jammed into his hair and she tugged hard, pulling his mouth off her breast and his body along hers until his chest crushed hers. "I can't stand the tingling pressure. It's almost painful. Touch me!" she panted.

Caine set his jaw and groaned. Her feminine smell had sent his senses into hyperalert, making him want her with a fierceness that would leave his brain sheer mush when he was done. She was so beautiful and uninhibited, her head thrashing back and forth in wild abandon. His own insides felt as if his wolf was shredding his guts from his chest all the way to his rock-hard crotch. He was burning from the inside out. Damn, he wanted nothing more than to fulfill her request and thrust his fingers inside her, deep and hard. But he had to keep it together for Emma.

He started to push his finger slowly inside her, but Emma bucked and his thick digit dipped inside.

Emma's breath caught on a pained gulp and Caine cupped his palm on her mound to keep his fingers from going to deep. Pinning her still with a tight hold, he spoke as calmly as he could. "Open your legs, sweetheart, and let me help you get used to me touching you."

As the tension released from her legs, her soft wet channel contracted around his finger, making his gut cinch and his body flash with heat. Caine clenched his teeth and closed his eyes for a second so he could focus. Slowly, he moved his finger deeper, pulling out and then sliding back inside.

Emma's hips began to move and she let out tiny whimpers of pleasure, begging, "Deeper."

Once Caine had plunged his finger to the hilt a few times and Emma changed her demands to, "Harder," he knew her body had finally adjusted.

Sweat coated his skin and Emma's, too, as he began to pump his finger in and out of her sex, adding another finger to the mix. Her smell was playing havoc with his mind. Caine planted kisses and then slid his tongue in a leisurely lap along the sensitive crease where her leg met her body. He needed to taste her, to implant her unique flavor in his memory so he could keep a tiny part of Emma to himself.

Emma cried out when he withdrew his hand, ceasing their intimate connection, but Caine's pulse thrummed in his head, a steadily increasing beat, drowning out everything but his desire to pleasure her in the most passionate and carnal way possible.

Dipping his head, he ran his tongue up her slick sex and shuddered, closing his eyes as her arousing taste exploded in his mouth and set his body on a knife's edge. Sharp and alert, he would readily accept the pain of holding back while he pleasured her. Spreading her thighs wide, he dove back for more, groaning as he slid his tongue inside, wishing like hell his cock could follow suit. Emma moaned and her musky sweet flavor coated his tongue, tasting like the most decadent dessert. She was pure heaven.

"Feels so good. More!" she demanded.

Caine thrust his tongue deeper before moving his lips to explore every intimate part of Emma…not a single place was left untouched. The moment he latched on to her clit, Emma jerked and her back bowed with her wailing cry.

"Don't stop, don't stop," she begged through ragged choppy breaths, her hips rocking at a faster pace.

Her excitement spiked his own and Caine had to mentally steel himself to keep from losing it. He was surer than hell that he'd have the worst case of nauseating blue balls when they were done, but this special woman was worth every ounce of suffering.

Let go, Em. Give yourself to me, he said in a low growl in her mind as he slid his fingers deep inside her and found her G-spot, upping the tension even more.

Emma screamed and yanked hard on his hair at the same time she began to convulse around his fingers. As her warmth flowed over him, Caine experienced a wild, jacked-up rush unlike any he'd ever had before. He counted every flutter around his fingers, relishing in each precious one, and again cursed the fates for keeping them apart.

He'd had his share of Lupreda women, felt their sweet sighs and soft feminine skin, experienced their bites of passion and demanding growls, but nothing came even close to the enthralling, erotic experience of watching Emma's passion unfurl and seeing her turn into the full-fledged wildcat he knew she'd be. Nothing got him off more than knowing he was the man responsible.

Caine moved up her sweet curves and gripped at her waist

with one hand while he pressed his lips against hers. Emma wrapped her arms tight around his neck and kissed him back with a wild fierceness that made his heart soar, telling him what their bodies already knew. They belonged together…like this. Loving one another, wallowing in each other's desires for days until they both couldn't walk, couldn't think, could barely breathe. Then they'd sleep to recover so they could rediscover each other all over again. Hell, yeah, that's what he wanted.

Hot tears stung behind Emma's tightly closed eyelids. Caine's kiss was so passionate and intense, she returned his fervor with every ounce of her soul. She couldn't believe how much she'd felt as he loved intimately on her body. The sparks flying between them, combined with his sexy voice floating through her mind and his talented mouth and tongue loving on her and tugging at her insides as if he were personally strumming them to life, sent her to a semiconscious plane she never knew existed.

"Only you," she whispered in wrenching sobs against his mouth.

Caine surprised her by growling low in his throat and thrusting his tongue deep into her mouth to the same rhythm of his finger still inside her…as if he were trying to imprint apart of himself on her forever. Emma knew she'd never look at herself the same way again. Caine had already left his impression on her, but the thought of being branded by the sexy wolf turned her on, and she met each of his thrusts with welcoming movements of her hips, holding him tighter against her.

When Emma crooned and undulated her hips, Caine withdrew his finger from her and slid his thumb along her slick folds. With each downward thrust back inside Emma's sexy body, he moved his thumb along her folds and applied circular pressure, bringing the tiny bit of flesh into play. The moment she began to purr between pants, the appealing sound rumbling softly in her throat was the ultimate aphrodisiac. He had to grit his teeth and force himself not to react or move or he'd go right over with her.

Instead, he shared, whispering every thought that went through his mind into hers. *I feel your hot body tightening around me, Em. Imagine it's me inside you thrusting deep. That's exactly where I want to be right now. Filling up your beautiful body with mine again and again. Come for me, sweetheart.*

Emma breathed heavily against his neck and then his shoulder as her body spiraled toward another climax. Caine gritted his teeth from the pleasurable pain he experienced as her nails dug deep into his shoulders, gouging him with each hitching breath she took.

Emma screamed and bit down on his shoulder to muffle the sound as she rode the waves of her powerful climax. The moment her tremors slowed, Caine pressed his lips to hers and spoke in her mind once more, his voice sounding hoarse like he'd yelled for hours. *In your heart and mine, you'll always belong to me.*

When Emma wrapped her arms around his shoulders and kissed and laved at the spot where she'd bitten him, his deep love for this woman clogged his chest as if someone had slammed a fist deep inside. He'd wanted nothing more than to bite her back; he'd even felt his canines descend while her body rocked against him, regardless of the silver around his neck. Caine barely held on, but he managed to keep his sharp teeth out of her skin, even though every fiber inside him, from his aching cock to his inner wolf, howled at him to claim her.

Staring into Emma's gorgeous eyes, full of love and passion, he realized he needed to back off for a bit or that's exactly what he would do. Caine ran his finger down her nose and tapped the end in a lighthearted gesture that was far from the intense battle that raged inside him. "Why don't you go sit by the fire and I'll see if anyone thought to stock the fridge for us."

Emma grabbed the soft throw blanket lying across the back of the couch and stood on trembling legs to wrap it around her before she moved to sit on the soft carpet in front of the warm cracking fire. Flames leapt high and sparks flew when a log shifted in the grate. The room held a pleasant smoky smell as she bent her knees, wrapping the blanket around her.

Caine's back was clearly in view while he peered into the fridge. Red claw marks marred his broad shoulders where she'd held on for dear life through her orgasm. Emma's stomach clenched from the vivid memories of the explosive climaxes Caine had given her, not to mention the fact she'd bitten the man. It was bad enough he'd been holding himself back, but why'd she go and tempt him even more by biting him?

Her cheeks flamed and her hands shook. She'd freakin' bit him. Laying her forehead on her arms, she blew out an unsteady breath. What must he think of her? She could still taste his blood and the salt from his sweat on her tongue and her body continued to react, clenching instantly at the memorable taste.

"Hey, are you asleep?"

She lifted her head and her heart jerked when Caine set a mug on the floor and sat facing her. Cinnamon apples and mulling spices wafted in the air while Caine stretched his long legs out beside her bent ones. Leaning back on his hands, he stared at her intently as if waiting to hear her innermost thoughts.

The position flexed his biceps and pulled his chest and stomach muscles tight, displaying his ripped body to perfection. He was beautiful, sleek and sculpted with firelight dancing in his intriguing hazel eyes. Their color appeared a lighter green than usual, but the swirling brown combined with the lighter green definitely affected her, knocking the breath from her lungs.

"You turned out the lights," she commented, blowing her hair out of her eyes.

He smiled and leaned over to brush her hair away from her face. But instead of pulling away, he ran his fingers through the strands, his reverent gaze following in their wake. "I wanted to watch you sparkle."

She lifted a hank of her hair to inspect it and saw the glittery strands. Awkward heat flooded her cheeks once more. "Why is my hair doing this?"

Caine's smile faded and his jaw flexed. "The Velius' fur was engineered to sparkle in the night, taking away their greatest hunting skill—the ability to hide in the darkness. Your eyes are the same, glowing golden in low light. My guess is the medicine you were taking was still inhibiting those attributes, and that's why I didn't notice a difference in you the first night in the club, even though your smell was definitely earthy."

The truthful tidbit of their race's history made her chest ache. Differences. They were different. And she was meant to be his prey. "What do feel when you look at me?"

Caine ran his fingertips leisurely along her brow, then slid his hand through her hair once more. "Aroused."

His honest, sexy-as-hell response made her skin prickle. "So my scent and the way I look doesn't make you want to hunt me?"

His lips tilted in the most devastating smile she'd ever seen—the kind that had "wicked" written all over it—making her toes curl and her body tingle all over. "I definitely want to hunt you. Not for prey, but to sink my teeth into your sweet skin like you did mine."

Mortified all over again, her cheeks burned and she spoke in a stuttering rush. "About that…I'm so sorry I bit you. I—I have no idea why I did that. I—"

Caine pressed his thumb against her lips and his eyes held a feral glint. "In the Lupreda world, biting you is how I would stake my claim and mark you as my mate, Emma."

His comment hit her hard in the stomach. Emma's pulse thundered in her ears. She'd never been more turned on in her life. She wanted him to bite *her*. Fiercely wanted it. More than anything, she wanted to be his mate. But when the hungry look in his eyes faded and his hand fell away, she knew he wouldn't bite her. Ever. How could he resist the sexual pull? She certainly couldn't. She knew he said he wouldn't have sex with her because of his zerker issue, but did he hold back from biting her because she was a panther and ultimately different? Her heart sank at the thought.

Caine picked up the mug of apple cider and handed it to her with a self-deprecating smirk. "Apparently, all I'm ever going to be able to offer you for sustenance is hot liquids."

As Emma sipped the hot cider, her gaze trailed over his beautiful body to the thick bulge pushing against the zipper in his jeans, and a sudden erotic thought shot through her mind. She took another gulp of the warm liquid and smiled behind the cup, plans forming. Being different could be *very* sexy.

* * *

Caine watched Emma drink the cider and his entire body pulsed to the beat of each swallow she took. To keep from reaching for her, he leaned back on his hands once more, loving this intimacy. He stored it up in his mind, inhaling deep and capturing her scent, memorizing all her sexy little movements for those long, lonely nights ahead of him once he turned zerker. It was only a matter of time. He couldn't see himself wearing the silver necklace forever, especially now that being with Emma wasn't an option.

She smiled at him over her cup and his heart soared. She was so damn beautiful and smart and sexy and…not his to have. The moment his mind started to wander down that unsettling path, Emma surprised him by setting her cup on the floor and shrugging the blanket off her shoulders.

Caine's breath literally lodged in his throat as she crawled across his legs and up his body, her luscious breasts still swollen from his kisses and the fire glinting off her soft skin. He suddenly ached everywhere at once, though the true pain centered in his groin—the one place Emma was studying with intense interest.

When she reached for the button on his jeans, Caine's movements were whip-fast. Catching her hand before she connected, he said in a strained voice, "What are you doing?"

Emma tried to pull out of his hold, then frowned when he wouldn't release her. "I'm unbuttoning your jeans."

"Not a good idea," he bit out, barely keeping a rein over his lust for the woman leaning over him.

Emma laughed, her voice washing over him in seductive waves, a siren's song. "Of course it's a good idea. I want to kiss you like you did me."

Caine closed his eyes briefly and ground his teeth, trying his damnedest to erase the mental picture of Emma giving him oral sex. His eyes snapped open and he growled, "As much as I would like nothing better than that, if these pants come off, I can't guarantee that I won't have you on your back in two seconds flat, taking you the way I really want to."

Desire flashed through Emma's golden eyes and they lit up with playful excitement. "Ooh, promise?" She reached for his pants button with her other hand.

"Emma," he warned, capturing that wrist, too.

Emma stared at him for several seconds. He could see her mind working behind those beautiful eyes of hers.

Caine didn't know how much more he could take. His inner wolf was snarling and snapping to get at Emma; her aroused scent was driving him wild with the need to join their bodies. When she sat back with a heavy sigh, parking her sweet ass on his leg, he released her wrists, heaving his own mental sigh, which sounded more like a groaning growl in his mind.

"Don't you want to keep your promise?"

Caine's gaze snapped to hers. "What promise haven't I kept?"

Picking up her cup of cider, she took another long sip, then set it down on the floor again. "The one where you promised me that I'll leave here a virgin tomorrow, but I wouldn't feel like one."

Caine realized she was referring to giving him oral sex as figuratively blowing away her all virginal innocence. Smart woman. Leave it to her to turn his words around on him, and it worked quite effectively as far as his inner wolf was concerned—the deviant, selfish bastard!

His gaze narrowed. "That wasn't what I meant, Emma. I was referring to your body, not mine."

A delicate eyebrow rose. "Are you saying that you want my first time giving oral sex to be with someone else?"

Caine fisted his hands on his thighs. "Hell, no! I don't want you to ever give anyone else—"

"Then what are you saying?" she interrupted, her voice breathless, her eyes wide.

Before she could think to pull away from him, Caine moved quickly, sliding his hand under her hair and cupping the back of her neck. As he held her captive, he ran his thumb along her jaw, tracing the delicate bone. "I'm saying you're dangerous and a worthy opponent in every respect."

A brilliant smile lit up her face, stealing his ability to think. He'd already lost thousands of brain cells during their earlier explosive lovemaking. "Is that a 'yes, you may continue, Emma'?"

Caine released his hold on her neck, his voice ragged and raw, his body raging for her to touch him. "Yes."

When Emma moved to settle between his legs on her knees, bending to unbutton his jeans, Caine's hand shook as he lifted it to her hair. The soft strands slid through his fingers in a sparkling flow of watery black silk, wrenching his gut even tighter. She was precious to him.

Every nerve ending in his body craved her electric touch with greedy anticipation and he found himself pushing her hair over one shoulder, exposing that sweet spot between her shoulder and her neck—exactly where he'd clamp down with his canines if he'd had the freedom to do so. His canines tingled, wanting to elongate. Caine ground his jaw and his fingers fisted in her hair as he mentally worked to keep his fangs from descending.

The sound of his zipper opening jerked his attention back to Emma. She lifted her head and laughed as she tried to tug down his jeans. "Um, a little help would be nice."

Caine gave a strained chuckle and after Emma moved to sit beside him and took a sip of cider, he shoved his jeans and underwear off his body. She sat quietly, her watchful golden eyes above the rim of her cup following his every movement.

The moment he tossed his clothes aside, she set down her cup. Leaning close, she breathed out a warm breath over his tensed stomach, then ran her cider-spiced tongue from his abs all the way up to his chest in one long, decadent lick. Caine held back a shudder of unadulterated ecstasy when she slowed to press a tingling kiss to his hard pectoral.

"You know, there are some benefits to being different," she murmured. Her lips barely grazed his nipple and an electrical current arced between them, shooting through his chest and straight to his rock-hard erection.

Hell, yeah, there were! Caine suppressed a groan of sexual frustration and curled his hands into fists, setting them back on the floor behind him. He wanted nothing more than to touch her, to run his hands along her soft, supple skin, to make her tremble from his sizzling touch, but the moment he connected, their humming attraction might be more than he could resist. He was an honorable man. He wouldn't take Emma against her will.

Then she glanced up and he saw the look in her eyes.

The problem was, it wouldn't be against her will. She wanted him sliding inside, taking her body and soul, biting her. Damn it to hell! Grinding his jaw hard, he locked his elbows to keep from moving one single inch. He refused to inhale through his nose or he'd catch the strong musky sweet notes of her arousal and his rigid control would shatter.

"Are you going to touch me?" she asked as she trailed more magnetic kisses back down his abdomen.

"Not a good idea," he managed to grate out.

A low, sexy laugh bubbled up and she continued her path downward. "You have a beautiful body, hard as a rock and sculpted in *all* the right places. And you taste like pure sin," she finished, planting a kiss along his erection.

His cock flexed and Caine shut his eyes to cut off the evocative picture of Emma bent over him. He jerked when her fingers surrounded his ridged shaft and his breathing instantly turned shallow.

The moment her tongue lapped up the moisture along the tip of his erection, Caine's head fell back and he growled toward the ceiling, tendons flexing in his neck.

But nothing prepared him for Emma's enthusiasm. The heat from her drink made their shocking connection even more erotic, and before he realized it, his hand was sliding through her hair, cupping the back of her head. Silk and heat made a heady aphrodisiac.

Caine groaned and rocked his hips, pressing deeper into her warm mouth, whispering encouraging words. At first Emma complied, taking direction, but she quickly adapted her own method—one that included a very talented tongue and strong-as-hell suction. She blew his mind, ratcheting up his heart rate, winding his insides tighter and tighter to a painful, pulsing throb.

Just when he thought he couldn't take it anymore, when he was sure he was going to explode, Emma began to purr; a deep, throaty vibration that rocked his world. The fast-paced sensations surrounded him, and the physical proof that Emma found pleasure in pleasuring him sent Caine right over the edge. He shuddered as his orgasm rushed over him in an all-over-body experience, slamming in thunderous, blistering waves of hot and cold flashes. Each heart-thudding jolt through his system was accompanied by his own groans and growls until he finished with a long guttural howl.

Emma jacked him up even more as she laved and tasted his body with slow reverence once he was fully spent. When stillness descended between them, she lifted her gaze to his, a sexy smile tilting her lips. "Different definitely has its fringe benefits. Wouldn't you say?"

Caine's pleased laugh echoed in the room. He pulled Emma into his arms and rolled her onto her back. "You're killing me."

Wrapping her arms around his neck, she gave an exaggerated sigh. "And here I thought I was entertaining you. I must work on my delivery."

Gripping Emma close, Caine buried his nose against her neck. Inhaling her earthy scent, he brought every bit of her deep inside himself. This beautiful, intelligent, quick-witted panther challenged every part of him—from his mind to his body. A howl of possession rumbled just below the surface, demanding he unfurl it for the whole world to hear. Caine swallowed the primal sounds that rose within him and remained silent, even as he ached to be the only man in Emma's life—now and forever.

Chapter 14

"The street Malac designated to meet with the other Velius is a dead end, flanked on three sides by abandoned buildings. We'll have to enter the buildings via back doors and come out through any open or broken windows," Landon commented as he stared at the blueprints on the polished mahogany table in the Lupreda's huge library.

"You know he's going to have men hiding in the buildings." Caine slid his finger down the paper. "This appears to be a narrow opening between these two buildings. It might be an option. We could slip through here unnoticed."

"Your wolf forms will make it harder to get inside the buildings. My men will enter first and leave doors open for yours while they go off to secure any men Malac may have positioned inside the buildings," Jachin commented from the cell phone's speaker.

As Landon agreed with Jachin's plan, Caine said, "I will be in human form, too, so I can help Jachin's Sweeper unit."

Landon jerked his attention to Caine, his brow furrowed. "You're stronger in your wolf form."

Caine's hazel eyes narrowed. "Once I'm a wolf, I'll stay one until daybreak. I want to take Emma safely to Jade myself. I won't let her out of my sight until I have to. Only then will I join you."

"I can take Emma," Kaitlyn offered.

"Thank you, Kaitlyn, but I would like Caine to take me to Jade." Emma took in all the Lupreda standing around the room. She'd watched them nod whenever Landon or Caine spoke, saw the respect in their eyes, and felt the closeness. Where had the Velius gone so wrong that they'd splintered so drastically? Did the panthers' individualistic nature make it hard for them to work together as one? Addressing the group of Lupreda whose gazes were locked on her, Emma said, "I want to thank all of you for offering your services. Malac will try to double-cross Jade and Roland. He needs my aunt so I'll cooperate with him. He has no reason to give her up, other than to set a trap for the other Velius. But I believe with your help, we'll be an unstoppable force—one he isn't anticipating."

After the meeting was over, several of the Lupreda crowded around the table to further strategize with Landon and Caine. Kaitlyn pulled Emma to the side. "I know you two are getting ready to go back to Caine's place. I have a request of you."

Emma nodded. "Anything. I appreciate everything you've done for me."

Kaitlyn's hazel-blue gaze shifted to the group at the table before she spoke in a low whisper. "I want you to talk to Caine. To convince him to come back to the pack."

Emma's eyes widened. "He's not part of the pack?" She'd seen the respect in the other Lupreda's eyes, the way they deferred to him, second only to Landon.

Kaitlyn shook her head. "He left over a fight with Landon about wearing the necklace. That part seems to have resolved itself, and I believe out of respect for what Landon has done for you, Caine will come back, but…" Kaitlyn paused then plunged on. "If today's any indication, I don't think he'll resume his role of Second."

"Why not? The other Lupreda seem to respect his opinion."

Kaitlyn shook her head, her expression sad. "I can tell by the way he held himself away from the others today, not approaching the group until it was time to discuss strategy. He's different. He only got involved when you were the center of the discussion, but not until then. In past Lupreda business discussions, he would have been right in there, side by side with Landon, butting heads over issues, giving his opinion. Challenging. Today, he's not the same and I'm worried."

Emma glanced up at Caine and Landon, their heads bent over the blueprints—two strong alpha men working together with a common goal. Peace. Her heart ached. She needed to make it right, to repay Caine for everything he'd done for her. "I'll do my best, Kaitlyn."

The Alpha's mate smiled. "Caine respects Landon, but he cares deeply for you. I know he'll listen to you."

Later that day, Caine entered the cabin via the back entrance, carrying the food he'd caught for an early dinner. When he didn't immediately feel Emma's presence in the house, he tensed. "Emma!" he called in a loud voice, setting the meat on a plate on the counter.

"I'm up here," came a muffled reply. She sounded like she was above him. The cabin didn't have a loft or attic, so there was only one place she could be. Caine washed his hands and walked out the front door.

The snow crunched under his boots as he stepped off the porch and turned his gaze to the roof. "What are you doing up there?" he said with a frown. Emma sat next to the stone chimney in the only spot on the roof that wasn't covered with several inches of snow. The fire from the night before had helped melt the snow near the chimney apparently.

"I found a good spot to enjoy the view before the sun sets."

She looked so adorable bundled in her coat with her arms wrapped around her bent knees. It was a good thing the roof wasn't a steep slope or she'd never have been able to stay perched up there comfortably. Caine started to ask how she got up there when he saw the disturbed snow along the edge of the porch roof. A single set of footsteps led diagonally up the roof toward the chimney.

"Come join me for a minute," Emma beckoned.

Caine stepped back and then took a flying leap. When he landed on the porch roof, Emma clapped. "You'll have to teach me that one! I got here the hard way."

Emma scooted over and Caine settled between her and the chimney. Leaning back against the stone wall, he pulled Emma against his chest and wrapped his arms around her waist, settling her in between his bent knees. "Just in case the pill doesn't work, after dinner, you'll need to take a shower to get my smell off you before we leave for the city."

Nodding, she sighed and leaned into his chest. "Hmmm, this is cozy."

Her soft hair, lifted by the cool mountain wind whipping

around them, ruffled in his face, reminding him of the torturous night he'd spent with her sleeping in his arms. They laid on the rug by the fire all night long. He couldn't bring himself to move her once she'd fallen asleep against him, nor did he want to. Instead, he'd pulled the afghan over them and rolled onto his back. Gathering Emma to him, he'd let her use his arm as a pillow. In turn, Emma had snuggled close and sighed contentedly in her sleep, making his chest wind tight with many regrets.

"It's beautiful and very peaceful here," she commented wistfully, drawing him out of his musings.

Caine took in the view from Emma's perspective. The sun sunk low in the deep blue sky, giving off streaks of vivid orange and purple mixed with muted pink far in the mountainous horizon. Vivid green poked through the snow-covered trees, letting winter know they would survive the heavy white blanket currently covering their limbs. A mixture of pine and Emma's earthy scent wafted around him in an alluring aroma. Kissing her temple, he stared at her profile and murmured, "Takes your breath away."

Emma's sigh sounded sad. She turned her head slightly and met his gaze. "I've been thinking about my aunt. I'm glad that doctor is sneaking her the meds she needs, but I'm still worried about her. I feel like all of this is my fault. She's old and fragile and…" She blinked back tears and Caine's arms tightened around her.

"She did this for you, Emma. I doubt she'd want you to feel guilty. We'll get your aunt back safely."

Emma's small hands fluttered nervously over his for a few seconds, then settled as she rested her temple against his jaw. "Thank you for trying to ease my worries…and for everything."

Strong emotions whipped through Caine, knocking the wind out of him with their intensity. He couldn't speak for several seconds, but his hold tightened around her reflexively.

"It was interesting and awe-inspiring experiencing your pack's dynamics today. I don't think the Velius have anything close to your cohesiveness."

"That's where you come in. They've waited a long time for a leader to show them the way."

Emma met his gaze. "I saw how your pack reacted to you and Landon—the Alpha and his Second giving direction. You both exude leadership, demanding respect with a mere look. It was fascinating to watch."

Caine stiffened. He'd felt so out of sorts among his brethren today, like he had no right to command their respect. "I'm a general member of the pack, yes, but I won't be Landon's Second any longer."

Emma frowned. "Why wouldn't you be? It's obvious how much you're respected."

Caine flexed his jaw and bitterness laced his words. "Because I have to be able to fight to keep that respect. Musk mode is no longer an option for me."

Emma raised an eyebrow. "Are you saying leadership is based on strength?"

"It is for my pack."

Both her eyebrows shot up. "Yet you expect me to lead my pride, and I'm not physically strong compared to some of my people."

"You'll have bodyguards." Caine frowned. He didn't like the direction she'd taken their conversation.

Emma ran her fingers along his jawline, her electric touch tempting him. "Leadership is about responsibility and making tough decisions no one else wants to make. It's about knowing you won't always be popular because of those decisions, even if ultimately they're in the best interest of the group's survival as a whole."

He cut his gaze to hers. "And you said you weren't a leader."

"Your pack looks to you because of your guidance, not because of your strength."

Caine clenched his jaw. "I can never be Alpha."

Surprise flitted across her face. "Are you saying that the Second in your pack is expected to be the next Alpha?"

"No. Neither has to do with the other. The Alpha chooses his Second based on his belief in that wolf's ability to lead in his stead if the need arose. It's a position of trust."

Emma tilted her head and squinted at him. "So why can't you be Second again?"

Because I want to lead, damn it! He shook his head at their circular conversation. As Second he would be leading. Landon always respected his viewpoints. Emma was right and she wasn't afraid to tell him he was wrong, even if she did so by directing him to the answer himself. *And that's why she'll make a great leader.*

Chuckling, he ran his fingers through her hair, letting her alluring scent loose. "I'm jealous your pride will have your shrewd leadership skills all to themselves."

"I'll bask in your compliment, even if I don't think I'm particularly skilled, just very determined." She closed her eyes briefly, purring at his touch.

Caine adored everything about her. Everything. "Although I don't know how our pack would deal with two women as strong-minded as you and Kaitlyn—"

Her eyes opened and amusement danced in their golden depths. "Feeling threatened?"

Caine let out a low growl and snapped his teeth close to her neck, making her gasp. "Try aroused, my little panther."

"Stay between Roland and Jade." Caine's hazel gaze locked with Emma's as they stood outside his truck, waiting to meet up with Jade. Five huge Lupreda paced in their wolf forms in the truck's bed behind them: Landon, Laird, Roman and two other males. Kaitlyn had parked behind them. She'd driven another seven wolves to town in Landon's truck and would stay in her human form to bring the truck into the alley if they needed her. They'd gotten a few strange looks by those who'd noticed the wolves in the dark, but then again, nothing surprised anyone in New York.

When Jade and Roland arrived, their SUV's headlights cutting through the darkness, another two vehicles, presumably more Velius, pulled up behind them. Caine's eyes narrowed. He started to reach for Emma as if planning to wrap his arm around her and keep her close. He stopped himself just short of touching her and spoke to her mentally. *I don't like leaving you in their care. Nothing about Malac is trustworthy. Despite what Jade says, I think she still harbors some hope he'll come around. He's unpredictable and out of control. Shift as soon as you can. You'll be able to defend yourself better in your panther form. We'll be right behind you.*

She nodded but didn't have a chance to say anything because Jade walked up. "Are you ready, Emma?"

Emma followed Jade and Roland back to their vehicle and climbed inside. Sandwiched between her people, Emma watched Caine get back in his truck. Even though she was with those of her own race, Emma had never felt so torn. Her heart ached and her palms began to sweat. *I already miss him, his warmth, his touch. How will I ever live without Caine?* she wondered. She didn't want to think about her future or the fact the Velius would expect her to produce more panthers to help propagate their race. Emma shuddered, despite the warm air blowing through the vents in front of her.

They were a couple of blocks away from the meeting place when a black panther darted across the street ahead of them.

Roland slammed on the brakes and Jade whispered with reverence in her voice, "Hawkeye."

The panther stopped briefly, his eyes and coat glowing in the darkness, before he bounded into a fast-paced run.

Even before Jade spoke, Emma could tell it was Hawkeye by the panther's massive size. As he disappeared between two buildings, she prayed Caine and the other Lupreda would catch his scent and recognize him as an ally. Once again, she found herself wishing the panthers had the ability to speak mentally like the Lupreda did. It would be so much easier to communicate with each other while in panther form.

Dirty snow had been plowed in six-foot piles on either side of the road as they parked their car on the street beside the building. Roland insisted on parking on the main road instead of in the alley. He wanted to be able to get away quickly and not be trapped by another vehicle.

After she'd shrugged out of her heavy jacket and exited the car, Emma shivered and tried to ignore the cold wind blowing around her as eight men exited their vehicles behind them. Her confidence bolstered, she acknowledged the deferential bow of the men's heads when they approached her. "Don't act unless you see me start to shift. Understood?" she whispered. She wanted to get her aunt to safety first before all hell broke loose.

"They're carrying the injections they'll need. They can shift almost as quickly as you. Your panthers will be behind you when needed," Roland assured her.

Once everyone nodded their understanding, Emma turned and accompanied Jade and Roland up the sidewalk that led to the alley.

The moment their group turned the corner, Malac stepped out of a black Hummer parked in the far back corner of the alley and beckoned to someone inside the vehicle.

Emma tensed but continued forward with her group past a few abandoned cars and a couple of Dumpsters. Trash showed through the dirty snow along the edges of the road.

Another man exited the back of the vehicle and helped Mary down. As Mary and the man holding her arm stepped under the streetlight's glow, Emma's temper flared when she saw the reason the man *had* to help her aunt down. Mary's wrists and hands were duct-taped together and a gag was tied around her mouth. Emma glared at Malac and started to stalk forward, ready to rail at him.

Roland's hand clamped tight on her shoulder. "Calm, Emma."

She jerked her gaze to Roland, shocked that he could see his sister treated so horribly and not react. "How can you watch—" Her words died off when she saw the look on the older man's face. Sheer hatred reflected in his eyes as he stared at Malac, who was currently talking to the man holding Mary.

Taking a deep calming breath, she returned her attention to Malac. He'd stepped away from his men and stopped several feet away from her. Sweeping the crowd behind Emma with a derisive look, he smirked. "I see you've brought a large part of the pride with you." Dark eyes flickered to the handguns Emma's men held. "I don't see any reason for such overkill. This is just a friendly exchange."

Emma had counted only three men other than Malac: the driver, who'd gotten out of the Hummer as they spoke; the man standing beside her aunt, holding her upper arm; and another man flanking the rear of the Hummer. Her gaze flicked to the surrounding buildings' broken windows, their kicked-in and broken graffiti-ridden doors.

She didn't think for one minute that Malac hadn't placed other men in strategic offensive positions inside the buildings, probably with guns in their hands. She knew he'd picked this section of town for its seclusion and abandoned environment, yet she was surprised she didn't see any homeless people hanging around. Then again, it was cold. The homeless people were probably huddled in a corner inside the buildings, trying to stay warm.

Running her hands down her thin blouse sleeves to stay warm, she locked gazes with Malac and kept her voice steady. "Once my aunt has reached the safety of her brother's side, I'll come with you."

Malac shook his dark head, his expression determined. He whistled and two sleek panthers jumped from the Hummer's open back window. She was surprised to see a light-colored, spotted jaguar walking alongside the pitch-black one. They quickly moved to flank Mary on either side. "The exchange will be an even one. You come forward at the same time my sentries escort your aunt across to her brother."

Emma recognized the diamond stud winking in the black panther's ear. He had to be the very young guard she'd passed in the hall at Malac's facility. The spotted jaguar must be the other young sentry she'd seen at the end of the hall. She remembered their detached expressions. Nothing but duty had shown in their eyes. Her heart thumped in fear for her aunt.

The wind whistled between the buildings, ruffling Mary's bobbed gray hair and flapping her coat open. Tears welled, spilling down her plump, wrinkled cheeks. The older woman was shaking her head "no," but one of the panthers nudged her forward with his shoulder. "It's going to be okay, Mary. Roland will take care of you," Emma said. *I just need to get her to safety first,* Emma reminded herself.

When Emma began to move forward, two of her own men stepped into place on either side of her, guns at the ready. They escorted her the same as the young male panthers were escorting her aunt.

Right before they were about to pass each other, a shot rang out from the direction of the Hummer. A man had popped up behind the passenger-side window and shot the guard on Emma's right. When the man stumbled back, she tried to steady him, but one of the panthers knocked her to the ground in the process of attacking the injured man. At the same time, the other panther went after the man on her left, who got off one shot before the panther struck.

Emma moved to the balls of her feet. A couple more of her men had rushed forward, only to stop in their tracks when Malac held an automatic handgun to Mary's head.

"You really didn't think I'd let her go, did you, Emma?" Malac taunted.

"Don't do this, Malac!" Jade said, raising her hand as she took a step toward them.

Malac jerked his gun upward with lightning speed and

fired, pegging the center of Jade's chest, saying, "Sometimes the traditional bullet just *feels* better." As the female Velius fell to the ground, blood spreading quickly from her gaping wound, he sneered, "You've always stood in my way. Not anymore."

Jade! Emma's gut wrenched when Roland caught Jade in his arms and fell to his knees. He gently laid her on the asphalt, his voice hoarse with worry. "Jade! God, can you hear me?"

Sheer hatred and rage rose up inside Emma, a rumbling, seething volcano ready to blow. Her claws itched along her fingertips and the tiny hairs on the back of her neck rose, sending a prickling sensation all over her body. At the same time she called forth her panther, she dove toward Malac in mid-shift.

Malac hadn't anticipated Emma's aggressive move. He was too busy enjoying Jade's suffering. The moment Emma slammed into him, her panther paw shoved at his wrist and the other paw landed on his chest. His gun skipped across the icy asphalt and Mary ducked out of the way, running toward her brother. Emma roared, digging her claws into the man's arm and chest as she sent him hurling across the road with a powerful shove.

Landing with a hard thud, Malac bellowed and jammed something into his neck. The second he jumped to his feet, a huge black wolf landed on the road between Emma and the man. Crouching in a battle stance, the wolf snarled and bared his teeth, challenging Malac.

His scent alone indicated to her it was Caine, but when she saw a silver chain hanging around the wolf's neck, she was surprised. *How was that possible?* Emma didn't have time to consider further because two other panthers suddenly attacked Caine simultaneously. They must've been hidden in some of the abandoned cars. One panther jumped onto Caine's back and the other rammed into his side with his shoulder.

Roaring, Emma started to pounce into the fray, when another huge panther shoved her to the side with his massive head, jumping between her and the panthers attacking Caine. Hissing at the panther who'd interfered, she tried to dive around his immense size, but the panther batted her away, blocking her path. Even if his size didn't give him away, Emma recognized his smell and his tactics. He was trying to keep her safe. Hawkeye.

Nodding to Caine, she pawed at the ground and Hawkeye flexed his powerful legs, jumping into the fight. One of the smaller panthers flew to the side, bleeding profusely at the neck, and while Caine fought the other one, teeth snapping and fur flying, Hawkeye went after the one he'd wounded.

Emma was so focused on Caine, she finally heard the roars, howls and guttural snarls all around her. The entire street was now filled with wolves and panthers fighting, claws and teeth ripping at fur, muscle and sinew.

And then her gaze landed on Malac who'd just finished shifting to his panther form.

An enormous black-and-brown wolf stood snarling at Malac. Landon's wolf stance bristled with challenge. He gave the man time to shift, yet he let him know by his bared teeth and fur standing on end that he planned to tear the panther apart.

Emma heard a distinct victory growl and turned to see one of Malac's panthers had a tawny-colored wolf pinned down with a locked bite on his neck. She knew she only had seconds to react or the panther would deliver a deathblow to the wolf's skull, killing him instantly. She wasn't sure how she knew this. She just did. Her instincts were that strong.

Bolting into a fast run, she thundered toward them. Before the panther knew she was coming, Emma leapt onto his back, digging her claws into his sides and grabbing hold of his scruff to yank him off the wolf. Her momentum took them all to the asphalt where they landed hard. Her ribs bruised, but Emma didn't stop. She released the muscle and skin along the panther's neck only long enough to grab hold of his head. Clamping her teeth hard, she crunched down to let him know she'd keep going and kill him if he didn't stop.

The panther thrashed and tried to throw her off, while keeping his hold on the wolf. Emma's claws dug into his sides. He wasn't giving up. He planned to finish off the wolf. He gave her no choice, damn it! She clamped down a bit harder and heard a slight crack—it was enough to get the panther's attention.

The moment he released his death hold on the wolf, Emma yanked her locked jaw and slammed his head to the ground. When the panther let out a grunt before he passed out, Emma loosened her jaws and scrambled to her pawed feet. His blood coated her mouth, and she could still feel how her teeth had embedded in his hard skull, nearly crushing it, but she refused to dwell on the sick feeling knotting her stomach—she'd almost killed someone, even if it was in defense of another.

She glanced up to see some of Jachin's men jumping from open windows. They each carried at least one man in their arms. The humans had to be Mafia working for Malac. The moment the vampires landed, they dumped the humans' unconscious bodies onto the road and then jumped into battle.

How can they tell whom to fight? Emma wondered, until

she saw Jachin nod to Caine, then point and direct his men. They must be speaking to each other mentally, she realized.

With Malac's men's numbers quickly dwindling, Caine, Landon and Hawkeye now stood in a semicircle facing Malac.

The Velius leader backed up a couple of feet, roaring at the panther and wolves to stay back.

Emma was surprised to see the original two panthers who'd flanked her aunt take flying leaps over Landon, Caine and Hawkeye to land between Malac and them. Simultaneously, the two panthers turned and crouched, ready to defend their leader.

Malac's eyes narrowed into slits, clearly pleased by the two panthers who'd put themselves between him and his attackers. He even nudged them until his defenders changed places.

Emma's gut tightened. She padded closer to the group. Something wasn't right, but she couldn't reason why she felt that way. Malac let out a challenge roar, seeming far too cocky as he walked forward a bit and placed himself in between the two panthers who were protecting him. They growled and flanked Malac even closer. Such blind devotion.

Malac let out an almost gleeful hiss right before he used his hind quarters to bump one of the panthers toward Caine and Landon, then quickly used his front paws to shove the black one into Hawkeye's path.

The moment Malac ran off toward the buildings, Emma reacted. She jumped onto Hawkeye's back, throwing him off balance. The huge panther stumbled while in mid-swipe. He'd intended to eliminate the panther in one blow, but Emma's interference lessened the impact of his attack and his paw only knocked the younger panther to the pavement, stunning him. Before Hawkeye could recover, Emma leapt off his back and crouched over the momentarily disoriented panther underneath her.

Hawkeye snarled at her and shook his head. Emma growled back, crouching closer to protect the young panther. She was going purely on her gut instinct with this one, but above all else, she knew she could *not* let Hawkeye hurt this panther.

Emma, Landon has gone after Malac. Do you want me to spare this one, as well? Caine's voice entered her mind. Emma glanced his way. The light-colored panther and Caine were facing off, circling each other, looking for an opening to strike. She nodded vigorously, hoping Caine would know to knock the beast out so he wouldn't be a threat to him or anyone else.

At that moment, the panther leapt toward Caine and the two animals rolled across the ground, ripping and snapping at each other with their claws and sharp teeth. In mid-turn, Caine began to shift and before the roll was complete, he'd fully shifted to his Musk form. Grabbing hold of the panther's muzzle with one powerful clawed hand, Caine slammed his fist into the panther's jaw, knocking out the animal.

Emma blinked at Caine in his Musk form. She'd been told the Lupreda couldn't shift to their werewolf form during the full moon, that the moon forced them from their human to their wolf half, unless they wore silver. When the panther underneath her began to stir and growl as if he planned to attack her, Hawkeye nudged Emma out of the way with his shoulder and slammed his massive head into the other panther's, knocking him unconscious with a satisfied grunt.

Caine gave Hawkeye a curt nod. The panther returned the gesture before he moved to stand beside Emma. Turning his black werewolf muzzle toward Emma, Caine spoke in her mind. *Hawkeye will keep you safe. I'm going to help Landon track Malac.*

After Caine jumped to an open window two stories above them and disappeared inside, Emma glanced around them. The battle appeared to be over. Wounded panthers, wolves and vampires were scattered along the street. Some leaned on cars, others lay on their backs panting and bleeding in the dirty snow, and a few, at least one or two from each race, were very still. Emma tried not to think about the losses as she padded up the road to see how Jade and Aunt Mary were doing.

A loud roar caught her attention right before something heavy landed on her back, slamming her to the ground. The wind wooshed out of Emma's lungs, quickly followed by horrific pain, but when Emma was unable to let out a moan or even move, panic set in.

Malac must've dived on top of her from the building above. Heavy thuds landed on the street next to them and Malac was yanked off her before the panther could do some serious damage.

Jachin, Caine, Landon and Hawkeye surrounded the panther. Blood oozed from several vicious wounds along his feline body, yet Malac didn't give up. He roared and swiped at them all with his deadly claws. Emma rolled onto her side and saw the vengeance in the faces and tense stances of her comrades. Each of them had his own reasons for wanting a piece of Malac, to pay him back for every bit of pain and suffering he'd caused.

When they all began to snarl at each other, Emma's heart jerked with worry. She gingerly moved her paws under her and started toward them when a loud shot echoed through the alley.

Malac paused mid-roar and then the panther crumpled to

the ground, unmoving and silent. A single bullet wound oozed blood from the center of his head.

"For my daughter!" Roland yelled, his frame quaking in anger and anguish. Dropping the handgun, he fell to his knees beside Jade and gathered her limp body in his arms.

Emma followed him and touched her muzzle to her aunt's leg. Mary shooed her toward Jade with a quiet but gruff, "I'm fine." Moving to Jade's side, tears filled Emma's eyes and she rubbed her panther whiskers along the female Velius' cheek. Jade touched her muzzle, then gulped in air. Blood seeped between Roland's hand, despite the pressure he was putting on her wound. Tears trickled down the woman's temples into her hair as she stared from Jachin to Hawkeye and then Landon and Caine, who'd all moved to stand on either side of Emma. Her forehead creased in pain and her words came out broken and winded. "We. Did. It. Right? Worked together for peace."

Emma's heart ached for the woman who'd led the panthers with such dedication and vision. Not everyone agreed with the methods she and Roland employed, but they all shared her desire for peace.

Kneeling down beside Roland, Jachin's blue gaze locked with the older man's and then Jade's as the vampire clasped her hand. "Yes, peace, Jade. We did it."

Silence descended on their small group once Jade took her last breath. No one said a word. No one moved for several minutes. No one could. Only the sound of Roland's soft cries and Mary's comforting words as she hugged her brother's shoulders filled the air.

When Landon jerked his wolf head up and stared behind her, Emma turned to see Kaitlyn in her human form kneeling beside the light brown wolf Emma had saved from the panther earlier. Emma remained in her panther form as she followed Landon and Caine over to Kaitlyn's side.

Kaitlyn's eyes filled with worry as she met her mate's gaze. "Roman's spine was badly wounded. He says he can't move." Tears spilled down her cheeks and she ran her hand over the wolf's head and ears. "He—he wants you to end it for him. He doesn't want to live like this."

When Landon looked up at Caine towering above them in his Musk form, Emma's chest tightened. Without hearing the words, she knew what he was mentally asking of his Second.

Chapter 15

I could end it for Roman with one bite, but in your Musk form, you could make it painless.

Caine glanced at his powerful Musk hands, and then he stared at Roman, the happy-go-lucky guy who wore T-shirts sporting "I'd rather be boarding than bored" logos. He understood why Roman would feel his life was over, but…what if he could eventually heal?

As if he knew the dilemma going on inside Caine's mind, Landon spoke to him once more. *This decision is entirely your own. As leaders, we have to make the tough ones. I consider you my equal in that respect. Whatever you decide for your packmate, I'll stand by you.*

Laird limped over to stand beside him and lifted his auburn wolf head to stare at Caine. *Don't do this. He'll heal,* he said, his tone sad, imploring.

What if he doesn't? He'll never forgive me, Caine said to Laird as he met Roman's deep brown gaze and thought of all the fun times they'd had together as friends.

Well? Roman finally spoke to Caine. *Get it over with, damn it!*

Caine flexed his jaw for several seconds, then shook his head. *You'll heal.*

Addressing Kaitlyn, Caine said, *We'll need to make a stretcher for him when we take him home. His neck needs to be immobilized so he doesn't have permanent damage.*

When Caine turned around, he saw that Hawkeye stood with all the remaining panthers behind him. Some were wounded and some were barely conscious, but their attention was focused on Hawkeye. Emma moved to stand beside Caine in a supportive stance.

In the blink of an eye, the panther shifted to his human form and spoke to the Velius with a deep authoritative voice. "Malac is gone. Too many events have happened for you to deny the prophecy's truth. The prophecy speaks of a leader… 'A leader is needed, you know this is true. Look not to one but two.' I know many of you believe I was the second leader along with Emral—Emma—but I'm feral, a loner who prefers his solitude, and that will always be true."

Sweeping his arm toward Caine and Emma, he continued. "They are your leaders. This wolf has proven he'll do whatever it takes to protect your Queen, and for that you should be forever grateful. Either choose to follow them or leave, but know that if you try to stir trouble with the other races as Malac has in the past—" Hawkeye's gaze narrowed "—I'll help Caine and the others hunt you down."

Caine was surprised by Hawkeye's declaration and his

support, but before the panthers accepted him, before he asked for Emma's decision, he wanted them to see him standing side by side with Emma—as he truly was…different from them in many ways.

Releasing his Musk form, Caine shifted back to a black wolf. He could never love Emma enough for the gift she'd given him—the ability to shift at will despite the silver chain. He realized what she'd inadvertently done after he'd heard the gunshot and dove out of the building window in his human form to help her. Without conscious thought, he'd shifted on the fly as he flew toward the ground, landing as a wolf to face Malac. He was no longer zerker.

With a nod of approval to Caine's wolf, Hawkeye morphed back to his panther form, and then turned and ran off down the road, disappearing into the night.

Caine slid his wolf muzzle along Emma's panther one. *Is this what you want, Emma? For me to be your mate and help you lead your pride? If you don't wish it, I'll understand and walk way. But if you do, I promise to protect you with every fiber of my being, even as I spend the rest of my days repaying you for the gift you've given me.*

Tears filled the panther's golden eyes staring back at him. Caine's heart stuttered and he waited for a sign. Tears could mean so many things. Stepping close, Emma ran her whiskers along his muzzle and leaned into him before she tucked her nose underneath his powerful jaw.

Caine clamped his jaw over Emma's muzzle, locking her against his neck in both a loving and possessive gesture. The sudden sensation of her purr vibrating against him made his throat knot and his chest swell with love and pride for this amazing panther and her acceptance. He knew they'd have a tough road ahead of them bringing the Velius pride around to a group who lived and breathed as one. But together, he and Emma could make it happen.

When Caine heard the Alpha's howl behind them, quickly followed by the other Lupreda, a bit of tension released from his body. Landon understood his decision and approved. The moment the Velius began their own deafening din of panther roars, Caine relaxed. Lifting his head, he released Emma and together they joined the primal chorus.

Emma stared at Caine as he drove them out to "their cabin" in the Shawangunks. He'd said it would be their getaway house when they needed a vacation from the city. And after the last two days, they certainly needed one.

Between Jade's funeral and those of several others they'd lost in the battle, as well as the various back-to-back meetings they'd conducted with the Velius, Emma and Caine had spent tons of time together—working—only to fall asleep in each other's arms exhausted the past two nights.

Mary had insisted Roland move in with her temporarily— that he needed to get away from the city for a while. According to her aunt, Casper hadn't left Roland's lap since the man had entered the house. Emma was relieved she didn't have to worry about them. Mary and Roland would take care of each other and would join their pride once more when they were ready. Now, if she could just get in touch with Hawkeye. She needed to tell him he had a family waiting for him to return.

After Emma had given Jared her notice, telling her boss that she'd stayed with her sick aunt at the hospital the past several days, she and Caine decided to start fresh in every respect. They would sell off Jade's and Malac's old proper-

ties and use the proceeds to build a new facility and a home
for the Velius, one that was conducive to group meetings and
activities.

The truck's headlights shone on Landon leaning against the
cabin's porch railing as they drove up. Emma glanced Caine's
way. "Since you called him to let him know you were staying
here for a few days, I'm sure he's waiting on you for a reason.
I'll go inside and let you two catch up."

Caine reached over and captured her hand as she started
to get out. Kissing her palm, he shook his head. "We're a team,
Emma. Whatever Landon has to say to me, he says to you."

His comment surprised her. "Are you sure? He's still your
mentor in many ways."

He smiled. "He's my friend first and foremost."

As Emma and Caine climbed the porch steps, Landon
pushed off the railing and addressed Caine. "You look good,
if a bit tired. Those Velius giving you hell?"

Caine laughed. "No more than the Lupreda would when
reorganization and reshuffling of duties occur."

Emma smiled at Landon. "I'm in awe with Caine's
ability to garner devotion and respect from my pride so
quickly—" She paused when another vehicle drove up
behind theirs and four Velius men climbed out, looking
focused and on guard.

Landon's eyebrow shot up as each man took a post around
the four corners of the house. Amusement laced his comment.
"I see how well you've gained their trust. That's a helluva
security detail."

Caine shook his head. "Emma is precious to them. Even
though she's safe here, it's hard for them to let go of old
habits and concerns." Stepping off the porch, Caine called out

to the men, "Your senses allow you more leeway. Spread out from the house a bit and you'll be more effective."

As the men quickly adjusted their positions, deferring to Caine's direction, Emma smiled. "You've taught him well, Landon."

Landon's green eyes crinkled with his deep laugh. "He's far too stubborn for me to teach him anything, Emma. You're seeing Caine's own leadership skills in action. Over the years, all I've done was to steer him away from crazy extremes."

"I guess that's *my* duty now." Emma snickered.

Smiling, Landon nodded. "Yes, it is. He'll keep you on your toes."

"It's great to hear how loved and respected I am," Caine snorted as he returned to Emma's side.

Emma wrapped her arm around Caine's waist, enjoying the feel of his muscular body against her side. "We're just teasing."

Caine pulled her close. "*He* was serious."

Landon's smile faded to a serious expression. "I've always known you'd make a great leader. I wouldn't have picked you as my Second otherwise. You make sound and fair decisions."

Caine's arm tightened around Emma. "How's Roman doing? He refuses to take my calls."

"He's healing slowly." Landon stroked his jaw, then sighed. "Only time will tell. I would've made the same decision you did for Roman. I told him so the night we brought him home."

Caine frowned. "Then why did you ask me to decide on his fate?"

Landon's gaze remained steady. "Because you needed to know what it felt like to have to make life-and-death decisions as a leader. Roman was your friend as well as your packmate.

Learning to separate yourself from your emotions so you can make that impartial call is the hardest skill to master."

Caine grunted, acknowledging his statement. "While you're here…" Lifting the silver chain off his neck, he held it out to the Alpha. "I'll give this back to you."

Landon curled his fingers around the silver chain, his brow furrowed. "Care to tell me how you were able to shift, not only with the silver around your neck, but in and out of Musk form, even though it was a full moon?"

Moving his arm to Emma's shoulders, Caine traced his fingers along her cheek. "It was the damnedest thing. I didn't know what Emma had done until I shifted on my way down from the second story of that building to defend her against Malac."

Emma glanced up at Caine as he continued. "I think I know what happened, though it's only a guess, because a panther has never mated with a wolf before."

Emma's cheeks heated under Landon's steady regard. He was watching them intently. "Mated? But we haven't. I mean you haven't—"

Caine chuckled and kissed her forehead; a soft electric touch to remind her how right they were for each other. "Remember when I told you that the Lupreda bite to mark their mates? You bit me that night, remember?"

Emma's face flamed brighter. "I have no idea why I did it," she mumbled.

"The desire to mate is fundamentally primal, Emma." Landon's light brown eyebrows elevated with his grin. "I find it amusing that you marked Caine and he hasn't marked you yet. He's always claimed to be a selfish bastard."

"I was *trying* to be honorable," Caine grumbled.

Laughing at Caine's annoyance, Landon's expression

turned contemplative. "It's intriguing that Emma's bite has apparently given you the ability to shift at will, though I guess I shouldn't be surprised. Kaitlyn and I still aren't sure if my mating bite gave her the ability to shift to a wolf, or if she has always had the ability because she was half Lupreda but was hindered by the silver chain she'd worn most of her life. Gabriel has been so busy in the city, he refuses to share anything about his human mate Abby until he brings her home in two weeks. It's driving Kaitlyn nuts not to know what changes, if any, have happened to her friend. It could answer the big debate between us."

Caine snorted, shaking his head. "You *like* thinking you had something to do with Kaitlyn's ability to shift. You're just jealous she can do so outside the moon's cycle."

Landon slid his gaze to Emma. "See what happens when he runs off to lead his own group? Complete insubordination."

Emma smirked. "Um, I think he's always been that way."

"Very true," Landon agreed. "As for you, it'll be interesting to see if Caine's mating bite changes you in any way."

Landon's comment sent heat shooting in rapid bursts throughout Emma's body, spreading to every nerve ending. She'd fantasized about feeling Caine's sharp teeth sinking possessively deep into her skin more times than she cared to count over the past few days, but she hadn't thought beyond the physical pleasure she knew the act would bring. The idea Caine might also be sharing something more of himself with her sent her emotions flying. Emma was left speechless.

The front door opened and Kaitlyn stepped out. "Oh, hi. I was just making sure you two had food since the last time you stayed here—" she cut her gaze to Landon "—someone forgot to make sure to have the Lupreda leave food for you."

Landon snorted. "Caine knows how to hunt."

"Not everyone lives on a steady diet of meat." Kaitlyn grabbed her mate's hand. "Come on, let's leave them to their evening." Nodding to Emma, she continued. "There's a pot roast and a salad in the fridge."

Emma smiled her appreciation, feeling like she'd joined not just one, but two new families. "Thanks, Kaitlyn."

"You're welcome." Kaitlyn stepped around them, tugging Landon off the porch with her. "Come by around ten tomorrow."

Growling, Landon moved with lightning speed, lifting his mate over his shoulder. Kaitlyn landed with an *oomph*.

"Put me down!" She pounded on his rear, sounding more embarrassed than angry.

"In case you haven't noticed, Kaitie, the boys took the truck when they left. I'm going to have to carry you back." Smacking her denim-covered rear, he grinned at Emma and Caine.

Kaitlyn kicked her feet in annoyance. "I can walk! Put me down."

Landon's grin turned downright sinful. "Oh, I will. In a bit." He turned to walk away and called over his shoulder, "Make that noon, Caine. I have a feeling Kaitlyn's going to be sleeping in."

"Landon!" was all they heard as the Alpha shot away in a blur so fast that Emma blinked in surprise.

"Um, wow!"

Caine leaned close. "Never leave a wolf wanting once he's had a taste. It makes us…antsy."

Emma's insides turned to molten liquid. "Have you felt antsy?" she asked in a whisper as she stared into the dark woods, mesmerized by imprint of Landon's blatant desire for Kaitlyn left behind in her mind.

Caine's voice was a husky rasp. "I've felt more than antsy. Each night I watched you sleep, I've burned."

Emma's gaze jerked to him. "You watched me sleep?"

Caine's eyes glowed a much lighter green. Sliding his hand into her hair, he skimmed her features as if he couldn't get enough of looking at her. "You murmur in your sleep and make the sexiest mewling sounds." His thumb slid an electric path across her jaw until it reached her lips. "It was very hard not to touch you."

Caine's touch, his voice, his intoxicating, musky smell and his mesmerizing gaze...everything about him enthralled her. "Why—why didn't you touch me? I thought you were just as tired as me and needed your rest. That's why I didn't—"

He pressed his thumb against her lips to cut her off. "I didn't touch you because I knew that when I did, I wouldn't stop. One night with you wasn't going to be enough for me, Emma. The next day, I'd resent the hell out of the panthers taking up our time. Call me a selfish bastard, but I want at least three uninterrupted days alone with you."

Emma swallowed, feeling a twinge of apprehension tighten her stomach. "Three days?" Caine had stamina unlike any she'd ever seen. More than one of the Velius had backed down during a debate with him, due to her wolf's sheer will. "I won't be able to move or walk or even think. I'll be—"

"All mine!" Caine's lips met hers at the same time he cupped the back of her head and pulled her against him.

Emma's heart raced from the possessive slant of his mouth moving across hers, his taste and the feel of his hard, muscular chest and strong arms surrounding her in a cocoon of steel. She kissed him back, her tongue sliding against his, loving the pent-up tension in his body, the sensation of his fingers fisting in her hair, while his other hand slid lower to clamp her butt hard through her jeans. Possessive, aggressive and all male.

His heart thumped steadily against her chest, slightly faster than it did each night while she'd fallen asleep in his arms. The fact that she could feel the rhythmic beat through their clothes only made her own heart ramp up even more.

Inside, Caine spoke in her mind right before he lifted Emma and carried her across the porch.

Emma didn't remember walking inside or Caine closing the door behind them. She was so caught up in kissing the sexy man, nothing else registered in her brain but him. Every single seductive, muscular inch of him.

Caine lifted his mouth from hers and placed his hand on the door behind her. Staring down at her, his breathing shallow, his voice carried raw emotion. "Lupreda don't often find their true mates, but when we do, the instinct to mark is near impossible to resist. I've fought my desire to make you mine for longer than I thought possible."

He closed his eyes briefly and his jaw tensed. "The thought of you being with someone else, touching another, giving him what I desperately wanted, tore me up inside. You'll never know how hard it was not to spread your sweet thighs and take everything you offered that night." Lifting her chin, he slid his fingers down her neck, his gaze following their path before his eyes returned to hers, serious and intense. "I *will* bite you, Emma, and I can't guarantee that it won't hurt. My feelings for you are too raw to deny you fair warning."

Emma loved this man so much he made her chest hurt. She respected his honor and integrity. She admired how ruthless he could be in the best interests of those he cared for, but more than anything she adored that he admitted he couldn't continue to hold back from her; that his feelings for her were that explosive.

Elongating her panther claws from the tips of her fingers, she dug them into his waist through his clothes. She didn't apply enough pressure to tear the material or break his skin, just enough to make him growl at her. "What makes you think I'm not going to bite you again?"

Not that I'm opposed to your bite—far from it, sweetheart, but it's my turn now. Caine gave her a feral smile and all four of his canines were on full display. Emma didn't bother holding back her gasp of excitement. Hell, she couldn't if she'd tried.

When she started to lift his shirt, Caine folded his fingers along the back of her neck and Emma's hands froze. Her gaze snapped to his, curious as to why he'd lock her in place.

Running his thumb down the side of her neck, Caine used his other hand to unbutton her shirt with slow purposeful determination.

As the cool air hit her, Emma's skin prickled and her desire rose. "Why are you holding me still?"

When the last button was freed, Caine pushed her shirt and jacket down her arms. Once they fell in a heap on the floor behind her, his eyes were the brightest green she'd ever seen them.

"You make me ache too much. I'm having a hard enough time keeping a rein on myself without your fueling my arousal."

"I want to touch you," she whispered, her voice desperate.

Caine gritted his teeth, sucking in a hissing breath before he shook his head. "I smell your desire spiking. It's like a freakin' red flag. If I let you touch me, we won't make it to the bed. I'll take you against this damned door!"

His ferocity and the obvious tension vibrating within him made Emma's stomach tighten and her sex throb. He was like a cobra, coiled and ready to strike. She loved him like this. Uncensored and edgy as hell! Her hands itched to slide over his hard back and heated skin. Her fingers tingled, ready to dig deep into his muscles and pull him as close as she could. A sly grin tilted her lips. "What's wrong with the door?"

Caine's guttural growl rumbled deep in his chest. "I want a chance to touch you, to make you so wet and needy that you can't stand it before things get primal and rough between us."

"I'm already there." Frustration laced her calm tone.

His gaze narrowed. "You're still a virgin and I'm not going to hurt you any more than necessary. End of discussion."

Damn his Alpha hide. Emma opened her mouth to speak, but Caine captured her lips in a head-reeling kiss, obliterating the argument she'd planned to make. *What was it again?*

Emma unleashed all the emotions that had built inside her over the past few days. She pressed her mouth to his and kissed him deeply, sharing the one part of her she seemed to have some control over. "I'm going to make you pay for holding me captive," she panted against his mouth, enjoying the feel of his canines brushing against her as he nipped her bottom lip.

Caine lifted his head and lines creased his forehead, his expression turning serious. "I promised you I would never use my power over you to hurt you in any way, but I *will* use it to keep you safe, Emma. Every damn time. You can rail on me later, if you wish."

Running his lips down her throat, he continued. "My job is to love you and protect you at all costs." He held his lips to the thudding hollow of her throat. *I feel how much you want this and the feeling is excruciatingly mutual, love.*

"Then, do something about it—" Emma cut herself off with a gasp when her bra suddenly fell away into two pieces, exposing her breasts.

Without pause, Caine dipped his head and captured a nipple between his lips. An electric jolt shot through her when his tongue rolled over the hard tip, then he began to suck.

Emma's knees went weak and her fingers flexed slightly, but that was all she could do…other than feel. God, she felt every humming sensation shooting through her system. The pleasure radiated from her head to her toes, pulsing to the erratic beat of her heart, landing with a thud in the center of her body. Need clawed with heavy, digging swipes at her sex, making her mewl and squirm under her skin.

When he slid his hand between her thighs, then cupped her denim-covered crotch with an aggressive hold, Emma whimpered, "Ca-can't take it. I don't care…just take me to—"

Caine didn't let her finish. He swiftly lifted her in his arms and strode across the cabin to the bedroom.

Chapter 16

The moment Caine set Emma back on her feet, she immediately pulled off his shirt. As the cloth fluttered to the floor, Caine unbuttoned her jeans, his hungry gaze lingering on her chest. Emma started to shove her jeans down her hips, but Caine snarled, halting her movements. Yanking hard, he ripped her pants and underwear right down the middle and gave a satisfied grunt as the two pieces slithered uselessly down her legs.

Standing naked in front of him, Emma's eyebrow shot up. "I still have shoes on, though I think it'd be easier on my clothes budget if you just slid them off instead of gnawing them apart."

Caine gave a dark smile and pushed on her shoulders, sending her flopping onto the bed. Emma's heart raced as he picked up her foot and removed her tennis shoe, but what she wasn't prepared for was the slow, sensual glide of his fingers along her calves as he pulled the torn pants and underwear off her legs. Tiny shocks of electricity mixed with heat.

Setting her foot on his chest, he did the same to the other leg, but didn't relinquish her foot when he was finished. Instead, Caine planted a soft kiss behind her toes and in the arch of her foot. Humming ensued between them, sending chill bumps scattering across her skin. Emma's breath caught as her lungs cinched. She was absolutely mesmerized by the site of Caine's sexy dark head bent over her foot, his big hands holding her gingerly, his warm lips traveling to her ankle where he kissed, then nipped at the fine bones.

All amusement fled, replaced by lightning heat snaking through her body in a swift awakening of passion and yearning that set her skin on fire. When he planted a sensual kiss behind her knee, then ran his warm tongue along the same spot, Emma discovered how erotic such reverent attention to her untapped erogenous zones could be.

Her toes curled on his hard, muscular chest and she stared hungrily at his broad shoulders as he moved his lips farther down her leg and nipped at the ultrasensitive skin along her inner thigh. When Caine pushed her foot up over his shoulder and went down on one knee beside the bed, Emma's fingers dug into the soft comforter under her. "Don't you want to—"

But she didn't get a chance to finish. Caine ran his tongue up her sex in a determined yet leisurely lap. When he went back for more, she set her other foot on his thigh and let her thoughts flit briefly onto a plane of blissful pleasure. Caine's growl turned into a groan as he thrust his tongue deep inside her, pressing hard against her body. Emma's heart raced and her pulse thrummed an erratic beat of stair-stepped excitement. Already her body was humming, tightening to a pitch of near orgasm. She didn't want to come without him this time.

Sliding her foot along his pants, she pushed her toes against his erection and whispered, "Take off your pants."

Caine shuddered, his intemperate gaze snapping to hers. *Demanding woman!*

His emphatic thought caused her to take notice and acknowledge his strength and primal urges lurking just below the surface. Emma squirmed from the invigorating power she derived knowing he was barely holding it together and could lose it any moment. The thought made her ache even more. "I'm not telling you anything you don't already want."

When Caine pulled away and stood to unbutton his pants, Emma propped up on her elbows and watched his dark, hooded gaze sweep over her naked flesh. She returned the favor, enjoying the play of muscles moving under his skin, the sexy dips and hollows of his chest and abs, down to the very nice line of dark hair that led to his very well-endowed erection that pushed against his abdomen when he stepped out of his pants.

A little apprehension mixed with her excitement, zipping through Emma as Caine placed a knee on the bed. But instead of moving over her, he caught her by surprise when he grasped her hand and pulled her to a seated position in front of him as he positioned himself at the top of the bed. Leaning against the headboard, Caine reached over and gripped her waist, lifting her as if she weighed nothing, and then settled her in front of him with her knees straddling his thighs.

"Hmmm, perfect," he murmured, his warm hands sliding to her upper back to press her body and therefore her breasts closer.

Not that she didn't enjoy the skin-to-skin contact. Caine's

warm body felt so good against hers, but in this position she was too high for them to—

Caine bent his head and captured a nipple between his lips, sending her concerns flying. Emma's pulse raced and her sex contracted at the exquisite pleasure his hard sucking was doing to her. Sliding her fingers through his silky hair, she clutched him close, then moaned even deeper when he clasped her other breast and ran his fingers teasingly across her nipple, barely touching her.

You're so ready I can smell the difference. Your musky scent is sweeter, his husky voice entered her head, raw and seductive.

Emma rocked against him. Spreading her legs slightly, she tried to lower herself onto his erection, but his arm locked her hips in the position they were, only allowing just the tip of his cock to penetrate her.

Releasing her nipple, he pressed gentle kisses against the inner curve of her breast. "There are other ways to orgasm, Emma. I'd like to show you."

Emma tried to move downward even more, to slide over him and lock them together in the most intimate way possible, but Caine's hold on her hips remained firm. "Why won't you let me go?"

His hazel gaze locked with hers and he slowly drew his thumb back and forth across her nipple, driving her libido through the roof. "Because it's your first time and I want you to be ready so you don't feel any pain. That's why."

Emma was trembling all over. She ached to the core, she wanted him that bad. "I'm in pain *now.* I'm beyond sure. I'm ready!"

Caine's chuckle sounded strained. Good, she wasn't suffering alone.

"Trust me, you'll enjoy this."

"Just let me—" Emma's demand broke into a moan of pleasure when Caine pinched her nipple. Her hips moved intuitively as shocking waves of desire splintered from her breast and straight to her core. Her muscles clenched tight, wanting more.

Caine captured her other nipple with his lips and began to tug, then nip at the tip. Emma's insides quickened with sexual excitement. Ecstasy coiled tight within her, tensing her stomach muscles, She rocked against him and the teasing tip of him barely inside her drove her into a frenzy of gnawing need. She pulled him closer and demanded with breathy gusts, "Feels so good. Don't stop."

Caine pressed his hips upward just slightly, penetrating then retreating in a tease that made her thigh muscles tremble as he spoke in her mind, his voice rough, aroused. *Come, sweetheart.* He gripped her hips and groaned, his own body a tense wire, ready to snap.

Emma screamed as wave after wave of pleasure began deep in her sex, swirling inside her. She rocked against his hard body, pressing herself shamelessly against him, trying to prolong the sensations clamoring through her. Anything to get closer to his magnificent heat and musky scent. Then she felt the slight pinch of him pushing inside her, stretching her walls, but she didn't care. She continued to move, loving every scent, every tremor, every touch between them. Finally she stilled and the only sound she heard was her harsh breathing and thudding pulse rushing in her ears.

A thin sheen of sweat coated her skin and Caine's expression was a study of intense concentration. She felt him, heavy and large inside her, his hands clamped bruisingly on her hips as if he couldn't let her go if he wanted to. "I guess I'm no longer a virgin," she whispered with a trembling smile.

"Not quite," Caine bit out, his voice full of gravel, the tendons on his neck and shoulders taut.

"I don't under—"

A tight, pinching sensation rippled through her walls, making her gasp.

Caine's gaze came into focus and concern etched his brow. His grip on her shifted, holding her up. "Sorry, Em. I meant to hold you in place."

Shock slammed through her when she realized the truth. Granted, she knew she wasn't sitting fully down, but still. Her eyes widened. "You're not all the way—"

He shook his head, his voice rough. "Not yet."

Emma's heart filled with love for his desire to take away her pain. Clasping his jaw, she whispered against his lips, "Distract me and make me *want* every painful twinge, my sexy mate."

Caine stared at the waning moonlight shining through the window, highlighting Emma's arresting eyes and sparkling hair. All he wanted to do was drown in this amazing woman. He loved her for her dedication to those she loved and felt responsible for, respected her steadfast resolve and admired her ability to keep him mentally on his toes, not to mention their amazing physical connection. He wanted to make her scream with sexual fulfillment, to make her his. Forever.

Running his hand through her hair, he spoke in a low voice. "I never thought I'd find someone who would make me question my path in life as you have. You excite me on many levels and challenge me on others. As far as I'm concerned, I'll never get enough alone time with you."

Emma kissed his palm and tears glistened in her eyes. "We'll have to make sure we take the time. Our pride will just have to understand."

Caine's chest ached with his deep love for this woman. She shared every part of herself and her race with him. Openly. Willingly and lovingly. Cupping the back of her head, he pulled her close and kissed her neck, sliding his lips along the soft skin. "I will take it slow and you tell me if something hurts. Okay?"

Emma wrapped her arms around his shoulders and buried her nose against his neck, nodding.

Sliding his hands up her sides, Caine lifted her off him and laid her back on the bed. Emma sighed and tried to pull him close when he leaned over her. "Not yet," he teased as he traced his fingers along the curve of her breast and down to her waist. When he bent and kissed her belly button, sparks zinged between them, making his lips tingle. Emma mewled, arching, pressing closer to his mouth.

Caine smiled against her skin. He reveled in the fact she couldn't get close enough. He understood the reaction. Their connection was so strong, it knocked him off-kilter while at the same time jacking him up.

He slid a finger deep in her sweet body and groaned when she clenched her muscles around him. He wanted nothing more than to sink deep into her heat, to make her scream and lose herself in her lustful urges, but he held back and nipped her skin where her leg met her body.

Emma's fingers tangled in his hair and she wrapped her leg around his neck. "Taste me again!" she begged, but he didn't need any encouragement. Her musky smell was driving him nuts.

Her flavor exploded on his tongue.

Emma thrashed and bucked, crying out. She was close. When he started to guide his finger inside her once more, she dug her nails into his shoulders and shook her head, panting as she pulled him up her body.

"Now!" she begged, locking her legs around his waist.

Caine leaned up on his elbows and guided himself into her. It took all his willpower not to ram deep, like he wanted. Emma wasn't helping his honorable goals. She was rocking her hips and making sexy moaning sounds. Driving him freakin' insane.

Take her, his inner wolf snarled.

Not yet. He tensed, holding himself back as he eased farther inside her, stretching her muscles. Withdrawing, he set his jaw and pushed deeper as ecstasy rippled through him. Emma's claws ripped at his skin. The bite of pain along with the smell of his own blood ratcheted up his desire.

A flood of heat shot through Caine's body, moving straight to his erection. Tiny pinpricks of molten pleasure-pain skittered across the thin sensitive skin along his shaft. His wolf was mating. If he didn't get this part over, she'd be in even more pain.

Caine spoke in her mind, right before he thrust all the way inside her. *You've taken my wolf to the edge. I have to now or I'll hurt you more.*

Emma tensed and gasped simultaneously. Preparing to mate, Caine forced himself to remain still. He kissed her jaw and whispered in a raw, ragged voice, "Are you all right?"

Undulating her hips underneath him, she panted. "I feel you stretching me and getting hotter." She keened, then kissed his jaw. "You are my other half. Make me scream again."

Caine swallowed the heavy emotions slamming through

him that she'd apparently gotten past any pain he may have caused. Running his lips along her temple, he stayed buried deep and slowly began to rock his hips. Each time her muscles tightened around his erection, a shudder of sheer pleasure rushed through him. *Mine!* he grated in her mind.

She let out an excited cry and met each of his thrusts with aggressive movements of her hips. "Yours. Always."

He ran his canines along the soft skin between her shoulder and her neck, needing to stake his claim, but he wanted Emma to ask for it. To know she understood and accepted everything that being his mate entailed.

Withdrawing from her, he pistoned deep once more and felt the beginnings of her body vibrating. She was so close. Tremors rocked his entire frame from his groin to his head. "I love you, Em. You are everything to me."

Tears slid down her temples and she fisted her fingers in his hair. "I love you so much it hurts to breathe sometimes. I want your mating mark. Bite me and make me yours," she sobbed, near frantic.

Caine pushed her hips deep into the mattress with his last thrust. At the same time Emma's gasp of pleasure and orgasm slammed through her, he sank his canines into her sweet skin and took the deepest level of possession for a Lupreda.

Her slick muscles fluttering around his erection, clasping even tighter, along with her heightened scream of passion, sent Caine spiraling into his own, explosive orgasm. With each pulse of his body sharing with hers, he experienced an intense bond and an even deeper emotional link to his mate. *Emma, mine.*

An hour later, Emma lay on her side, running her fingers along Caine's hard chest. Propping up on his elbow, he traced his knuckles gently over his bite wound on her shoulder. "Amazing!"

"What?" Emma lifted her head slightly and tried to see what he saw but couldn't. She'd need a mirror. "What is it?" she asked, glancing his way.

He smiled and tiny lines crinkled around his eyes. "You're already healed. All that's left behind are faded red marks."

Her brow furrowed. "Isn't that the way it works?"

Caine's eyebrows rose. "If my saliva could heal you, then yes, I would've licked your wound to close it and you'd already be healed. But we both know my saliva doesn't heal a panther, so this means your wound closed and healed on its own."

Emma adopted the same position, propping up herself. "I thought panthers didn't heal as fast as a wolves."

Sweeping her hair over her shoulder, Caine leaned close and kissed her forehead, then slid his lips to her temple. "Maybe that was my mating bite's gift to you—giving you the ability to heal quickly."

She smiled mischievously. "Do you think I can shift to a wolf now?"

Caine snorted and ran his fingers across her hip. "Was I able to shift to a panther?"

Laughing, Emma shook her head. "It'll be interesting to see what other changes, if any, develop within me."

"Indeed." Caine's finger made tiny swirls around her belly button.

The contemplative tone of his voice drew her attention. She looked at him, but Caine's gaze was fixated on her stomach.

He was thinking about children. Grabbing his wrist, Emma kissed his palm then flattened his hand against her belly.

"We're truly going to be merging our races one day and then our differences won't matter."

Caine gripped her rear and scooped her under him with a deep growl. "They never did, my little panther. Not to me." Sliding his gaze down her body, his feral smile held all kinds of naughty promises. "I can see all the ways we're the same, but learning all the ways we're different…now that's something I look forward to exploring with you in intimate and excruciating detail for the rest of our lives."

* * * * *

Silhouette Desire kicks off 2009 with
MAN OF THE MONTH,
*a yearlong program featuring
incredible heroes by stellar authors.*

When navy SEAL Hunter Cabot returns home for some
much-needed R & R, he discovers he's a married man.
There's just one problem: he's never met his "bride."

Enjoy this sneak peek at Maureen Child's
AN OFFICER AND A MILLIONAIRE
Available January 2009
from Silhouette Desire

One

Hunter Cabot, Navy SEAL, had a healing bullet wound in his side, thirty days' leave and, apparently, a wife he'd never met.

On the drive into his hometown of Springville, California, he stopped for gas at Charlie Evans's service station. That's where the trouble started.

"Hunter! Man, it's good to see you! Margie didn't tell us you were coming home."

"Margie?" Hunter leaned back against the front fender of his black pickup truck and winced as his side gave a small twinge of pain. Silently then, he watched as the man he'd known since high school filled his tank.

Charlie grinned, shook his head and pumped gas. "Guess your wife was lookin' for a little 'alone' time with you, huh?"

"My—" Hunter couldn't even say the word. *Wife?* He didn't have a wife. "Look, Charlie..."

"Don't blame her, of course," his friend said with a wink as he finished up and put the gas cap back on. "You being gone all the time with the SEALs must be hard on the ol' love life."

He'd never had any complaints, Hunter thought, frowning at the man still talking a mile a minute. "What're you—"

"Bet Margie's anxious to see you. She told us all about that R and R trip you two took to Bali." Charlie's dark brown eyebrows lifted and wiggled.

"Charlie..."

"Hey, it's okay, you don't have to say a thing, man."

What the hell could he say? Hunter shook his head, paid for his gas and as he left, told himself Charlie was just losing it. Maybe the guy had been smelling gas fumes too long.

But as it turned out, it wasn't just Charlie. Stopped at a red light on Main Street, Hunter glanced out his window to smile at Mrs. Harker, his second-grade teacher who was now at least a hundred years old. In the middle of the crosswalk, the old lady stopped and shouted, "Hunter Cabot, you've got yourself a wonderful wife. I hope you appreciate her."

Scowling now, he only nodded at the old woman—the only teacher who'd ever scared the crap out of him. What the hell was going on here? Was everyone but him nuts?

His temper beginning to boil, he put up with a few more comments about his "wife" on the drive through town before finally pulling into the wide, circular drive leading to the Cabot mansion. Hunter didn't have a clue what was going on, but he planned to get to the bottom of it. Fast.

He grabbed his duffel bag, stalked into the house and paid no attention to the housekeeper, who ran at him, fluttering both hands. "Mr. Hunter!"

"Sorry, Sophie," he called out over his shoulder as he took the stairs two at a time. "Need a shower, then we'll talk."

He marched down the long, carpeted hallway to the rooms that were always kept ready for him. In his suite, Hunter tossed the duffel down and stopped dead. The shower in his bathroom was running. His *wife?*

Anger and curiosity boiled in his gut, creating a churning mass that had him moving forward without even thinking about it. He opened the bathroom door to a wall of steam and the sound of a woman singing—off-key. Margie, no doubt.

Well, if she was his wife...Hunter walked across the room, yanked the shower door open and stared in at a curvy, naked, temptingly wet woman.

She whirled to face him, slapping her arms across her naked body while she gave a short, terrified scream.

Hunter smiled. "Hi, honey. I'm home."

* * * * *

Be sure to look for
AN OFFICER AND A MILLIONAIRE
by USA TODAY *bestselling author Maureen Child*
Available January 2009
from Silhouette Desire

CELEBRATE
60 YEARS
OF PURE READING PLEASURE
WITH HARLEQUIN®!

We'll be spotlighting a different series
every month throughout 2009
to celebrate our 60th anniversary.
Look for Silhouette Desire® in January!

Collect all 12 books in the Silhouette Desire®
Man of the Month continuity, starting in
January 2009 with *An Officer and a Millionaire*
by *USA TODAY* bestselling author
Maureen Child.

*Look for one new Man of the Month title
every month in 2009!*

REQUEST YOUR FREE BOOKS!

2 FREE NOVELS PLUS 2 FREE GIFTS!

Silhouette®

nocturne™

Dramatic and Sensual Tales of Paranormal Romance.

YES! Please send me 2 FREE Silhouette® Nocturne™ novels and my 2 FREE gifts (gifts are worth about $10). After receiving them, if I don't wish to receive any more books, I can return the shipping statement marked "cancel." If I don't cancel, I will receive 4 brand-new novels every other month and be billed just $4.47 per book in the U.S. or $4.99 per book in Canada, plus 25¢ shipping and handling per book plus applicable taxes, if any*. That's a savings of about 15% off the cover price! I understand that accepting the 2 free books and gifts places me under no obligation to buy anything. I can always return a shipment and cancel at any time. Even if I never buy another book from Silhouette, the two free books and gifts are mine to keep forever.

238 SDN ELS4 338 SDN ELXG

Name	(PLEASE PRINT)

Address	Apt. #

City	State/Prov.	Zip/Postal Code

Signature (if under 18, a parent or guardian must sign)

Mail to the **Silhouette Reader Service:**
IN U.S.A.: P.O. Box 1867, Buffalo, NY 14240-1867
IN CANADA: P.O. Box 609, Fort Erie, Ontario L2A 5X3

Not valid to current subscribers of Silhouette Nocturne books.

**Want to try two free books from another line?
Call 1-800-873-8635 or visit www.morefreebooks.com.**

* Terms and prices subject to change without notice. N.Y. residents add applicable sales tax. Canadian residents will be charged applicable provincial taxes and GST. Offer not valid in Quebec. This offer is limited to one order per household. All orders subject to approval. Credit or debit balances in a customer's account(s) may be offset by any other outstanding balance owed by or to the customer. Please allow 4 to 6 weeks for delivery. Offer available while quantities last.

Your Privacy: Silhouette is committed to protecting your privacy. Our Privacy Policy is available online at www.eHarlequin.com or upon request from the Reader Service. From time to time we make our lists of customers available to reputable third parties who may have a product or service of interest to you. If you would prefer we not share your name and address, please check here. ☐

SN08R

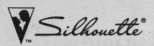

MIRA®

The chilling
Flynn Brothers trilogy
from bestselling author

HEATHER GRAHAM

SAVE $1.00

DEADLY NIGHT
DEADLY HARVEST
DEADLY GIFT

Coming October 2008.

SAVE $1.00 on the purchase price of one
book in the Flynn Brothers trilogy
by Heather Graham.

Offer valid from September 30, 2008, to December 31, 2008.
Redeemable at participating retail outlets. Limit one coupon per purchase.
Valid in the U.S. and Canada only.

52608517

5 65373 00076 2 (8100) 0 11566

MHGTRI08CPN

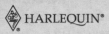

nocturne™

COMING NEXT MONTH

#55 THE DEVIL TO PAY • MICHELE HAUF
Bewitching the Dark

Vampire phoenix Ivan Drake's soul belonged to the
Devil Himself, and he had no choice but to enforce
Himself's wicked law. But when Ivan was sent
to claim the *Book of All Spells* for his master, he
wasn't prepared for his encounter with the book's
enchanting protector. With his soul already the
property of another, would he be willing to lose his
heart, as well?

#56 ALPHA WOLF • Linda O. Johnston

Major Drew Connell had created an elixir that
allowed werewolves and other shape-shifters of the
Omega Groundforce to shift at will—and someone
was out to steal it. A werewolf himself, Drew exposed
his secret to beautiful veterinarian Melanie Harding
when she saved his life. Could Drew and Melanie
protect the elixir before its powers were used to
create ultimate evil?